One Fete
in the
Grave

The Liv & Di in Dixie Mystery Series by Vickie Fee

Death Crashes the Party

It's Your Party, Die If You Want To

One Fete in the Grave

One Fete
in the
Grave

Vickie Fee

KENSINGTON PUBLISHING CORP.

http://www.kensingtonbooks.com

KENSINGTON BOOKS are published by

Kensington Publishing Corp.
119 West 40th Street
New York, NY 10018

All Kensington Titles, Imprints, and Distributed Lines are available at special quantity discounts for bulk purchases for sales promotions, premiums, fund-raising, and educational or institutional use. Special book excerpts or customized printings can also be created to fit specific needs. For details, write or phone the office of the Kensington special sales manager: Kensington Publishing Corp., 119 West 40th Street, New York, NY 10018, attn: Special Sales Department, Phone: 1-800-221-2647.

Kensington and the K logo Reg. U.S. Pat & TM Off.

ISBN-13: 978-1-4967-0066-7
ISBN-10: 1-4967-0066-X
First Kensington Mass Market Edition: June 2017

eISBN-13: 978-1-4967-0067-4
eISBN-10: 1-4967-0067-8
First Kensington Electronic Edition: June 2017

10 9 8 7 6 5 4 3 2 1

Printed in the United States of America

For my sweet Southern mama, Jean

Chapter 1

There were a series of deafening explosions. Babies were crying. A dog was howling. And out of the corner of my eye, I could see the outline of a man, no doubt intoxicated, relieving himself in the bushes.

It was the annual Fourth of July fireworks celebration in Dixie, Tennessee, capping off a daylong festival.

I was lying on a blanket next to my husband, watching the pyrotechnic display. The fireworks were being ignited in a field just the other side of Tiptoe Creek, which runs through Centennial Park. Balls of fire raced through the night sky directly overhead looking as if they would fall on us and set the crowd ablaze.

Larry Joe reached into the ice chest, pulled out an unlabeled brown bottle, and popped it open. If anyone asked, he'd say it was root beer. It wasn't root beer. But alcoholic beverages were technically illegal in the public park. On holidays, the law turned a blind eye to such infractions, as long as people made an effort to be discreet.

He tilted the bottle toward me in a gesture that asked, "Want one?" I shook my head. Words would be useless at this point competing with the ear-piercing explosions, now being accompanied by the high school band playing a John Philip Sousa tune. The fireworks show had started tentatively with lapses between the colorful explosions and crescendoed to rapid-fire bursts stacked one upon another like a deck of cards.

An impressive multicolor firework erupted as the band reached a rousing conclusion. Everyone clapped and cheered. A moment later, an even more impressive display lit up the velvet sky. The crowd remained silent for a few seconds to see if this truly was the finale before bursting once again into cheers and applause.

Eventgoers started streaming toward the exits. The row of bouncy houses that had earlier been buoyant with the energy and laughter of children was now in various stages of deflation. The aroma of fried foods, from funnel cakes to pronto pups and catfish, clung to the humid air even as vendors packed it in and shuttered their walk-up service windows.

Larry Joe and I stood up and started gathering our blanket, ice chest, and other supplies: sunscreen, sunglasses, mosquito repellent.

Suddenly, a woman's scream pierced through the noise of the crowd. The clapping tapered off as the hysterical screaming persisted. Everyone looked around for the source. I could see Sheriff Eulyse "Dave" Davidson and Deputy Ted Horton making their way to a row of porta potties beyond the vendor booths.

Helen Maples was standing outside one of the portable outhouses screaming her head off. I assumed she had entered the facilities and had an unfortunately intimate encounter with a snake or some such thing. But I was wrong.

The sheriff opened the door and there sat town councilman Bubba Rowland, with his pants around his ankles and a large red circle staining the front of his shirt.

This wasn't the first time Bubba had been caught with his pants down. But it certainly looked like it would be his last.

Deputy Ted closed the door on Bubba and started cordoning off the area around bathroom row. The sheriff spoke with some of the security volunteers and reserve deputies before making his way to the stage microphone. Dozens of people had clearly seen Bubba through the open door, and that information had spread like wildfire within moments, so Sheriff Dave didn't skirt the issue.

"We're investigating the death of Councilman Bubba Rowland," he said into the microphone. "Anyone who talked with Mr. Rowland, and, of course, anyone who noticed *anything* that seemed suspicious, make your way to the stage area so we can take your statements. Everyone else may leave in an orderly fashion, but please give your name and phone number to one of the volunteers who will be standing at the exits with clipboards to take your information. Thank you."

Dave came down the stage steps and made a bee-line to where I was standing. He nodded to Larry Joe before turning his attention to me.

"Liv McKay, you're up first on the interview list."

"Why me?"

"Because every time a dead body shows up in this town you're within spitting distance of it. And for once I'd like to ask you some questions before you launch your own little investigation."

I opened my mouth to protest that accusation, but he cut me off.

"And . . . since you were the events coordinator for the festival, you're probably in the best position to fill me in on any incidents or unpleasantness that went down today. I'm especially interested in anything that involved Bubba Rowland, as you might expect."

Larry Joe started to walk away, but Dave stopped him.

"Larry Joe, just a couple of quick questions while I've got you here."

"Okay, shoot."

"Have you been around the festival much today? Did you help out in any particular area?"

"No, this was Liv's baby. I was at work most of the day. I did stop by and eat lunch here on the grounds with Liv and I came back shortly before the fireworks show tonight. I was here at the park for a while last night helping them set up the stage."

"Did you have any conversations with Bubba Rowland today?"

"No. He waved at me as I walked through from the parking lot this evening and I returned the favor," Larry Joe said.

"All right, thanks. I think we're good."

Larry Joe wandered off to start picking up litter on the festival grounds.

"Okay, Mrs. McKay, follow me."

Generally, Dave calls me "Mrs. McKay" only when he's interrogating me. I'm not sure why he calls my husband "Larry Joe" during questioning, but I'm always "Mrs. McKay" when someone drops dead in my vicinity.

I fished a Diet Coke out of the ice chest at my feet, trailed Dave to the stage area, and took a seat in one of the folding chairs.

"That big bloodstain on Bubba's shirt makes natural causes seem unlikely," I said. "Is it too much to hope it was suicide?"

"Not unless Bubba managed to shoot himself in the back," Dave said. "There's a bullet hole through the back of the porta john. My best guess is someone with a rifle positioned themself in that strip of woods," Dave said, motioning toward a stand of trees and underbrush.

"You've been here pretty much all day, right?" Dave asked.

I nodded before adding, "Feels longer."

"So tell me every time you remember seeing Bubba today and who was with him at the time."

"We started things off with the 5K run. I'm pretty sure Bubba wasn't here for that," I said, envisioning the overweight councilman with a limp, who kept putting off knee-replacement surgery.

I related to Dave what I remembered about an altercation between Bubba and the man who was running against him for his seat on the town council in the upcoming election. Webster Flack is a staunch conservationist who represents a passionate group of protesters with ecological concerns about a proposed residential/commercial development. Bubba had strongly advocated for the development, in which—not coincidentally—he was one of the major investors. Flack and his placard-toting followers had recently picketed in front of Bubba's building supply company and were strongly suspected of leaving behind some unflattering graffiti on the side of the building.

Flack had rented a booth at the festival, as had other candidates running for the council. Difference being, instead of just passing out pamphlets that touted his stellar attributes and qualifications, Flack had additional literature, signs, and posters pointing out Bubba's many moral shortcomings. Bubba naturally took issue with this and the two men had had a loud and ugly name-calling confrontation, followed by some chest-thumping.

"Your deputy broke it up before any punches were thrown," I said. "I overheard bits and pieces, but Ted could give you more details."

"All right," Dave said, scribbling something on his notepad. "Who else did you see talk to Bubba?"

"Bubba spoke to half the people at the festival at some point," I said incredulously. "He was in full-on campaign mode, shaking hands and kissing babies." After pausing to think for a moment, I said, "Oh, there was some unpleasantness with Bubba over the Miss Dixie Beauty Pageant results."

"I heard some people thought Cassie Latham should have won," Dave said. "What did Bubba have to do with it?"

"I heard part of a conversation Pageant Director Rosemary Dell had with Bubba," I said. "She started out talking in a hushed tone, but she looked livid. As I walked past, she was giving him a piece of her mind in a very loud stage whisper. Apparently she overheard part of a conversation Bubba had with one of the judges and accused him of trying to influence the outcome of the pageant in favor of his niece, Jennifer Rowland—who ended up winning, as you know."

"When was this?" Dave asked.

"Shortly before the pageant started."

"And where were they?"

"Standing near the contestants' tent."

"What's your take on the accusation? You think there's anything to it?"

"I don't know if Bubba interfered with the judging or not. I do know that I felt certain Cassie would be the hands-down winner after the talent portion. I think most other people did, too. Did you hear her performance?"

"No, I can't say that I did."

"Jennifer Rowland played a number on the piano that any third-year piano student could have managed. Cassie, on the other hand, sang a song she wrote herself that I believe could land her a recording contract in Nashville if the right person heard it."

Dave made another entry in his notebook.

"Do you know if Cassie or her family has lodged a formal complaint? Did you hear anybody else take issue with the pageant results publicly?"

"I don't know about anything official, but later, after the pageant, Lynn Latham, Cassie's mother, had a tearful encounter with Bubba. She walked past me crying, and obviously drunk. I didn't hear much of what she said to Bubba except, 'Why?' Bubba, talking loud enough that I could hear him from a distance, was acting solicitous and told her he understood she was disappointed, but she should be proud that her daughter was named first runner-up.

"I think someone must have gone and found Lynn's mama and alerted her to the situation, because in a minute Nonie Jones came over and said something to Lynn before putting her arm around her and leading her daughter away."

"When and where was this?"

"This was maybe an hour or so after the pageant results were announced," I said. "Lynn came up to Bubba. He was standing by the Coca-Cola stand with a bunch of other men, sipping Cokes spiked with whiskey from under the counter."

I sat back and massaged my temples. I had a throbbing headache.

"I can't really think of anything else at the moment. It's been a long day," I said.

"Okay. Thank you, Mrs. McKay," Dave said. "Go home and get some sleep. But come by the office sometime tomorrow afternoon, so we can continue our little chat."

Apparently, Sunday was not going to be a day of rest for me.

"You're too good to me," I said, before turning to walk back to where we'd left the ice chest, blanket, and other items on the grass.

I scanned the park and waved to Larry Joe to signal I was ready to leave. Since we had driven separate vehicles, I assumed Larry Joe had hung around only to see if I needed help with anything. He came over and took charge of the ice chest, while I gathered up the blanket and other small items. I'd have to come back tomorrow to make sure everything was cleaned up and hauled away, but I was more than ready to call it a day.

When Mayor Virgil Haynes had asked me to take on the job of event coordinator for this year's Fourth of July festival my gut instinct was to say "no." I should have listened to my gut. I honestly tried to say no, in a roundabout way. I quoted a price for my services as a professional planner that I believed the town council would never go for. They approved it without batting an eye. That should have been a warning.

I was serenaded by cicadas as I walked to my car.

Past ten-thirty, the air was still thick with humidity and my SUV, which had been parked in the sun all afternoon, was stuffy and hot when I opened the door and climbed in. I started the engine and cranked up the air-conditioning. In the enclosed car, I was overwhelmed by the scent of mosquito repellent I had liberally doused on myself. Summer in Dixie—and all across the South— means heat, humidity and mosquitoes. With two reported cases of West Nile virus and one case of Zika virus in western Tennessee so far this season, local stores were selling a lot of DEET.

Once I made it past the traffic leaving the festival area, the streets were dark and quiet as I drove the short distance to our house on Elm Street.

I was dead on my feet by the time I made it home. But my shoulders were aching and my head was throbbing. I took some aspirin and told Larry Joe, who had made it home just ahead of me, that I was going to take a quick shower.

I pinned up my cocker spaniel blond hair, as my mama has dubbed my dishwater blond locks, because I didn't think I could stay awake long enough to blow-dry it. I stripped and stepped into the downstairs shower—the only working shower in the slightly dilapidated Victorian we call home, which is in the midst of never-ending renovations.

The hot water from the massage showerhead pelted against my neck and shoulders, smoothing out the kinks. The aspirin had helped my headache, as well. I slipped on a nightshirt that was hanging on the hook and slowly ascended the stairs to the bedroom.

I crawled into bed with Larry Joe, who woke up just long enough to lean over to kiss me before rolling over and snoring like a bear. I was too tired for the snoring to bother me. I was asleep almost as soon as I closed my eyes. During the night I awoke in a sweat when the image of Bubba Rowland's blood-soaked shirt invaded my dreams.

Chapter 2

I usually try to make it to church on Sundays and Larry Joe tags along occasionally. But after an action-packed Saturday that ended with an ugly bang, I didn't even bother to set the alarm.

By the time I made it to Centennial Park to check on things, a volunteer crew was breaking down the last of the tents and a Cub Scout pack was haphazardly picking up litter. All the porta potties had been hauled away, except the one in which Bubba had been discovered. It was still festooned with crime scene tape. We wouldn't be getting our security deposit back on that one.

I spotted Deputy Ted Horton and a couple of reserve deputies combing through the strip of woods where Dave thought the shooter had been positioned. I made the rounds, thanking the volunteers and chatting for a moment with the weary den leader before getting into my car and driving to Sunrise Mobile Village.

When I pulled onto the gravel parking pad my best friend shares with her neighbor, I found Di Souther sitting on the small deck in front of her trailer reading the Sunday newspaper. Her strawberry blond hair was pulled back in a ponytail and she was wearing cut-off denim shorts, her legs showing off the sunshine she soaks up as a mail carrier with a walking route.

"Any good sales in the paper?" I asked as she opened the door and motioned for me to go through.

"Nothing worth driving all the way into Memphis for," Di said, folding up *The Commercial Appeal*, the Memphis daily, and laying it on the dining table.

"There's still coffee if you'd like a cup," she offered.

"Thanks. I could use it," I said. I poured myself a cup and doctored it with a splash of milk from the carton I retrieved from the fridge before taking a seat on the sofa.

"I'm glad I didn't stick around for the fireworks show last night, since it ended kind of ugly, with the dead guy and everything," Di said.

"Did you talk to Dave?" I asked.

"No, a neighbor rushed over to tell me the news this morning as soon as I stepped out the door to grab the newspaper. If somebody was going to get killed, I guess it's not a huge surprise it was Bubba Rowland."

"Yeah. He had his fans, of course. Enough to keep getting reelected to the council. But there were also plenty of people who won't be shedding any tears over his death."

"He lived next door to your mama, didn't he?"

"Uh-huh. They always got along fine, although she was a lot closer to Bubba's wife, Faye, who passed away a couple years ago."

"Okay, Sherlock, you were on the spot all day watching the action. Who do you think knocked him off?"

"You're as bad as Dave. I was the very first person he questioned last night after Bubba was discovered. He accused me of always being on hand when a body turns up."

"There is some truth to that, you know," Di said.

Unfortunately, she was right. I had discovered a couple of corpses in a client's garage once. And I had also stumbled over a body during a businesswomen's retreat last fall. But it's not like it's a hobby.

"I could speculate about all the many people who had some beef with Bubba. But I honestly have no idea who killed him, and I'm not inclined to care all that much."

Di gave me a doubtful look.

We chatted for a bit and she told me there were rumors circulating that the supervisor at the post office was thinking about retirement.

"Would you be interested in applying for the position?"

"Honestly, no," she said. "Not that I'd have a real chance of getting the job, anyway. But I don't think I'd enjoy being stuck in the office all day. I enjoy my route."

* * *

I left Di's place and went home.

Larry Joe and I were expected for lunch at Mama's at 1:00 PM, along with my mother- and father-in-law and Earl.

Earl Daniels is my mama's boyfriend, although she'd never call him that. She says he's just a good friend. But he eats supper at her house most evenings that they don't go out for dinner, and he always accompanies her to social events.

When I got home, my marginally handy husband was upstairs banging on pipes. After over a year of messing around with the plumbing in the upstairs bathroom, he briefly had it up and running around Thanksgiving, as he had promised me he would. The comfort and convenience of having a working bathroom upstairs was short-lived. In a matter of a few weeks we had a water leak. Larry Joe disconnected the plumbing to figure out what the problem was, and more than six months later he's still trying to figure it out and repair the water damage.

I ventured upstairs to change into a skirt, since I knew Mama and Larry Joe's mom would still be wearing their church clothes.

"Honey, you need to clean up and get ready to go over to Mama's for lunch. And put on a button-front shirt, not a T-shirt. Mama's doing a fancy Sunday dinner. Your mom and dad are going to be there, too."

"Aw," he groused. "It's the Fourth of July weekend. I figured she'd just have Earl throw some burgers and dogs on the grill. Why is it a dress-up affair?"

"I don't know, but that's what she said. Maybe she figured after spending all day at the park and eating festival food yesterday we'd like something different today. Honestly, I'm happy to sit inside in the air-conditioning. We lucked out yesterday with fairly mild temperatures, but it's supposed to be hotter today."

Larry Joe was bent over his toolbox when I passed by the bathroom on my way to our bedroom. I leaned in the doorway and smacked him on the seat of the pants.

"Stop griping. You know you like my mama's cooking. I think maybe she wanted to do something nice because she knows how busy I've been lately with planning the festival and how busy you and your dad have been breaking in the new garage supervisor."

Larry Joe and his dad had finally found a suitable new supervisor for McKay Trucking Company after a series of troubling events last year, including the murder of two employees. The whole wretched affair had put us all through the ringer, with two employees getting killed and Di and me ending up with a rifle to our heads. And the stress of it all had put Daddy Wayne in the hospital with a heart attack.

I phoned Mama just before we left the house to see if she needed me to pick up any last-minute items from the store.

"No, hon, we're good to go. I'm so excited y'all are coming over," she said, sounding almost giddy.

"Okay, Mama. We'll see you in a few."

I was a little puzzled why Mama seemed so excited. It's not like Sunday dinner at her house is a rare occasion for us.

We usually come through the back door, but Mama had the front door propped open so we entered the house through the living room. Mama hollered from the kitchen, "Come on back." We walked through to the den, where my in-laws were chatting with Earl.

My mother-in-law came over and gave me a hug.

"Hello, Miss Betty."

I'd called Larry Joe's mom "Miss Betty" since I was a young girl and I hadn't seen any need to change it when she became my mother-in-law. On the other hand, his dad had graduated from Mr. McKay to Daddy Wayne after the wedding.

"Oh, Liv, you did just a wonderful job with the July 4th celebration this year," she said.

"Well, thank you, but I think finding a dead body after the fireworks show might have thrown a bit of a wet blanket on things."

"Bubba Rowland always was nothing but trouble," she said.

I was a bit surprised by my usually charitable mother-in-law's remark.

Realizing how harsh she must have sounded, she added, "Of course, it's terrible him ending up like that."

"Bubba was an ass and everybody knew it," Daddy Wayne chimed in.

My father-in-law's remark came as no surprise to anyone.

I hugged Earl and Daddy Wayne before slipping into the kitchen to check on things.

Mama, who at nearly six feet tall towers over me, was wearing a purple chiffon dress with a pleated skirt and oversized dangly purple earrings. The purple nicely accented her striking emerald green eyes and color-enhanced jet-black hair.

She was transferring a bubbling sauce into a gravy boat and told me I could start carrying the serving bowls and platters into the dining room. Mama had outdone herself. Offerings included a maple-glazed ham, green bean casserole, home-made mashed potatoes with gravy, pan-fried okra, deviled eggs, and a sweet potato casserole. It looked more like Thanksgiving than a typical Sunday dinner.

After she had finished with the gravy, she found me by the table and cinched me into a bear hug, smooshing me to her ample bosom.

"I'm just tickled pink you're all here," she said. "I'm going to run to the powder room and put on some lipstick. Tell everyone to start gathering around the table."

I called from the kitchen doorway for everyone to come in for lunch. When they came through, it suddenly struck me that Earl was actually wearing a tie. Earl rarely wears a tie except to funerals. Mama's schoolgirl excitement and Earl wearing a necktie made me think something was up.

We all held hands while Earl said grace, then tucked into our feast.

Larry Joe mentioned something about Bubba's murder and Mama interrupted.

"I'm going to ask you men not to ruin our beautiful dinner by talking about Bubba."

They moved on to talking about baseball. Larry Joe and his dad are die-hard Cardinals fans and try to make it to one home game in St. Louis every season. We also usually go to at least a couple of games at AutoZone Park in Memphis to see the Redbirds, the Cardinals's farm team, in action.

Mama and Earl seemed to be sharing knowing looks all through dinner. After the meal, Miss Betty and I helped clear the table. Then Mama shooed us into the den and called for Earl to help her serve dessert.

Earl carried the plates, forks, and napkins and Mama brought in a triple-layer chocolate cake—the recipe that had earned her a blue ribbon at last year's July 4th baking competition. They set the cake and plates on the ornate antique buffet that had belonged to my grandmother. Earl cleared his throat before saying, "Can I have everyone's attention for a moment." He and Mama stood there holding hands. Earl's ears were bright red.

"We wanted you to be the first to know that Virginia and I are engaged to be married."

Miss Betty jumped up and said, "How wonderful! I'm so happy for you both."

My mother-in-law rushed over to hug Mama and I trailed behind her in a bit of a daze.

Mama, who is generally not very good at keeping secrets, had given no indication that an engagement was on the horizon. Not that I was unhappy about it. It had been nearly five years since my daddy had died and she and Earl had been seeing each other steadily for more than two years.

The men walked over and shook hands with Earl, offering congratulations. Even my curmudgeonly father-in-law seemed genuinely pleased by the news.

Mama held out her hand to show off an engagement ring with tiny diamonds surrounding a marquise-cut emerald. Miss Betty and I admired it and I thought how romantic it was for Earl to choose a ring that matched my mother's eyes. Earl is a thoroughly nice guy, but romantic isn't a word I'd use to describe him. Then it dawned on me that my mother wouldn't have left something as important as an engagement ring up to Earl. I hugged Mama, who looked at me with misty eyes and said, "You are happy for me, aren't you, Liv?"

"Of course, Mama," I said sincerely. "Earl is a wonderful man, and I know he'll take very good care of you."

"I know. But I may need your help to make your sister understand."

That was a huge understatement, but I forced a smile and said, "I'm sure Emma will come around."

After cake and a bit of chitchat, Larry Joe and I said our good-byes.

In the car, Larry Joe said, "Wow, I didn't see that coming, at least not this soon. Had your Mama given you any indication?"

"Of course not. If she had, don't you think I would have told you? I think they're a good match, though. Anybody who can put up with my mama is at least a minor saint. Unfortunately, I don't think my little sister is going to share that view."

"She'll come around," Larry Joe said.

"That's what I told Mama, but I'm having some trouble believing it myself. Emma was such a daddy's girl. She's not going to take to the idea of somebody replacing him."

"Earl's not trying to replace your daddy. Part of the problem, I think, is that Emma hasn't spent time around Earl like we have, and seen how well he treats your mama," Larry Joe said.

"You and I know that, but I don't think that's the way Emma will see it," I said. "She's never been happy about Mama spending time with Earl, which is ridiculous. But that's Emma for you."

Larry Joe pulled his truck into the garage at our house. He headed for the back door and I walked over to the SUV.

"I'm going down to the sheriff's office," I said. "He wanted to continue our little conversation from last night. But honestly, I don't know what else I can tell him. I already told him that I saw Bubba have run-ins with Webster Flack and Rosemary Dell, as well as trying to calm down a very upset and visibly tipsy Lynn Latham. I was run off my feet yesterday and didn't exactly keep tabs on what Bubba was up to."

"I'm going to take a nap and then catch up on some work while you're gone," Larry Joe said.

He paused and then turned to me, resting his hand on the back door handle. "Honey, you ought to be prepared for Dave to ask you some questions about Earl. It's not exactly a well-kept secret there was no love lost between Earl and Bubba."

"You can't honestly believe Earl had anything to do with Bubba's death," I said, feeling protective of Mama's new fiancé.

"Now don't get riled up, Liv. You know I don't think Earl killed Bubba. But he's bound to be a suspect, especially after the shouting match he and Bubba got into a couple of weeks ago at that town hall meeting."

Earl and Bubba were longtime adversaries. Earl owns a building and supply center, providing lumber, hardware, plumbing, and electrical supplies to builders and do-it-yourself homeowners. Bubba, along with his brother Bruce, owned a rival business in town. The competing stores often had price wars. If one offered a 10 percent discount, the other would advertise 15-percent-off deals. But Bubba went beyond the expected rival business antics. He abused his position on the town council and as liaison to the planning commission. He would vote for and lobby for developers who bought from his company and delay or try to deny approvals for builders who bought supplies from Earl.

"Earl had every right to get mad at that meeting,"

I said. "Bubba was acting like a horse's patoot. And Earl wasn't the only one to have a heated exchange with the late councilman."

"I know that and so does Dave. But considering the long history of bad blood between the two of them, Dave has to look at Earl as a suspect. You just need to prepare yourself for the likelihood that Dave may ask you some questions about Earl and try not to get all worked up. That's all I'm saying."

I knew he was right, but I didn't have to like it. Then an even more frightening thought occurred to me.

"You don't think Dave will question Mama, do you?"

"I imagine he'll talk to all of Bubba's neighbors at some point," Larry Joe said.

I thought about that unsettling possibility during the short drive to the sheriff's office.

The last of the after-church lunch crowd were coming out of Town Square Diner. Ladies in summer dresses, some wearing hats, and men in suit trousers and suspenders, who had shed their jackets in the ninety-plus-degree temperature, were spilling onto the sidewalk. While the diner stays busy, most of the rest of the businesses in Dixie's charming downtown are closed on Sundays. The courthouse in the center, surrounded by one-way streets on three sides, anchors the town square, which boasts a beauty salon, bakery, drugstore, and barbershop, along with a thrift shop and a storefront church.

I pulled up and parked in front of the sheriff's office, which is located on a corner across the street from my Liv 4 Fun party-planning business, of which I am sole proprietor and the only full-time employee.

I was relieved when Dave asked me to come into his office instead of the interview room. I'd had the displeasure of spending some uncomfortable hours in that room being grilled by Dave when he felt Di and I had overstepped certain boundaries. He'd actually had the nerve to accuse us of breaking and entering once just because we happened to take a look around inside a suspect's camper when he wasn't at home.

I took a seat in one of two blue vinyl chairs that faced Dave's desk. He sat in a big, swivel office chair and shuffled through some papers before looking up.

"Have you thought of anything else that might be pertinent to Bubba Rowland's murder?"

"No, I can't say that I have."

"You said that you saw, at various points during the day, Webster Flack, Rosemary Dell, and Lynn Latham having words with Bubba. Is that correct?"

I nodded.

"Do you remember seeing any of them just before or during the fireworks?"

I assumed this meant Dave believed Bubba had been killed during the fireworks, which made sense since the fireworks explosions would have masked the sound of a rifle blast.

"Let me see. They introduced all the winners from the day just before the fireworks show. Cassie Latham, as first runner-up in the Miss Dixie pageant, was seated onstage next to Jennifer Rowland, as well as the winners from the cooking contests and the 5K winners in the different age divisions. The winners' families were seated in folding chairs near the stage. I do remember seeing Lynn Latham sitting in the audience, still looking sadsack, when I walked through to stake out a spot to watch the fireworks.

"Rosemary Dell must have been seated nearby, too, because they called her up to the stage to introduce Jennifer and Cassie and thank the pageant sponsors. I don't remember seeing Webster. But just before the fireworks started, the winners left the stage and the high school band started setting up.

"Some people stayed and had turned their folding chairs toward the creek. But a lot of people got up and wandered off to get drinks and snacks, or to look for friends to sit with or to use the facilities. It was just starting to get dark by then and little kids were running around waving those glow sticks. It was pretty much mass confusion. It settled down a bit when the fireworks started. But as it seemed we were approaching the finale, some people started gathering up their lawn chairs and blankets and heading to the parking lot to beat the rush.

"Once the fireworks started I can't say I know

where anyone was except Larry Joe, who was sitting on the blanket next to me."

"You don't recall who else was near you? Did your mama and Earl sit with you during the show?"

I remembered what Larry Joe had said about Dave viewing Earl as a suspect and tried my best to sound casual.

"No. The fireworks are a bit too loud for Mama's taste. She had told me before the winners were recognized that she was going home."

"Do you know if Earl left with her?"

"Mama had driven her own car. I don't know when Earl left. I do know he spent a good part of the day directing traffic and helping line cars up in rows where they were parking on the grass."

"Did you actually see him in the parking area or did you just know he'd be working there?"

"I was parked on the festival grounds in one of the reserved spots. I did see him over by the grass parking area when I left just after lunch. I ran by my office for a few minutes to cool off and to pick up some extra judging sheets."

"How long were you gone?"

"About twenty minutes or so, I guess."

"Did you leave the festival area any other time during the day?"

"I drove an older lady in the golf cart over to the Methodist church. As you know, we had set up the fellowship hall as a cooling station for folks to hang out in the air-conditioning and drink bottled water. Since it was a relatively mild day we didn't have any real heat-related emergencies, but some elderly people did take advantage of the cool space."

"How long were you there?"

"I went twice during the day, once to transport the older lady and once to use the facilities, which are a little more comfortable than the porta potties."

"When was the last time you remember seeing Bubba?" Dave asked.

I thought for a moment.

"He was standing next to the stage when they introduced Jennifer as the new Miss Dixie. Everyone clapped, but I remember him whistling and yelling out something like, 'That's our girl,' looking over his shoulder, and giving a smile and a wink to her mama and daddy, who were sitting in the folding chairs just behind him. Carrie looked displeased with his lack of decorum, but no one ever accused Bubba of being a class act."

"Do you recall having a conversation with Bubba at any time during the festival?"

I stared at the wall and tried to visually scroll through the events of the day.

"No, not really," I said. "I spoke to him a couple of times in passing. That morning he shook my hand and thanked me for organizing this year's festival. I think that was after the 5K and just before the judging started for the kudzu jelly competition."

Dave jotted something down on his notepad.

* * *

I was in Dave's office for over an hour before he let me go. Some questions he asked two or three times, slightly rephrasing them each time. As much as he irritated me at times, we were lucky to have someone like Dave as the sheriff of Delbert County. Before coming to Dixie, he had worked with the Metro Nashville Police Department for twelve years, the last few as a homicide detective.

Since I knew Larry Joe was working, if he wasn't still napping, I called Di to see if I could drop by. I was dying to tell someone about Mama's engagement.

I parked in front of Di's trailer and tapped on the unlocked front door before letting myself in.

Di was making strawberry daiquiris in a blender.

"I knew you were supposed to continue your interrogation with Dave this afternoon, so I figured you might like one of these," Di said as I set my purse on the table and plopped down on the sofa.

"Believe it or not, I've got bigger news than a murder investigation," I said. Di turned off the blender and turned to face me.

"Guess who's sporting a great big engagement ring?"

"I give up."

"Virginia Walford, although I guess she'll be Virginia Daniels after the wedding."

"Your mama and Earl are engaged? That's wonderful!" After a pause Di added, "That is wonderful, isn't it?"

"Yeah, I think so," I admitted. "I'm just afraid

my little sister's going to give Mama a hard time about it."

"Emma's so busy with her own family, raising a baby and a preschooler, she shouldn't have time to run your mother's life. What's her problem with Earl, anyway?"

"He's not her daddy."

"That's going to be true of anybody your mama marries," Di said, bringing over a frozen daiquiri and setting it on the coffee table.

"I know. It's ridiculous."

I took a sip of the frosty concoction, which really hit the spot on a hot July day.

"So, have they set a date, and has your mama already got you busy planning the wedding? I expect she'll have some definite ideas about what she wants."

I sat there wordless, staring off into space for a moment. "She *is* going to expect me to plan the wedding, isn't she?" I finally said as the reality of it hit me.

"I think you can count on it," Di said.

The two of us erupted in a fit of giggles as we speculated on some of the outrageous ideas Mama might come up with for her wedding.

Little did I know.

"You want another glassful?" Di asked.

"Give me about a third of a glass more. I'd better pace myself since I have to drive home."

Di ripped open a bag of pretzels and brought them over.

"Here. This will soak up some of the alcohol."

* * *

I left after a couple of hours. On the drive home I was seized by the abject terror of having Mama for a client. This must have been written all over my face because as soon as I walked into the den, where Larry Joe was sitting at the computer, he said, "Did Dave give you a rough time with the questioning?"

"No, it's worse than that. Di pointed out the obvious. Mama is going to expect me to plan her wedding. I don't know why it didn't occur to me right away. Can you imagine Mama as a client? Especially for a wedding," I said.

My head began to throb at the thought of it.

"Actually I had thought of that, but I decided it was probably better not to mention it."

Chapter 3

When I awoke Monday morning, I rolled over and opened a bleary eye to peek at the alarm clock. It was 9:00 AM. I was usually at the office by now, but what's the point of being your own boss if you can't bend the schedule now and then.

I padded down the stairs and into the kitchen. What I needed was coffee. Lots of coffee. I knew Larry Joe had long since left for work. He usually gets to the office at the family trucking business by seven o'clock. I hoped to find that he had left me at least some coffee dregs. To my surprise there was a full pot. He had left a note, saying he had set the timer on the coffeemaker to start brewing at 8:00 AM. He didn't think I'd rouse before then. He was only off by an hour, but the warming plate stays on for two hours, which meant the coffee was still piping hot.

I retrieved a giant mug from the cabinet, filled it

with coffee, and added a splash of milk. I quickly sucked down the contents of the first mug for the caffeine hit. For the second mugful I sat at the kitchen table and savored it as I checked e-mail and messages on my phone. Some mornings I would be disappointed to find no messages. But today I figured no news was good news.

It was a quarter past ten when I pulled into a parking space on the square. My office is above Sweet Deal Realty and accessed via a street-front glass door that opens onto a steep staircase. Before heading up to my office, I stepped into the real estate office. Nathan Sweet, my landlord, was nowhere to be seen, but agent Winette King was at her desk and on the phone. From what I could hear it sounded like she was scheduling a house tour for prospective buyers. She waved and motioned for me to take a seat. Winette looked fresh pressed in a lavender jacket. She was absently fiddling with a pen, drawing attention to her immaculate manicure. I looked at the distressing state of my own fingernails, which I had painted a bright red for July 4th, but which were already starting to peel.

"Mornin', sunshine," Winette said in a singsong voice. "You're late getting in today, even for you. But then you had kind of a busy weekend, what with the festival and the murder and all."

"The murder had absolutely nothing to do with me," I said, feeling peeved that everyone seemed to think my presence at an event somehow invites homicide.

"No, of course not. But still . . . it's funny how you always seem to be on the spot when a body turns up. I'm surprised Sheriff Davidson hasn't hired you to work like one of those hounds that sniffs out corpses. What're they called?"

"Cadaver dogs," I said. "I actually stopped in to share some happy news with you, but I'm not sure I care to anymore," I said, getting up from my chair.

"Oh, don't be that way, Liv. I'm just having fun with you. What's your good news?"

"It's not exactly *my* good news, but I am happy about it. Mama and Earl got engaged."

"Oh, glory be," Winette said, clapping her hands together. "I'm so glad your mama has found her a good man. They're in short supply, you know."

"Yeah, we're very fond of Earl. At least most of us are."

"Uh-oh," Winette said. "Who's not on board with this engagement?"

"Emma. She's always viewed Earl as an intruder trying to take her daddy's place, I'm afraid."

"*Humpf.* You need to set little sister straight right quickly. She's got a husband and two young children, but she thinks your mama should live all by herself in a big, empty house keeping vigil over her daddy's memory. That's nothing but selfish," Winette said, quickly cutting to the heart of the matter, something she has a gift for. "So have they set a date for the wedding?"

"Honestly, I didn't even ask. I was so surprised by the engagement announcement. Earl gave her quite a rock, though, a great big emerald framed with diamonds."

"Ooh, Lordy. Next time I see her I'll have to ask to take a look at it."

"I doubt you'll have to ask."

Before going up to my office, I made a quick stop in the ladies' room. This amenity is included in my rent since there's no restroom upstairs. It's not the most convenient arrangement, but the rent's cheap. I walked out the front door of the real estate office, turned left, walked a few steps, and unlocked the street entrance to my office—which is the only entrance or exit other than the fire escape out back. The green awning over the front door is emblazoned with "Liv 4 Fun." I had to choose a short business name since the plate glass door is the entirety of my street frontage.

I took a seat at the desk in my paneled office with acoustical tile ceiling and checked voicemail. There was a panicked message from Heather Mann, a client for a baby shower coming up this weekend.

"Liv, this is Heather. I'm worried we won't have enough food for the shower. Everyone we invited has RSVP'd that they're coming. And my Aunt Rose is a big eater. Call me back when you have a chance. Thanks."

Click.

I pulled out the folder for the baby shower and looked over the menu and guest list. I knew the planned brunch menu would more than adequately feed a crowd, including a pregnant woman and her ravenous aunt. But I needed to reassure my nervous client, who was dealing with hormonal ups and downs along with the usual hostess anxiety. I decided to hand off that task to my assistant, Holly, who was scheduled to come in around noon. You wouldn't guess it to look at her, with her somewhat eccentric fashion sense, but Holly has a calming effect on people, including me. She could always make me believe that even a seemingly impossible task was doable.

I caught up on some paperwork and printed out some invoices that needed to be sent out. I stuffed and stamped the envelopes and left, locking the door behind me. As I struck out across the town square, heat shimmered in waves above the sidewalk. The day was another scorcher. I paused to drop the invoices in the mailbox in front of the courthouse, before continuing across the one-way street on the opposite side of the courthouse to the diner.

"Hey there, Liv," Mabel said as I stepped up to the counter. Customers and waitresses buzzed past. Town Square Diner was always packed for lunch, with friends, acquaintances, and sometimes even complete strangers sharing tables during the rush. There was a brisk take-out business, as well.

"Hi, Mabel. I see business is booming, as usual. I'd like to order two chef's salads and two large sweet teas to go."

"Sure, hon. You want ranch dressing with that?"

"I'll take one ranch and one bleu cheese."

Mabel retrieved two salads, made fresh that morning, from the under-counter fridge and rang up my bill.

"You tell your mama I'm pleased as punch for her and Earl. They're a cute couple," Mabel said as she handed me change.

"Thank you, I sure will."

I wasn't all that surprised Mabel Cross had already heard about the engagement since nearly half the town passes through her doors each day, but I was looking forward to telling the good news to Holly.

Back in the office, I cleared space on my desk for our lunch. In a couple of minutes I heard Holly clicking up the stairs. She breezed in wearing a black sleeveless top with black and white hound's-tooth capris. Oversized orange sunglasses sat atop her white, pageboy-styled hair, and an orange pedicure peeked out from her strappy white sandals. Holly's fashion vibe could be described as Jackie Kennedy, the Onassis years.

"Awlright, darlin'," Holly said, her *r*'s polished smooth by a proper Southern finishing school. "Let's get to work. Oh, by the way, my congratulations to your mama and Earl. I'm so happy for them."

"Did you run into Mama this morning?" I asked,

feeling a little let down I didn't get to reveal the big news to Holly.

"No, hon. Sylvia called me earlier and mentioned it."

I should have guessed that Mama's friend, Sylvia, had already spread the news like the town crier.

Holly intuited my disappointment. "I'm sorry, darlin', I didn't mean to steal your thunder," she said before adding, "You are pleased about the engagement, aren't you?"

"Yes, I am. Little sister is another story, though. I think Emma is going to need some convincing."

"Your mama can be pretty persuasive."

"That she can," I acknowledged.

After we finished lunch, I filled Holly in on Heather's concern about lack of food for the shower and asked her to make a reassuring phone call. Holly is amazing. By the time she hung up, she had even me wondering if we'd have too much food.

Holly is a dream assistant and one I could never afford if I had to pay her based on her resumé. Fortunately for me, she enjoys the work. She's the widow of a retired admiral and has entertained diplomats and military brass around the world. She's also from an old and moneyed Dixie family. While Holly is completely down to earth, her pedigree reassures some of our snootier clients.

The two of us reviewed the details for the baby shower set for Saturday. We had a meeting scheduled with Heather at 3:30 PM. While Heather's sister, Tiffany, was listed as the hostess on the shower invitations that were sent out, for propriety's sake, Heather is our actual client—the one writing the checks. Tiffany is the official hostess, since it would be considered improper for a mom-to-be to host her own shower. But it was Heather's desire to do a gender-reveal party, and she didn't trust anyone other than her sister to keep her mouth shut about whether it was a boy or a girl until the shower. Plus, Heather said she wanted food other than grocery store cake and some stale mints and mixed nuts, which are standard fare at many church hall showers put on by the ladies' auxiliary.

Many of our clients prefer to let me and my part-time and as-needed staff, which, in addition to Holly, includes Harold the electrician and Kenny the carpenter, both all-around handymen, handle everything. Other clients, like Heather, hire Liv 4 Fun to plan the event and source materials, while they do most of the work themselves. This saves the client a good bit of money. While I enjoy the huge, over-the-top events we put together, I also really enjoy helping clients throw a fabulous party on a very modest budget.

For the shower decorations I had ordered discount-priced supplies and given Heather and Tiffany a short training session on how to put things together. Now Holly and I were going by to check on their progress.

* * *

Tiffany greeted us at the front door and Heather walked behind her, approaching us sway-backed and tottering as if she were being pulled along by the baby in her bulging belly. I couldn't help but worry she might go into labor before or during the shower. I leaned over her stomach to give her a shoulder hug.

She and Tiffany were eager to show us their craft projects. I'm always a little worried at this point. Even though we try to make any decorating projects as simple as possible, some people are just challenged when it comes to cutting or gluing and such. But Heather and Tiffany were rightfully proud. The little favor bags with take-home treats for the guests looked adorable.

The supplies we had given them were heavy-duty white lunch sacks, entwined pink and white ribbon, pale pink cardboard, and darker pink tulle. From those materials they had crafted little tulle tutus, topped by cardboard ballerina tops on the side of each bag. They had punched holes in the tops of the bags and pulled ribbon through the holes so it could be tied into a bow to secure the goodies once they were inside. They had also filled baby food–sized jars with pink and white jelly beans and affixed pink-checked labels that said "Heather's Baby Shower," along with the date. The other items for the gift bags were rubber ducky–shaped soaps, which I'd gotten at a real bargain on clearance from a wholesaler. The sisters had already filled and tied up the bows on all but a couple of the bags.

A fun element of this shower—one that I'd never

done before—is that it would announce that a baby girl is expected. Holly and I were sworn to secrecy—even the grandmothers didn't know yet. So little pink items that would give the secret away, like the ballerina gift bags, would have to be hidden away until the right moment.

We went over the rest of the arrangements for the shower and where everything would be positioned. We told Heather we would be there an hour and fifteen minutes before the shower to help put the finishing touches in place.

After we said our good-byes to Heather and Tiffany, I dropped Holly off by the office to pick up her car and then I started toward home. Just as I pulled into my garage, my phone dinged, alerting me that I had a new text message. It was from Sheriff Dave.

Please e-mail me the names of any professional photographers or videographers who covered any of the events on July 4th, as well as a list of any people you can recall shooting photographs, and especially video. —Thanks, Dave

Gee, thanks, Dave, I thought as I unlocked the back door and stepped into the kitchen.

I sat down at the kitchen table and phoned Di.

"Hi, are you home already?" she said before I could say hello. Caller ID can be both convenient and scary.

I told her about my assignment from Dave.

"Do you know if he's just looking for pictures from around the time of the fireworks show?" I asked.

"No, my understanding is he wants as much information as he can get about who connected with Bubba during the day, as well as who was where around the time of the shooting," Di said. "Terry's calling everybody who gave their name and number, but my guess is Dave wants you to help with at least a partial list of people who took photos but left before the fireworks."

"I'll give it some thought, but I'm guessing half the people there shot pictures, at least with their cell phone cameras. That's going to take the sheriff's office untold hours to wade through."

"Yeah, Dave's already scheduling overtime for Ted and Neal and Terry and sorting out schedules for reserve deputies to work their max hours this month," Di said.

As sheriff of Delbert County, Dave serves a big area with a small staff. Hartville is the largest city in Delbert County and the only one with its own police department. The sheriff's department covers all the unincorporated areas of the county, as well as providing contract coverage to the towns of Dixie and Atford. The sheriff's office is located in Dixie, the county seat. There's a substation in Atford, which could barely even be called a town at this point, but it's still incorporated. Deputy Neal Ford generally operates out of the substation. Deputy Ted Horton and dispatcher Terry Deacon work out of the Dixie office. Dave also depends on a cadre of volunteer reserve deputies. Fortunately, Delbert County has a pretty low crime rate, but when something like a murder happens it's all hands on deck.

"Sounds ambitious. I'll do whatever I can to help."

After I got off the phone with Di I surveyed the contents of the refrigerator to figure out what Larry Joe and I could have for supper. I devised a perfect plan.

"Honey," I said when Larry Joe answered his cell phone. "Could you pick up dinner on your way home?"

"Any requests?" he asked.

"Surprise me," I said.

If he showed up with anything other than plates from Taco Belles or Town Square Diner, I'd actually be surprised. I spent most of the time until Larry Joe got home cleaning the wilted and moldy items out of the fridge, before making a fresh pitcher of sweet tea.

I pulled a notepad out of the junk drawer and had just started on my list of known photographers and videographers from the festival when I heard the garage door open and Larry Joe's truck pulling in. Larry Joe came in with our take-out dinners. I could tell from the bag it was from Taco Belles. No real surprise there.

I poured sweet tea over ice and my husband set Styrofoam containers on the table for each of us—

catfish tacos with chipotle tartar sauce for me and beef fajitas for him.

After we said grace I scribbled a couple more names on my list.

"I see you're taking names."

Larry Joe leaned over and took a look at my notepad.

"Is Roger Martin in trouble?" he asked, squinting his eyes and reading a name off my list.

"That'll be up to the sheriff to decide. He wants me to make a list of everybody I remember shooting video or taking pictures the day of the festival. Along with interviewing witnesses he's got his deputies poring over photos and footage trying to get some kind of timeline about where Bubba was and who he talked to throughout the day."

"That's a tall order," Larry Joe said.

"Yeah. And there's no way it's going to be complete—no matter how many pictures and how much video he gathers."

"No, but I think it's still a clever idea," Larry Joe said. "Most cameras have a time stamp feature and that's a lot more reliable than witness estimates of time or memories about who all was where at any given time."

"True. After dinner I'll finish my list and let you look it over and see if you can think of anybody else to add before I send it to Dave."

Larry Joe told me how his dad had been in an awfully good mood today.

"He's never in a good mood, especially on a

Monday. That old geezer's up to something, I know it," he said.

Daddy Wayne has always been on the crotchety side, but even more so since his heart attack. Larry Joe and his mama have been after my father-in-law to cut back his hours, per doctor's orders. But he's having none of it. Still, I wanted to give him the benefit of the doubt.

"Maybe he's starting to relax a bit now that y'all have hired a new supervisor," I offered.

"Naw. There's more to it than that. I'm going to keep an eye on Dad this week."

After supper Larry Joe wandered into the den to watch TV. I finished my list and had him look it over. After he added a couple of names, I typed the list into an e-mail and uploaded the few photos I shot on Saturday—I had been too busy to take many pictures—and hit SEND.

I was walking to the den to snuggle up next to Larry Joe and watch some mindless TV when my phone buzzed. It was Mama.

"Liv, I just got off the phone with your sister. I'm going to need you to call and try to talk sense to her. She was trying to think up every reason in the world I shouldn't get married or why I should at least hold off on a wedding. Hold off? We haven't even set a date yet."

I'd been hoping Emma would be a grown-up and I wouldn't have to give her a talking-to. Wishful thinking, apparently.

"I'll call her in a day or two after she's had some time to take it in," I said.

"I'd be obliged. Call me after you talk to your sister. Oh, and I'd like us to get together for lunch one day this week if you can, so we can start tossing around some ideas for the wedding. I feel so lucky having a daughter who's a professional planner. Bye."

Lucky wasn't the word that sprang to mind for me.

Chapter 4

It had taken me three nights' sleep to feel rested after the festival on Saturday. The emotional drain of the murder and the ensuing interrogations, in addition to the fatigue of a long day on my feet tending to one mini crisis after another, had left me exhausted. But by Tuesday I was feeling almost normal and even made it to the office by eight o'clock.

I made some phone calls and notes, preparing preliminary plans for a retirement party for the CEO of a local company. I had a teleconference call with the CEO's secretary and the human resources manager, who were in charge of the party, scheduled on Friday.

I heard footsteps on the stairs and assumed it was probably Winette. I looked up to see the sheriff standing in my doorway.

"Liv, could we talk?"

"Dave Davidson, I swear if you badger me with one more question . . . You're going to have to arrest me. I'm done. I do have a job besides being your professional witness, you know."

"It's not about the case. It's personal," he said, hat in hand with his eyes downcast.

I didn't apologize, but I did feel contrite.

"Okay," I said and motioned for Dave to come inside. He skulked into the office and took a seat facing me across the desk. He declined my offer of a Coke or bottled water. He seemed reticent to speak.

"What is it, Dave?"

"Liv, you and I go way back. I mean when I'd spend summers in Dixie with my grandparents, I used to play baseball with Larry Joe and the other guys. And you girls would be sitting in the grass stringing daisies. Remember? And there was that time I smoked one of my granddaddy's cigars and threw up on your book bag."

"I remember," I said. "Good times."

"Anyway, I know I shouldn't ask. It's probably not fair, but . . ." Dave said.

"What? Spit it out."

"Never mind. Forget it."

Men infuriate me. I knew, of course, he wanted to ask me something about Di. But I was afraid for a moment he was just going to drop it.

Finally, he said, "It's about Di. Here's the thing. I'm crazy about her. You know that. But just when it seems like things are good between us, she pushes me away. And she insists we practically sneak around to see each other, as if we have something to be ashamed of. Honestly, sometimes I think she's embarrassed to be seen in public with me. I shouldn't ask, but you *are* her best friend. Has she told you anything that would help me figure out what's going on with her? I'm at a loss here."

I struggled for a moment with my conscience. I didn't want to betray Di's confidence. But she was acting insane and Dave and I did go way back, what with him having barfed on my book bag when I was eleven.

"Honestly, Dave, she doesn't share a lot of details with me about your relationship. But I do know this—Di has some crazy idea that if it gets out around town in a really public way that you two are a couple, it will hurt your reputation or reelection chances or some such."

"Why the hell would she think that?"

"Apparently because her ex is in prison. She thinks that taints her somehow in other people's eyes."

"That's just dumb," Dave said.

"Yeah, well . . ."

"What should I do?"

"I don't know that I'm qualified to give advice."

"That never stopped Dear Abby. Besides, you're happily married. And who else am I going to ask? If you have any suggestions I'd like to hear them," Dave said with pleading eyes.

"Okay, here's what I think. But if you tell Di I said so, I'll never speak to you again."

"Understood."

"I think you need to make some kind of grand romantic gesture. You know, like in *An Officer and a Gentleman* . . ."

"You mean that Richard Gere movie that makes women get all weepy?"

"That's the one. When he walks into the factory in his uniform and sweeps Debra Winger off her feet and carries her out while all her friends are clapping and cheering—*that's* a grand romantic gesture."

He bit his lip, seeming to mull over what I'd said for a long moment.

"If I stopped Di on her mail route and picked her up and carried her to the cruiser, people would probably think she was under arrest."

This clueless man is a detective, I thought to myself.

"I'm not saying you should do what Richard Gere did. You'll have to come up with your own romantic gesture. And I don't know specifically what that would be. But if I were to dream something up and tell you what to do, Di would never buy it anyway. It'll have to come straight from your heart and fit the moment.

"Just give it some thought. And don't you dare let on to Di that I told you about her crazy insecurities where her ex-husband is concerned."

"No, no, of course not. Thanks, Liv. I think."

Dave stood up with a puzzled look before leaving,

and I could hear him slowly descending the stairs. I felt a growing knot in my stomach, hoping I'd done the right thing.

About noon I decided to amble down the block to the farmer's market on the corner, thinking I should eat something healthy for lunch for a change. I ran into Rosemary Dell coming out of the market with a sackful of produce, baby lettuce leaves peeking out the top of the bag.

"Hi, Rosemary. I see you're buying some veggies."

"Yes, Suzanne has some beautiful vegetables right now, peak of season. Have you recovered from the festival yet? That must have been a long day for you as events coordinator."

"It wore me out, but I'm okay now. How about you? There's been quite a bit of grumbling about the pageant results. But, I'm sure you've gotten an earful about that."

"Goodness yes. What a mess. But I had a long conversation with the judge I saw talking to Bubba Rowland and he flatly denies that his decision was influenced in any way. And I went over all his judging sheets and everything looks right."

"So you're satisfied everything was on the up-and-up?"

"As satisfied as I can be. Of course, that doesn't mean everyone else is satisfied, but I can't help that. Cassie and her family haven't filed a formal complaint about the results. And honestly, with Bubba's untimely demise I think it would be better just to let things be. Nobody would feel good about taking Jennifer's crown away from her under the circumstances. But Cassie will still meet the age eligibility requirements to enter again next year and, between you and me, I plan to ask an anonymous benefactor to pay her entry fee since her family doesn't have a lot of money."

"That sounds like a good plan all around," I said.

Rosemary waved to someone down the block and said a hasty good-bye. I entered the market and looked over the many enticing choices on offer. I settled on a luscious-looking apple and a small wedge of goat cheese from a local farm.

"Hi, Liv. Looks like you're planning to eat lunch at your desk today. Busy?" Suzanne Bagley asked as I placed the items on the counter next to the register.

"There's always plenty to do when you have your own business, as you well know. But honestly, I'm just trying to eat something healthier for a change."

"I hear you. By the way, I was so pleased to hear about your mama and Earl's engagement."

"Thanks, Suzanne. We're very fond of Earl. He's a brave man to take on my mama."

Suzanne tossed her head back as she laughed.

"So what's her engagement ring look like?"

"It's a great big emerald surrounded by little diamonds—pretty impressive."

"Good for her. Extend my congratulations to her and Earl, will you?"

"Sure thing. Thanks, Suzanne."

I went back to my office and pulled a package of rye crackers out of the desk drawer to go with my cheese and apple. After lunch, I gave Mama a call and arranged to meet with her the next day to get the ball rolling on planning her wedding. I figured there was no point in putting off the inevitable.

Chapter 5

I arrived at Mama's a day later and slipped in through the kitchen door, which is never locked. The creaking of the back door brought Mama stepping lively from the family room. She gave me a hug.

She fixed us bacon, lettuce, and tomato sandwiches—with tomatoes fresh from her garden—homemade pimento cheese on celery stalks, some grapes, and fresh-baked brownies.

I'd initially planned to ask her to meet me at a restaurant, some neutral ground as opposed to her home turf. But Mama talks loudly and I didn't really want other people to hear every outrageous idea she might propose.

"I've jotted down a few preliminary ideas," she said as she pulled a folded stack of notebook paper as thick as a deck of cards from her apron pocket and placed it on the table beside her plate.

I tried not to look worried.

Mama put some coffee on to brew just before we sat down to lunch. She was pretty quiet as we ate, but after she'd wiped the brownie crumbs from her chin and poured us each a cup of coffee, she launched into a rather long list of "preliminary ideas."

"Earl and I both have already had the big, traditional church wedding, so we want to do something different the second time around."

Mama said she wanted to have the wedding on Earl's property. He has a farmhouse with a large wraparound porch, a big barn where he stores tractors, and a large man-made pond with an island in the middle of it. It truly was a lovely spot for an outdoor wedding.

"The pond is really the best feature of the property, so I think we should play that up. I'm thinking we should have one of those gondolas ferry Earl and me and the minister out to the little island. It's too small for a crowd, so the guests will have to watch the ceremony from the banks.

"I'd like the bottom of the boat to be wide enough that Earl and I can stand side by side as the gondolier rows us across. I think that would look elegant. Plus, if we sit down, the back of our clothes will get wrinkly. And wrinkles aren't attractive.

"Now I suppose we'll need some kind of sound system on the island, so the guests can hear us exchange our vows," she said, staring off into space and tapping the capped end of a ballpoint pen against her chin. "It doesn't need to be anything big or elaborate, though."

Mama talks loudly enough that people could probably hear her in the next county without a sound system, but Earl and the minister might need some amplification, so I jotted down "sound system" in my notebook.

"Oh, and I want some swans swimming in the lake. I've always thought swans were so classy. The shore kind of slopes down to the lake, so we'll probably need some planks or a little platform on the bank to make a flat surface to put out some chairs for the guests. Just those folding slatted wooden chairs will be fine, nothing too fancy.

"And if the front of the gondola had some kind of carved figurehead on it, you know, kind of like a Viking boat, I think that would be a nice touch. Don't you think so, Liv?"

I had refilled my coffee cup a few times while Mama had droned on for what seemed like hours. I'd sucked down so much coffee I could barely blink. Sugar. I needed sugar. I helped myself to another brownie, sat back down at the table, and forced the corners of my lips to curl up into a smile.

Mama moved on to the reception.

She envisioned refreshments on the expansive porch, with people circulating around the porch and through the house. After that, there would be a dance in the barn.

"We'd like the music to be a mix of lively two-stepping, some slow dances, and some line dancing—so no one feels left out if they come stag. Fun and casual, but classy," she said emphatically. "I'm not talking about a hoedown in overalls and flour sack dresses. And there will be a live band, naturally."

Naturally.

"Liv, you haven't been saying much. You're the pro, so jump in here with any ideas."

I cleared my throat and searched for the right words.

"Like I told you on the phone, Mama, the first meeting is really just a chance for clients to tell me their vision. From this conversation I'll try to create a plan that incorporates all the things that are most important to the client as best I can.

"You haven't mentioned how many people you plan to invite. Since you're talking about using the house and porch for the reception, I assume you'll want to keep the guest list somewhat intimate."

"*Hmm*, I suppose we can comfortably handle about sixty people," she said.

I was relieved. This was a much lower number than I had expected. "That sounds doable."

I gathered up my notes and told her I thought we had made a good start.

"We can talk more specifically about food, and decorations and invitations and such, later on. You should start working on a guest list, and be sure to get a list from Earl."

Mama and I said our good-byes and I drove back to the office. After getting settled at my desk and returning a couple of phone calls. I typed up my notes on Mama's wedding wish list and e-mailed it to Holly. I thought about discussing it with her over the phone, but wasn't sure if I was ready to actually say some of the items on the list out loud just yet.

I had asked Holly to feel free to get back to me with any initial thoughts or comments she had. In a few minutes an e-mail notification from Holly popped up on my phone screen.

Just remember, Liv, pretty much anything is possible with enough time to source and plan.

I think she was trying to make me feel better.

In a minute, another e-mail from Holly came through.

Have your mama and Earl settled on a date?

The answer was "no." A date, even a tentative one, was something Mama had refused to commit to when we met. This caused me some concern.

I tried with limited success to put Mama and Earl's colorful wedding plans out of my mind and concentrate on other projects. I called the bakery to confirm the specialty items for the baby shower this weekend. I phoned Heather to make sure everything was going smoothly on her part—and to see how her doctor's appointment went and if he thought the baby would hold off on her grand entrance until after Saturday.

I was ready to pack it in for the day when my cell phone buzzed. It was Larry Joe.

"Liv, I'm afraid I won't be home for dinner. Dad and I are taking a prospective client out to Red's

Steakhouse. I'm hoping some red wine and a juicy porterhouse are going to pay off with some new business."

"Okay, honey," I said. "I'll keep my fingers crossed."

I had no intention of cooking dinner for one. Chinese food suddenly sounded like a winner. I phoned Di and invited her to join me, if she didn't have plans for supper.

"That sounds great, if you don't mind waiting until after my yoga class."

"No, that's fine."

"You got wine, or should I bring some?" she asked.

"Actually, we have a couple of bottles of Riesling in the fridge. I'll see you in a while."

I killed some time wrapping up a bit of paperwork and then phoned the restaurant and placed my order. They said it would be ready for pickup in about fifteen minutes.

I ran in and paid for my takeout order and drove home. The aroma of garlic and ginger was intoxicating. I was starved by the time I made it back to the house. Di pulled into the driveway just behind me.

"Hey," she said, catching up to me in the garage. "What's Larry Joe up to for dinner?"

"He and his dad are wining and dining a potential client. Are you seeing Dave tonight?" I asked as I opened the door and stepped into the kitchen with Di right behind me.

"I doubt it," she said. "He has that whole murder investigation thing going on. I talked to him briefly and he said he thought they were making progress. So I guess that's good news."

After pouring each of us a glass of chilled wine, I joined Di at the kitchen table and we dug into the takeout containers.

"Oh," I said, holding up my hand as I swallowed a bite of garlic ginger chicken. "Guess who I saw walking hand in hand into the Chinese place?"

"Who?"

"Ted and Daisy."

"So they're still an item, huh?"

"I guess so," I said. "Doesn't Dave ever mention them?"

"Hah. Can you imagine Dave talking about Ted's love life?"

Di and I both laughed at the suggestion. The two of us had played at least a small role in getting the deputy and an odd little wallflower named Daisy together last fall.

After dinner we moved the conversation, along with the second wine bottle and glasses, into the den. Di plopped down in the recliner and I kicked off my shoes and stretched out on the sofa.

"Planning any interesting parties these days?" Di asked.

"I'm not sure interesting is the word for it, but I met with Mama today and listened for an hour and a half while she described the dream wedding she envisions for herself and Earl."

"Do tell."

I gave Di a rundown of the major points on Mama's wish list.

"A ferryman with a Viking gondola, an elegant hoedown," Di said between snorts and unladylike guffaws. "And your mother and Earl exchanging vows on their own little fantasy island." She broke down laughing again.

"Don't forget I have to somehow set up a sound system on that fantasy island in the middle of a pond—stocked with swans."

"Oh, stop it," she said, doubled over. "My ribs are hurting."

I sat up and poured some more wine into my glass.

"Feel free to drink straight from the bottle," she said.

I shot her a withering glare.

"Listen," she said, after regaining her composure. "At some point you'll have to guide your mom toward some sensible wedding plans."

"You've met my mother, right?"

"Maybe you can enlist Earl's help. He's a sensible man."

"I'd always thought so. But he did ask my mama to marry him."

Di refilled her glass and chinked it against mine. "Here's to the happy couple," she said.

The wine kept flowing as we tried to think of even more ridiculous ideas for the wedding—which wasn't easy.

After a while I heard Larry Joe come in from the garage. He followed the laughter into the den.

"Evening, ladies. Sounds like y'all are having a good time."

"Yeah, it's been fun," Di said, rising from the recliner. "But I think I'm going to call it a night." She walked through the doorway into the kitchen.

Spying the two empty wine bottles on the end table, Larry Joe said, "You need a ride home?"

"No, I'm fine. Your wife drank her share and most of mine."

"Is something wrong?" he asked, casting a look of concern my way.

"Your mother-in-law gave Liv her wish list for the wedding," Di said before bursting into laughter again.

"I can hear you, you know," I said.

"Good night, you two," Di said as she made her exit, still giggling.

Larry Joe lifted my legs up a bit, sat on the sofa, and plopped my calves onto his lap.

"I'm cutting off your alcohol, lady. Looks like you've had enough," he said, giving me a little slap on the thigh. "You think you can make it up the stairs?"

"Sure. Nothing to it," I said, placing my thumb against my finger and making a failed attempt at snapping.

I was only slightly unsteady. With his hands on my shoulders, Larry Joe walked behind me, guiding me up the steps.

After escorting me to the bed, he disappeared into the bathroom. The phone on the nightstand rang. We rarely get calls on the landline, so I picked it up without thinking.

It was my sister.

"Hi, Emma," I said wearily.

"How come you didn't call to warn me about Mama's engagement? Engagement, hah—the very idea is ludicrous."

"I don't see that there's anything ludicrous, or surprising, about Mama and Earl getting engaged. Mama's been widowed for more than four years and she and Earl have been spending time together steady for the past two years. What's surprising is that you've chosen to remain oblivious to reality."

I don't usually speak so harshly to my little sister, so maybe it was the wine talking.

I guess she was taken aback since she was quiet for a long moment.

"What's realistic about Mama getting married at her age? She had a long, happy marriage—more than forty years. That should be enough for her."

"Emma, Mama may not be a spring chicken, but she doesn't exactly have one foot in the grave, either. And you don't get to decide what's enough for her. You're being just plain selfish."

"Am I? I'm just trying to preserve my daddy's memory for my children. I don't want them growing up calling some other man 'Granddaddy.'"

"Emma, you're not preserving Daddy's memory for the kids. They have no memories of him. He died before they were born. That's just the sad truth. You're trying in some misguided way to preserve Daddy's memory for yourself. So you expect Mama to keep vigil over his memory and live in a big house by herself, while you live in a home filled with the love of your husband and two young children. And I call that selfish."

She hung up.

The last time I remember Emma hanging up on me was when she and Hobie were engaged and I told her I thought he was a horse's patoot. I'd had to eat those words, but I had no intention of taking back what I'd said about Mama and Earl.

Larry Joe walked in and sat down on the side of the bed.

"I couldn't help overhearing some of that," he said, reaching across and taking hold of my hand.

"You think I was a little tough on Emma?"

"Maybe. But I think someone needs to be a little tough with Emma, and your Mama shouldn't have to deal with that. She'll come around."

I hoped he was right, but I had my doubts.

Chapter 6

Thursday I woke up to a throbbing headache. After two aspirin and a Diet Coke I took a cool shower—the weather forecast was calling for temps in the upper 90s. I ate a piece of toast and grabbed another Diet Coke for the road. I drove slowly to the office with the air conditioner on full blast. Usually, I stop in the real estate office to say hello, but I wasn't feeling all that sociable.

I finished up the itemized invoice for my work on the Dixie Fourth of July festival to turn in to the mayor's office. The board would meet Tuesday night and I wanted to be sure my bill was on the list for approval. I felt that I'd more than earned that check.

After placing the bill in an envelope, I was just about to run it over to city hall when my cell phone buzzed. Caller ID showed it was my mother. Against my better judgment I answered anyway.

Mama was rattling on a mile a minute, but she

was boohooing so loudly I couldn't make out what she was saying. All I could decipher was something about Earl and "I can't believe it."

She was so upset I could only speculate that Earl had had a lucid moment and broken off their engagement. I told her I'd come right over. My mama can be a drama queen at times, but a broken engagement truly would be a big deal and I couldn't stand the thought of anybody breaking her heart.

I drove the few blocks to her house, located on the opposite side of the town square from where Larry Joe and I live. I hurried into the house and didn't have any trouble finding Mama since I could hear her sobs as soon as I opened the door. I walked through to the den and found her lying facedown on the sofa, soaking a blue chenille pillow with her tears.

I sat down on the end of the sofa by her feet and patted her gently on the back. She sat up and blew her nose, honking into a wad of Kleenex. I gave her a moment to compose herself.

"Mama, you were so upset I couldn't understand much of what your were saying on the phone. What happened?"

"Sheriff Davidson has lost his mind—that's what happened. He marched Earl out of here in handcuffs after saying he was arresting him for murder. Murder—can you imagine! I should've stopped him. I should've pushed his sassy butt onto the sofa and sat on him until he came to his senses."

I brought up that image in my mind's eye for a moment.

"But I was in shock and Earl was talking all calmly, telling me everything was going to be okay. I just can't believe it. The law waltzed in here and hauled off my *fee-AHN-say* like he was a common criminal."

She started tearing up again.

"Mama, tell me exactly what Dave said. Did he say he was taking Earl in for questioning, or arresting him on suspicion of murder?"

"When I opened the front door, the sheriff said he had a warrant for Earl's arrest. He waved some paper in my face and pushed past me. He said something to Earl and then told the deputy to read him his rights. I ran over and hugged Earl's neck and he was telling me to be calm, that it would be all right. Then the sheriff and the deputy ripped him from my arms and took him away," she said before splaying herself across the sofa and placing the back of her hand to her forehead.

She started to cry, going limp for a moment. Then she suddenly sat up straight as if she had a steel rod in her spine.

"Liv, you and I know dang well Earl Daniels never killed anybody, not even somebody like Bubba Rowland, who probably needed killing. You've been able to steer the sheriff in the right direction a couple of times in the past when he had his sights set on an innocent person. I need you to do that for me now."

"Mama, I'll do what I can, of course, but . . ."

Before I could finish, she took me by the hands, looked earnestly into my eyes and said, "I hate to ask you to get involved in this, but your mama's future happiness depends on it."

No pressure there.

"And I'm sure you've been worried that I might be getting a little carried away with the wedding plans. But I swear to you on a stack of Bibles, if you clear Earl's name we'll have just a small, simple wedding. It won't be any trouble at all for you."

I knew Mama's idea of a simple wedding might mean settling for one swan instead of a flock. But the fact that she made the offer let me know how desperate she must be feeling.

I gave her a big hug. "You just leave it to me, Mama." I pulled back and gave her a stern look. "And I mean that. You leave it to *me* and behave yourself. The first thing we have to do is get a lawyer and see if we can get Earl released on bail. I'll have Larry Joe call Bill Scott, the attorney for McKay Trucking. He doesn't practice criminal defense, but he'll know who we should talk to.

"I'd better get going and see what I can find out," I said, rising from the sofa. I gave Mama one last admonition to lay low for now, knowing it would be a temporary reprieve, at best.

I called Larry Joe from the car and filled him in on Earl's arrest. Within fifteen minutes he called back saying that Bill Scott had a friend in Memphis who was a top-notch defense attorney and that he would phone him personally. A little over an hour later the attorney was on his way from Memphis to meet with Earl.

I had gone back to my office, thinking work would keep my mind occupied. Not to mention, I had a lot of items to check off my list for the baby shower this weekend.

After I had talked to Larry Joe the first time, I had called my mother-in-law to let her know what was going on. She had offered to go over and be with Mama, for which I was thankful. Miss Betty is a kind and sensible person, who seems to exert a certain calming influence on my mother.

In a bit, I called Holly, who exerts a certain calming influence on me. I told her about Earl's arrest and that I might need to lean heavily on her for the baby shower, depending on what happened with Earl.

"Awlright, darlin'," she said. "Don't you worry about a thing."

The district attorney didn't seem to think Earl was a danger to the general public, so he didn't object when bail was set at $250,000. Fortunately, it wasn't a problem for Earl to post bail out of his retirement savings.

I had called Mama to let her know that Earl would be released on bail shortly and that Larry Joe and I would pick him up at the jail. But before we returned Earl to Mama, we detoured by our house. I wanted to get as much information from Earl as I could without Mama interrupting constantly.

We settled Earl into the recliner in our den and Larry Joe poured some Jack Daniels over ice and handed it to him. I wondered if Earl's line of Daniels was any relation to Jack's, but decided not to ask. After letting Earl sip on his whiskey for a minute and offering to fix him something to eat, an offer which he declined, I started with the obvious questions.

"Earl, I know there was a long-running feud of sorts between you and Bubba. But I know Dave well enough to know he wouldn't arrest you for murder based solely on that. What kind of evidence does he think he has against you?"

"He never told me. But he kept asking me a lot of questions about my rifle, so I'm thinking that must be the key thing."

"Did he get a search warrant and confiscate your gun?" Larry Joe asked.

"Didn't have to. He asked me on Tuesday if he could take in my rifle from the gun rack in my truck to compare ballistics on the bullet that killed Bubba—and I gave him my permission."

Larry Joe threw his hands in the air and paced back and forth a few times.

"Why in the world would you do that?"

"That's just what that attorney asked me. I guess the answer is, I didn't kill Bubba so I didn't feel the need to hide anything."

"Earl, why did you have the rifle in your rack?" Larry Joe asked. "It's not hunting season."

"My brother-in-law has been having some coyote trouble. They've gotten some of his chickens more than once lately."

"Okay, so the rifle was in the gun rack in your truck in the grassy lot where you were helping with parking. Were you ever away from the parking lot during the day for any significant length of time?" I asked.

"Yeah, I left for lunch," he said.

"Okay, so who was watching the lot while you were gone? Maybe they broke into your truck and took the rifle."

"Nope. Don't think so," Earl said.

"Why not?" Larry Joe asked.

"Because I took my truck with me when I went to have lunch with your mama," he said, looking over to me.

I could tell Earl wasn't going to make this easy.

"Do you remember seeing anybody loitering in the general vicinity of your truck or ducking into the woods?"

"Nope. But it wouldn't make much difference."

"Why not?" Larry Joe said. I could tell he was trying his very best to sound patient.

"'Cause I always lock my truck."

"You could have forgotten to lock it this once," I offered.

"Nope. I didn't forget," he said.

I decided to approach this from a different angle.

"Earl, did you see anybody passing through or near

that parking area around the time of the fireworks? Specifically, did you see Webster Flack or Lynn or Cassie Latham or Nonie Jones?" I asked, tossing out a few possible suspects.

"I did see Lynn Latham leaving just before the fireworks, even waved at her. But she told the sheriff it wasn't her," Earl said.

"Did Leonard see her?" I asked, referring to the man I had seen working the parking area with Earl.

"No. He'd left already. His sciatica was giving him grief, so I told him to go on home and I'd manage without him."

Earl turned to Larry Joe and asked, "Could I trouble you for another splash of whiskey? Then I'd better be heading out before Virginia starts to worry."

It was getting late and I knew Earl'd had a rough day.

"You can bring that whiskey with you, if you want, and I'll run you over to Mama Walford's," Larry Joe said.

I couldn't help wondering what Larry Joe was going to call Mama when she changed her name from Walford to Daniels.

The two men started toward the kitchen. Earl paused in the doorway and looked back at me.

"Virginia got all excited telling me about the wedding plans you two are cooking up. Do me a favor, Liv, and keep your mama busy with wedding planning so she's not worrying herself over me. Give her whatever she wants and I'll write the checks. I just want her to be happy."

They left and I could feel hot tears spilling over my lower lashes. Earl wanting Mama to have the wedding of her dreams—her crazy, outlandish dreams—was just about the sweetest thing I'd ever heard and it made me want to give him a big hug. Knowing that he was going to do absolutely nothing to help me rein her in made me want to wring his neck.

Since I often have these kinds of conflicted feelings where Mama is concerned, maybe she and Earl really were perfect for each other.

Chapter 7

Friday morning I parked on the square in front of my office. When I got out of the car, I could see through the front window that Winette was sitting at her desk. I decided to pop in for some coffee and a chat, if she had the time.

"Mornin', glory," she said as I walked in, jangling the bell on the door. Winette is definitely a morning person.

"Good morning. Can I steal some of your coffee?"

"There's a fresh pot. Help yourself."

Next to the sink and counter that housed the coffeemaker, there was a gleaming stainless steel logo on the wall for Residential Rehab. RR is a worthy nonprofit that brings together volunteers to do house repairs and maintenance for the elderly and disabled in our community. Winette is its chairperson and tireless advocate. I was especially proud of the logo that Winette's son, Marcus, a college student studying architecture, had designed. I had coordinated with a local fabricator to donate his time to fashion the stainless steel sign from Marcus's design and Mr. Sweet paid for the materials. Since Winette often holds RR board meetings, as well as meetings with volunteers and benefactors here, it was the perfect spot for the sign.

I poured my coffee and took a seat in the chair facing Winette's desk.

"How's your mama holding up?" she asked.

"Pretty good under the circumstances. Fortunately, Earl was able to make bail pretty quickly. I don't think Mama would have handled it well if he were locked up right now."

"I don't for a minute believe Earl Daniels is a murderer, but I know Sheriff Davidson must have had some kind of evidence before he'd arrest him."

"Unfortunately, it appears Earl's rifle was the murder weapon. Since there was a well-known and long-running feud between Earl and Bubba, somebody decided to use that to frame Earl for murder."

"*Mmm-hmm.* I sure do hope the sheriff can get to the bottom of things in a hurry."

"You and me, too. Winette, I've been meaning to ask your take on the proposed development that Webster Flack and his crowd are so dead set against. What do you think about it?"

"I don't have an opinion on the conservation aspect. All I know is that the city attorney said the development won't violate conservation areas or protected wildlife habitats—at least from a legal perspective. I *can* tell you from a real estate perspective, I have some doubts," she said.

"What do you mean?"

"It's too big, for one thing. When you add together the larger single-family homes, the zero lot lines, and the condos, I think it's more units than they'll be able to sell in ten years."

"Are they going to build in phases, filling up as they go?" I asked.

"My understanding, and I could be wrong on some of this, is that they plan to build the condominiums and a good number of the zero-lot-line houses on spec and then custom build the single-family homes as the lots sell.

"But it's not just the housing. It's a mixed-use development, meaning there's a retail component as well. And I'm all for having convenient shopping where it makes sense. But again, the plans don't add up to me. They're proposing a coffee shop, a dry cleaner, a bakery, and a car wash to start, with other stores possibly later on," Winette said.

"You don't think that will work?"

"I don't know about the coffee shop, but most people who live in this development are going to be commuting to work, some nearby, but many to Hartville and Memphis. People might drive through for coffee on the way to work in the mornings, but they're not likely to hang out and buy a second or third cup. We already have two dry cleaners in town, and most people drop off and pick up dry cleaning on their way to and from work. I guess some folks might switch to using the one closer to their house, but a lot of people, me included, are pretty loyal to their dry cleaner when they find one that does a good job. And car washes are small-margin businesses for profits. And lots of people around here just use a garden hose and wash their own cars anyway.

"I don't know. It just doesn't sound like something that would fly around here. And I can tell you, confidentially of course, that Mr. Sweet didn't invest and you know that man never misses a chance to make a dime, which tells me he doesn't think it's a sound investment. It makes me wonder if the developer is just incompetent or up to something shady."

"Will Sweet Deal Realty be involved in selling the properties?"

"No, and as far as I know neither will any of the other local real estate agencies. The developer has a real estate broker's license."

The phone rang and Winette answered a call. I waved and walked out the front door. Strolling next door I thought about what Winette had just told me. Bubba being heavily invested in what Mr. Never-Misses-a-Deal Sweet deemed an unsound investment was puzzling. And I couldn't help wondering if it had some connection to why Bubba was killed.

* * *

I went upstairs to my office and tried to immerse myself in work to get my mind off of Earl's arrest and Mama's broken heart, at least for a little bit.

I had a conference call scheduled for early in the afternoon that I needed to prepare for. Phillip Clenk, the CEO of a local company, was retiring in late fall and the staff wanted to put together a big send-off for him. There had been a few e-mail exchanges with the CEO's administrative assistant, but this would be our first conversation.

I'd looked at the company's Web site to get some sense of the company's style and some background on the retiring boss. All I was able to discern was that the company seemed conservative and that the CEO was approximately the same age as Methuselah. Not very helpful, but I felt certain I could scratch potato sack races off the list of possible party activities.

The administrative assistant, Miss Payne, brought the human resources director, Hal Banks, into the teleconference call. After introductions, I told them to call me Liv and Hal was comfortable with being on a first-name basis. Miss Payne preferred to be called Miss Payne.

Since Miss Payne was a buttoned-down type and was clearly in charge of the party arrangements, I decided to take my cues and clues from her.

"Mrs. McKay, Liv, Mr. Clenk is a serious and accomplished man and what we're looking for is a very dignified affair to mark his retirement. Wouldn't you agree, Mr. Banks?"

Not surprisingly he agreed with everything she said and I got the feeling he was just there to take notes. I could tell this party was going to be a lot of fun.

There would be a dinner—nothing spicy, because Mr. Clenk has a delicate constitution. There would be a PowerPoint presentation highlighting his many accomplishments. And there would be tasteful gag gifts to add a touch of "whimsy."

After Miss Payne ended the call, I phoned Holly to give her an update.

"I just got off the phone with the CEO's secretary. Her instructions for the retirement party are clear. There will be no fun allowed. She basically wants a wake."

"Even a wake can be fun if there's enough alcohol on offer," Holly said.

"I don't see that happening on this one, but we'll hope for the best. I did ask if Mr. Clenk had any pastimes he enjoyed outside of work, looking for something to grab hold of."

"And?"

"He collects stamps. Any ideas?"

"Let me think it over and I'll get back to you," she said.

I wrapped things up at the office and turned my thoughts to Earl's predicament.

I intended to grill Dave about arresting Earl, but I knew if I stormed into the sheriff's office he'd just ignore me. I called Di and she suggested it would be better to talk to him away from his lawman lair, where he's in charge. She said that he was coming over to her place in an hour and that I should "drop by" shortly thereafter to have a go at him.

I wrapped things up at the office, keeping one eye on the clock, anxious to put Dave on the ropes. In an hour, I locked up and drove over to Di's place. After I tapped on the door, Di let me in and I tore into Dave without bothering to exchange pleasantries first.

"Dave, you can't actually believe that Earl killed Bubba Rowland. I understand that you'd need to bring him in for formal questioning, but to charge him with murder is ridiculous."

"Look, Liv, I know you're very fond of Earl, that he's practically family—I like him, too. But I can't ignore the evidence. Ballistics tests show his rifle is the murder weapon."

"I know Earl gave you permission to test the rifle," I said. "But how come you zeroed in on his rifle as the possible murder weapon to begin with? Was it just a fishing expedition?"

"No, several witnesses remembered seeing a rifle in Earl's truck and it was parked beside the woods where the killer was most likely positioned when he shot Bubba."

"Earl's truck was parked all day at the festival. Anybody could have taken the rifle out of it."

"It's not that simple," Dave said. "Earl insists he always locks the truck and there were no signs of a break-in."

"So he forgot for once, or somebody—maybe somebody at his company—had a key made or took his spare."

"Maybe. But that he had a rifle in his gun rack is a little suspicious in and of itself. People don't usually keep a gun inside their truck outside of hunting season," Dave said.

"Earl explained that, too. His brother-in-law has been having coyote trouble. They've recently gotten into the chicken coop—more than once."

"That's what he says," Dave said. "But there are other problems with his story."

"Like what?"

"You know I don't have to talk to you about the case, don't you? Probably shouldn't even be discussing it," he said.

"Is this the part where you tell me to butt out and mind my own business, because I think we both know that's not happening. Like you said, Earl's practically family."

"Okay, okay," Dave said. "Just calm down, take a seat, and I'll walk you through the crux of it. His attorney already knows this anyway."

I propped my bottom against the edge of the dining table and crossed my arms. That was as relaxed and calm as I could manage at the moment.

"His truck was parked right next to the woods where the shooter was when he fired at Bubba. Earl worked that area, helping with traffic, and Leonard Cates worked with him most of the afternoon. But just before the fireworks started, Earl told Leonard to go on home, that he could handle it, thereby eliminating a witness."

"Leonard's sciatica was acting up," I said. "He was

in a lot of pain, so Earl told him to go home. I'm sure Leonard confirmed that. How could Earl possibly have planned for Leonard's sciatica to flare up so he could get him out of the way?"

"Maybe Leonard's sciatica flares up with regularity, maybe it just provided a convenient excuse. The fact remains that Earl dismissed a witness shortly before the shooting. And Lynn Latham, the person he claims to have seen and waved to, and who could provide Earl at least a partial alibi, says she doesn't remember seeing him," Dave said.

"Maybe she doesn't want to admit to being anywhere near those woods at the time of the murder because she's a suspect," I said. "She had good reason to want Bubba dead. She believed he caused her daughter to lose the Miss Dixie pageant; she was overheard by witnesses confronting him about it. And the winner of the Miss Dixie Beauty Pageant gets entry into the Miss Tennessee Star Teen pageant, which, with her talent, could possibly land her a recording contract in Nashville."

"She may have had motive, but how did she retrieve Earl's gun without him seeing her? Earl said himself that he saw her leave," Dave said. "And getting back to motive, Earl definitely has a strong one. There were plenty of people who didn't like Bubba, but most people don't commit murder because someone rubs them the wrong way. Bubba's activities on the council and planning commission may have been costing Earl a substantial amount of money—Earl certainly believed so. And construction in the area has been pretty slow for a couple of years. Providing materials for this new development could put a lot of money in somebody's pocket."

"Or maybe, because Earl and Bubba had a long-running and public rivalry, somebody decided Earl would be the perfect person to frame for murder."

"Earl had motive and opportunity, and his rifle is the murder weapon. Some others may have had motive, but there's no evidence that anyone else had the opportunity. I had to arrest Earl. It's up to the D.A. and the grand jury now."

"So you're just going to stop looking for the real killer?"

"Liv, you—both of you"—he shot Di a look—"should know me better than that. Ted and I will continue to check out every lead. We're still digging through photos and videos. But some of that photo evidence has already confirmed that Earl's rifle was in the rack in his truck earlier in the day, but late in the afternoon it was gone."

"Do those photos show who was around Earl's truck in the afternoon?"

"That's one of the things we're specifically looking for," Dave said. "Unfortunately, it's not like we're looking at a constant stream of surveillance footage from a security camera. It's just random photos and video shot by eventgoers who have turned them in as we requested. Some of them are time stamped; some aren't. We're doing our best to put together a timeline."

"So what about these photos showing Earl's truck?"

"Some of the pictures were taken of a vintage Corsair that was parked directly across from Earl's truck earlier in the afternoon. The guy who took them said he has been looking to buy a Corsair to restore. Earl's truck is in the background of some of the photos, and they clearly show the gun in the rack. There's also some video shot by a man of his wife with the grandkids shortly before dark. They were mainly coming for the fireworks but wanted to buy the little ones some glow sticks and junk food before the show started. Grandma wanted pictures of the kids in their matching outfits before they got cotton candy or whatnot all over them. So they shot some footage in the parking lot as soon as they got out of the car. They were also parked in the row across from Earl's truck and their video shows from two different angles that the rifle was not in the rack at that time."

"So Earl was toting a rifle around and nobody noticed? Why would he take it out of the truck before he intended to use it?"

"I can only speculate about that," Dave said. "But he could have taken it out of the truck at a convenient time when nobody was around and hidden the rifle in some brush in the woods. We do know Earl had a digital camera on him with a telephoto lens. He said he had been shooting some photos and hoped to get some nice ones of the fireworks. But looking through a zoom lens would also have allowed him to keep track of Bubba. When he saw

Bubba heading for the porta potty, he could have seized upon the opportunity to shoot him during the fireworks when the sound of the rifle blast would be masked by the explosions. He could have entered the woods, retrieved the rifle, which had a scope on it, aimed and fired, then slipped out and placed the rifle back in the truck."

"That's nothing but a load of bull crap," I said, so angry I could feel myself shaking.

"I've got to get back to work," Dave said, getting up from the sofa and putting on his hat. "Liv, I know you're not going to let this go. But Earl has an attorney, a good one I might add. Share any information you think will help Earl with his lawyer and let him build a defense. And if you run across any real evidence, you had better tell me about it right away."

Di opened the door for him to leave. Dave touched her arm gently, and she flinched.

I slid into a dining chair. She sat down across from me at the blond wood table.

"Things don't look good for Earl, do they?"

"Do you want me to be encouraging or honest?" Di asked.

"Both."

"Okay. He's not sunk yet. But I hope his lawyer is as good as Dave says."

Chapter 8

On Saturday morning, I figured Heather and Tiffany would have plenty to do getting ready for the shower, so I told them I'd stop by the bakery and pick up the cake on my way. When I walked through the front door of Dixie Donuts and More, the aroma of fresh, hot doughnuts prompted a sudden, overwhelming craving. I justified taking the time to buy two glazed doughnuts and a cup of coffee by telling myself I'd had a light breakfast and I'd need my strength to be in top form for the shower.

Bakery owner Renee brought the cake from the kitchen and set it on the counter/display case next to the cash register. I had planned to pay for the cake and add it to Heather's bill, but Renee said Tiffany had paid in advance when she ordered it.

I opened the box to inspect the cake before leaving. It's never wise to take a cake order on faith only to discover later that your box contains a SpongeBob SquarePants cake when you were expecting a sweet baby shower confection. The short two-tiered cake featured a pink marzipan ballet slipper and a blue sneaker. Underneath the mismatched footwear were alternating blue and pink letters that read, "It's a . . . " When the cake was sliced, a luscious pink shade of strawberry cake hidden under the frosting would reveal it's a girl.

I put the cake box on the passenger side floor-board of my car and wedged it in tightly with small boxes to keep it from sliding around. I phoned Heather to tell her that I was on my way and that I'd need someone to hold open the front door for me so I could carry in the cake.

Holly was already on-site overseeing the decorations. Things were shaping up.

We unboxed the cake to a chorus of *oohs* and *aahs* all around.

"Liv, does this look even to you?" Holly called out from the living room. She and Tiffany had strung a clothesline across the curtain rod in the bay window.

I suggested some slight adjustments and the two women hung a few small toys and baby items from the line. Adorable little outfits would be clipped to the line later as Heather opened her gifts. Packages from Tiffany ensured the gifts to be opened would include a pink tutu and frilly dress. The gift table positioned beneath the clothesline featured a stuffed pink elephant and blue rhino, which matched the cute zoo animals theme in the nursery.

While Tiffany and Holly decorated the living

room, Heather and I worked on setting out items for brunch. The menu included ham with mini biscuits, made by Heather's mom; cheesy grits, which were being kept warm in the oven; granola and Greek yogurt parfaits topped with fresh strawberries and blueberries, chilling in the fridge; mini bagels, which would be offered with an assortment of flavored cream cheese spreads; and juices and coffee. Holly would be making omelets to order, something she had a flair for.

Heather looked tired and the shower hadn't even started. I encouraged her to take a seat in the living room and prop her feet up on the ottoman until the guests arrived.

"We're in really good shape," Holly reassured her.

"Are the favor bags tucked away safely?" I asked. "We don't want anyone to sneak a peek at those little pink tutus until after the reveal."

We heard a car door slam.

"Here's Mama, even though we told her not to come early," Tiffany said after peering out the front window.

"It's fine," I said. "We're just about ready to roll and the other guests will be arriving soon."

Normally with a budget party like this where we were only hired to do the planning, Holly and I would just come by to oversee the setup and give the hosts one last boost of confidence, and then slip out before the party began. But since Heather was so hugely pregnant she could hardly move, and probably shouldn't be on her feet too much, Holly and I had decided between ourselves that we would stay and be hands-on for this one. Tiffany had also given us some indication that there could be a bit of a power struggle between Heather's mom and mother-in-law. Hopefully, we could serve as a buffer and keep them in neutral corners. Most people may not realize it, but managing contentious family situations is an integral part of a party planner's job.

About fifteen minutes later the other guests began to arrive. Everybody hugged Heather, who had managed to dislodge herself from the easy chair. Tiffany collected gifts and placed them on the gift table. Holly got everyone started on beverages.

The juices would actually play a part in a shower game called My Water Broke. Ice trays of different sizes had been filled to varying degrees. A miniature baby doll had been placed in each ice tray slot. The ice cubes would be dropped in the chilled juices and would melt at varying rates. Once a cube was completely melted, releasing the baby, the guest was to yell, "My water broke!" The first one to do so would win a prize.

Our plan called for serving the food first. As a party planner I've learned that the earlier in the day a meal is scheduled the more important prompt service becomes. People get cranky when they're hungry. Heather had been right about her Aunt Rose having a big appetite. She was working on her second plate before everyone else had been served. But I wasn't worried about running out of food.

Holly was whipping up omelets with the speed and efficiency of a short-order cook.

After everyone had eaten, we played a couple of

the usual games—passing around a bag that people reach into to feel baby-related items and guess what they are, and having guests suggest possible baby names beginning with certain letters of the alphabet.

Holly and I were busy in the kitchen. Tiffany walked over and touched my arm. "Liv, Heather wants you and Holly to join us for the games. Come on in here and sit down. We'll work on clearing up later."

Holly sat in an empty chair near the gift table and I squeezed into a tight spot on the end of the sofa. I spoke to Heather's mom, who was sitting in a chair beside the sofa, but I was honestly more interested in the gossip that the women next to me on the sofa were dishing out.

"I heard Heather's mother-in-law was against the marriage," a woman known to me only as Deena said in a hushed tone. "Didn't think Heather was good enough for her baby boy."

"Well, Heather didn't exactly live like a nun before she and Josh got together," the other woman, a chubby redhead replied. "'Course Josh ain't no prize, either. But I guess he and Heather are a pretty good match."

"Yeah, and at least Heather knows who her baby's daddy is, which is more than I can say for that Weems girl Josh used to run around with," Deena said.

"Oh, I know it. That child's father could be any one of a half dozen men in Delbert County."

Oddly enough, there's more than one Weems family in Delbert County, so I was trying to figure out which one they were talking about. I finally decided I should be ashamed of myself for listening to idle gossip and began chatting with Heather's mom.

In the pass-the-bag-and-fondle-the-contents game, everyone was stumped by something called baby bangs. It's a fringe of hair attached to a delicate hair band that makes it look like the baby has more hair—an infant toupee, basically. It's completely ridiculous but was good for a few laughs at the shower.

Heather had decided she wanted to reveal the cake before opening the gifts to allow people to savor dessert while she was unwrapping presents and so everyone could chat about the big "It's a girl" revelation.

I was helping Holly in the kitchen and listening to the background of laughter going on in the living room when I heard someone yell, "My water broke!" I grabbed the gift bag we had designated for the winner of that game and walked into the other room. As I passed Heather I saw she had suddenly stopped laughing and put her hands to her belly. I also noticed a puddle on the hardwood floor between her feet and realized she was the one who had called out about the water breaking—and she wasn't talking about the game. I'm not an expert on these matters, but I know enough to know when a pregnant woman's water breaks it's time to get her to the hospital.

I placed my hand on Heather's shoulder and told her everything would be okay. Tiffany had gone into the bedroom to gather up the party favor bags.

"Holly, get Tiffany. Tell her she needs to take Heather to the hospital."

Chaos momentarily broke out as Heather's mom and mother-in-law took in the scene, panicked, and then tried to compete for who should be in charge. Holly ignored them both and seized control.

Holly clapped her hands to get everyone's attention.

"Ladies, it looks like this sweet baby girl has decided she's ready to make her grand entrance," she said.

Holly instructed Heather's mom to go and fetch Heather's packed bag for the hospital and her mother-in-law to call her son and tell him to meet them at the hospital because he was about to become a daddy.

"Tiffany, you take Heather to the hospital in her car. Mamas, the two of you should follow in one of your vehicles, so one of you will be able to drive Heather's car back here later on. She and Josh won't need both their cars at the hospital, and Tiffany can ride back here with her mom."

Heather started toward the front door, with her sister at her arm. She stopped, surveyed the mess, and said, "We need to at least put away the food."

"You go have that baby—we'll take care of everything here," I assured her.

All the guests peered out the window as Tiffany backed out of the drive and drove off toward the hospital. A couple of women said hasty good-byes, but everyone else asked what they could do to help.

I started assessing which food items to put in the refrigerator, which to wrap and send home with guests, and which items should go in the trash. Holly supervised sorting through the baby gifts and picked out the things that the baby might be able to wear right away, such as the smallest sleepers. We put those and some receiving blankets in the washing machine so they would be laundered and ready to use.

Other gift items were taken into the nursery. Toys and books were put on shelves. Diapers and wipes were placed on the changing table. Once the laundry had run, we folded all the cute little clothes and put them in what seemed to be the appropriate drawers in the nursery.

Some of the ladies were taking down the decorations and putting them away, while I finished washing up the last of the dishes. After everyone had gone and Holly had taken one last look around to satisfy herself that everything looked right, we both left and headed for home.

In some ways it felt like it had been a full day, but it was only about one-thirty when I got home. I put the few goodies I had brought home from the shower in the fridge, grabbed a Diet Coke, kicked off my shoes, and went through to the den.

With my feet up on the sofa and my beverage on the table beside me, I checked messages on my phone. There was a message from Di wanting to know if I was up for a run to the mall in Hartville this evening.

I replied, **Shopping sounds like fun. I'll swing by your place. Sixish?**

She responded almost instantly with a thumbs-up.

There was also a text from Larry Joe, whom I could hear hammering away on something upstairs. It said, **What should I do about lunch?**

I texted back, **Fix yourself a sandwich. I'm in the den.**

Shortly, I heard my husband stomp down the stairs and into the kitchen.

"Hey, babe," he said. "I'm fixing myself a sandwich like you told me to. You want anything?"

"I'm good."

In a few minutes he came into the den with a beer and a pile of turkey lunchmeat, lettuce, tomato, cheese, and pickles stuffed between two slices of white bread.

"How'd the shower go?"

"It was pretty exciting. Heather went into labor. She's at the hospital now."

"Wow. You really know how to put on a party."

"What about you, are you making progress on getting the shower upstairs operational again?"

"Yes, ma'am. I estimate you will be luxuriating under a massage showerhead within two or three weeks."

I had my doubts, but tried to seem positive.

"Honey, if you think that sandwich will tide you over, we'll have supper about five. I'm meeting Di around six to go to the mall."

He went back to doing whatever it is he does for hours to the upstairs plumbing and plaster. I dozed off and on to the droning of some old movie starring Elizabeth Taylor on TV.

I made an uninspired supper of spaghetti with store-bought marinara sauce, but it did say "organic" on the label. After tossing a small side salad to go with it, I called to Larry Joe that supper was ready. He couldn't hear me for the racket he was making and I was too lazy to traipse up the stairs. I texted him.

What did people do before cell phones?

Larry Joe and I sat down to supper. He said grace, nicely remembering to pray for God to watch over Heather and the baby. After the "amen," he launched into a sermon.

"Liv, before you and Di start conspiring to get Earl off the hook by finding Dave another murder suspect, I just want to say . . ."

I tensed up, expecting Larry Joe to lay down the law about how I needed to keep my nose out of it.

"I'm behind you on this one hundred percent."

I'm sure the surprise registered on my face.

"But . . ."

Somehow I knew there'd be a "but."

"I want you to be careful. And if you hear anything that could point to another suspect, you need to tell Dave and Earl's attorney right away—no digging up the dirt on your own. And don't keep me in the dark, either. I might even be able to help. Okay?"

"Okay. You can even tag along with us to the mall

if you'd like. I imagine we're just going to do some window shopping and toss around ideas about possible suspects."

"I think I'll take a pass on that and let you and Di scheme in your own peculiar way. But let me know what you come up with."

"You've got it."

I gave Larry Joe a quick kiss, grabbed my purse, and started toward the door. Then I stopped, turned around, grabbed him, and gave him a big hug and kiss.

Di was watching out the front window of her trailer and hurried out the door as soon as I pulled up. She climbed in and buckled up.

"I like that top," Di said about the blue and white summer blouse I was wearing.

"Thanks. Mama gave it to me for my birthday."

"She did good."

"She has her moments."

"How's she holding up?" Di asked.

"She seems to be mostly in denial. But that's probably a good thing. Maybe it will keep her from meddling in the investigation."

"Right. She should leave the meddling to us."

"My thoughts exactly."

"So what's our plan?"

"Before we come up with a plan, we need to come up with a list of likely suspects."

"There's a long list of people who didn't much care for the man," Di offered.

"Yeah, but which of them is better off financially now that he's gone? That seems like a good place to start."

We made the uneventful trip from Dixie to Hartville ruling out everyone we saw during the fireworks. I pulled into the mall driveway and parked near a side entrance. A group of giggling teenaged girls fluttered past us as we approached the door.

"Are we shopping for anything in particular?" I asked.

"No. Why?"

"You were the one who suggested we go to the mall."

"Oh, I just thought it would be nice to get out for a bit. And the mall's air-conditioned. I wouldn't mind looking for some earrings."

"Cheap or expensive?"

"Definitely cheap."

We strolled past the jewelry store and into an accessory shop with lots of costume necklaces, bracelets, and earrings.

"These are different," Di said, holding up a pair of earrings featuring crystal skulls with red eyes.

"Those are definitely you," I said.

We were the only customers in the store, but we didn't dare mention possible suspect names out loud. We might be out of Dixie, but we were still within the boundaries of Delbert County.

"Ooh, what about these for your mama?" Di said as she held up a pair of earrings featuring swans with really long necks. "They'd go perfect with the swans in the pond."

"I'm not sure I should encourage her."

Di couldn't decide on earrings, but she ended up buying a cute little denim and rhinestone purse before we left the shop.

"Maybe we could scout for a wedding dress for your mother. What does the bride wear to an outdoor, Viking, gondola, classy hoedown wedding?"

"Beats me, but I'm sure Mama will have some definite ideas about it."

"Your mama did promise to go with just a simple wedding if you clear Earl's name."

"I wouldn't bank on that. Did I tell you Earl actually asked me to keep Mama occupied with wedding plans so she wouldn't worry about him? He basically said he wants her to be happy so just give her the wedding she wants and he'll sign the checks."

"That's really sweet," Di said.

"Yeah, it's sweet. But it doesn't make my life any easier. You know I gave up the wedding-planning part of my business because I just couldn't deal with all the drama. And that was planning weddings for relatively sane, reasonable people."

"I think you deserve some ice cream," Di said as we approached the food court.

We each ordered a hot fudge sundae.

"Let's stroll down to the empty end of the mall, where the JCPenney used to be," I said.

We sat on a bench next to the vacant storefront, where we could talk in relative privacy.

"Okay," Di said. "What about Webster Flack? You said he almost came to blows with Bubba the morning of the festival. He was dead set against that new development and he was also trying to win Bubba's seat on the town council. And he, or some of his group anyway, spray painted obscenities on the side of Bubba's building."

"All that really proves is that they can't spell. I'm not sure Webster gains anything by Bubba's death. The development will almost certainly still go through."

"He'll be running unopposed for Bubba's spot on the council, won't he?"

"I'm not sure about that, either," I said. "I should find out. There may still be time for someone else to file to run in the election."

"What about Bubba's brother?" Di asked. "Were they close? They co-owned the business, so now I suppose it all goes to the brother."

"Yeah," I said, mulling that over for a moment. "But if their arrangement is like that of most businesses, they both drew a salary. Bruce would have more control over the business now, I guess, but he won't be in for a big financial windfall unless he sells the business, which would surprise me. And as far as I could tell they got along."

"*Hmm*," Di said. "I've got nothing."

"Me neither. I'll call Dorothy, the mayor's secretary, Monday morning and see if it's too late for someone to file to run against Webster in the general election. And I'll ask Earl if he knows about Bubba and Bruce's business partnership or whose bank account might get fatter from the new development now that Bubba's out of the way."

Chapter 9

I usually go to the 10:15 service at Dixie Community Church. But I had set the alarm for 6:20 so I could make it to the 8:00 service, the one Mama and Earl usually attend. I wanted to be there to show my support, and Larry Joe, whose church attendance is sporadic at best, actually got up early to go with me.

"Are you sure your mama and Earl are going to services today? Did you talk to her?" Larry Joe asked as he fixed himself a bowl of cereal.

"I didn't talk to her about it, but I'm certain she wouldn't do anything that might give the slightest impression she thinks Earl is guilty. Besides, not everyone in town has seen her engagement ring yet."

I was wearing a sleeveless pink floral dress and Larry Joe was clad in khakis and a golf shirt when we strolled into church at five minutes to eight. The building is mostly free of adornment, with only the pews and the cross on the façade indicating that it's a church.

Mama and Earl were sitting in their usual spot. Mama's friend Sylvia, who generally gets on my last nerve, reluctantly scooted to the end of the pew to let me sit next to Mama, with Larry Joe next to me. Earl was seated on Mama's left and she had her arm draped over his, prominently displaying her bedazzled left hand.

A lady with a wobbly warble had the solo in the choir special. I thought I was going to have to pinch Larry Joe to keep him from laughing. The tone became decidedly somber when the pastor launched into a sermon on being prepared to meet our maker.

After the final amen, lots of people came over to offer their prayers and words of support to Earl. However, I couldn't help but notice a few people attempting to skulk past us avoiding eye contact. It may not have been Christian of me, but I was taking names in my head.

We begged off from going out to eat with Mama and Earl. I felt Larry Joe and I had performed our duty by putting in a rare appearance at the early service. I heated us up a breakfast of leftovers from the baby shower brunch. There were still remainders after Holly and I had left ample portions of what would keep in the fridge for Heather and Josh and boxed up and sent home as much as the guests were willing to take with them.

I warmed up the ham on biscuits in the microwave,

along with some cheesy grits, and spooned some Greek yogurt and fresh strawberries into small bowls.

We ate mostly in silence as Larry Joe read the sports section and I flipped through the entertainment section of the Sunday paper.

My phone buzzed and caller ID indicated it was Heather.

"Hi, Heather. I've been thinking about you. How are you doing?"

"Oh, we're doing just fine."

I could hear some sweet coos and gurgles and envisioned that she was holding the baby close to her face.

"I was in labor for kind of a long time and they ended up keeping us overnight. We got home a couple of hours ago. I just wanted to thank you and Holly for taking charge and keeping my mom and mother-in-law in line, and for staying and cleaning everything up. That was so sweet of you."

"Oh, don't be silly. Glad to do it. So tell me about the new arrival. How much did she weigh? Who does she look like? And what's her name?"

"She weighs eight pounds six ounces and is twenty inches long. I'm not sure who she looks like, although Josh's mom thinks she looks like her. And her name is Haley."

"Aww, she sounds just perfect. I can't wait to hold her. You take care and try to sleep while she's sleeping."

After I hung up with Heather I filled Larry Joe in on the baby's stats.

"More than eight pounds is a good size for a newborn, right?"

"Yes, it is," I said. "I'm sure she looks nicely filled out—and probably won't be wearing those new-born-sized sleepers she got at the shower for very long."

Larry Joe said he was heading to the golf course to play nine holes. After he left, I loaded the dishwasher and was wiping off the table when the landline rang. It was my sister.

"Hi, Emma. I have to ask, why are you suddenly calling me on the landline instead of on my cell?"

"Because I want to know that you're home and able to talk privately and not sitting in a restaurant or some public place. I need to talk to you about Mama—even if you don't want to hear it."

I knew I'd been a little rough on her the other night. Then again she had hung up on me, and no apology seemed to be forthcoming.

"Liv, I just got off the phone with my friend Nicole, who called to let me know—since apparently my own sister doesn't feel the need to let me know what's going on—that Mama was at church this morning with Earl. She said she was kind of surprised to see them there this morning after Earl's arrest and everything. Imagine my surprise. Nobody bothered to tell me that Earl had been arrested—for murder, no less."

I never did like Nicole, who was one of Emma's best friends in high school. I had thought she was catty and low class even back then. Her phone call to Emma did nothing to change my opinion of her.

"Emma, Earl Daniels did not kill anyone. I know that in my heart of hearts, and so does Mama. She's standing by his side through this difficult time. And Larry Joe and I intend to do the same."

"You are unbelievable. What kind of spell does this man have y'all under? Don't you see that we have to protect our mama from this man, at the very least until he's been cleared of a murder charge? Or have you completely lost your mind?"

"You were dead set against Earl anyway. His arrest is just a convenient excuse for you to take aim at him."

"Convenient excuse? Is that what you call it? Liv, if you won't talk some sense into Mama I'll have no choice but to drive down to Dixie and do it myself. I was wondering if maybe we should talk to the doctor about her medication. But I'm beginning to wonder if I should talk to the doctor about you."

I hung up on her.

I hoped the talk about her driving down to Dixie to pester Mama was just an idle threat. I was so stirred up after Emma's phone call that I couldn't sit still. I busied myself with cleaning the bathroom and mopping the kitchen.

After finishing my frenzied round of chores, I flopped onto the sofa in the den and flipped mind-lessly through cable television channels. After a few minutes of that nonsense I pulled myself together.

You need to get busy clearing Earl's name, I thought.

I grabbed a notepad and pen from the kitchen drawer and started a list of what I knew so far, which was "not much."

Larry Joe came in from his golf game and took a quick shower. I decided turning on the stove or cooktop in this heat was out of the question. So, I put some corn on the cob, still in the husks, in the microwave and set about slicing tomatoes and other vegetables fresh from Mama's garden. I tossed a salad that inluded butter lettuce, raw zucchini, squash, and carrots, peeled off the husks and buttered the steaming hot corn; and called to Larry Joe that supper was ready.

I made my salad a vegetarian affair, but added some chopped ham to Larry Joe's, since we had some leftover ham and biscuits from brunch and he's definitely happier when there's a bit of meat on his plate.

"This salad's good, honey," Larry Joe said. "And I think these tomatoes are perfectly ripe."

"Yeah, I think we've hit peak on this summer's tomatoes. How was your golf game?"

"My score's nothing to brag about. But the men in the clubhouse all seem to believe in Earl's innocence—or at least that's the line they're feeding me."

"*Mmm,* did you notice how *some* people at church this morning were making a point of slipping past us without speaking to Mama or Earl?"

"I did. But try not to let it worry you. There're always a few. So have you and Di zeroed in on any likely suspects yet?"

"Not really, but that reminds me. Do you know if anybody involved in this new development might get a bigger slice of it now that Bubba's out of the way?"

"No, but it's altogether possible Bubba was accepting bribes or kickbacks from the developer to push through approvals on the town council. If that's the case, he'll be able to keep more cash in his wallet now. That kind of thing would be hard to prove, though. I'm sure Dave is digging into the financials."

"Bubba was a major investor in the development, too, wasn't he? Will his share go to Bruce now, or mean a bigger slice of the pie for the other investors?"

"Nobody's made any money yet. I don't know how much cash Bubba had actually put in, but I doubt the developer would have any trouble lining up other investors. I'll ask a couple of golf buddies who'd probably know something about it."

"Do you know anything about this developer? He's not from Dixie. What's his name, something Rankin?"

"Aaron Rankin," Larry Joe said. "I met him at the country club. I think he hit up a number of his investors out on the golf course. And he's from Memphis, but somebody told me he has relatives in Hartville."

"See if you can find someone who knows him personally, maybe knows his family over in Hartville, will you?"

"I'll try. But what are you thinking? Is he a suspect?"

"At this point everybody's a suspect. But something Winette said has been bothering me. She seems to think this development plan doesn't add up. She said they're overbuilding the residential and the kind of retail in the plans doesn't seem practical. Even more telling, though, she said Mr. Sweet, who never misses out on a good real estate investment opportunity, passed on this one. It makes me wonder if this Rankin guy is a bit shady."

"I'll see what I can dig up. Even if he didn't kill Bubba, if there's a chance he's playing fast and loose with some of our friends' life savings, he needs to be found out."

I nodded sullenly and took a big swallow of iced tea, cupping the glass with both hands and enjoying the feeling of the cold condensation under my fingers.

"I'm going to call Dorothy at the mayor's office in the morning and ask if Webster Flack gets to run unopposed now that Bubba's gone, or if there's still time for someone else to get on the ballot," I said.

"That's a good idea."

"I figure it's worth checking. But honestly, I think Webster and his band of protesters are just morons."

"Nothing to say morons can't be dangerous," Larry Joe said.

After supper Larry Joe said he needed to catch up on some paperwork, so I told him I'd probably run over to Di's if she was around.

I picked up my phone and suddenly had the brilliant idea that if I walked through the festival grounds it might prod my memory about something from the day of the murder. Di was amenable to meeting me at the park for a stroll.

I arrived first and was standing beside the World War II veterans' memorial when I saw Di pull up.

"It's not as hot as it was earlier, but still we'll probably want to stay mostly in the shade," she suggested.

Fortunately, the paved walking track that snaked through the park was at least partly shaded by large white oaks for most of its one and a half miles, and by this time of day the shadows were beginning to lengthen.

"I thought a walk couldn't hurt," I told Di. "But I'm also hoping returning to the scene of the crime might help me remember something that would help with the investigation. I mean, I was here all day. I'm bound to have seen or heard something that I'm just forgetting."

"Okay, sounds like a plan. So what was set up in this area?" Di asked.

"The information booth was here," I said, taking a wide side step onto the grass beside the beginning of the walking track and slicing both my hands downward in a vertical karate chop.

This was the spot where I had stowed my clipboards and bag of tricks—miscellany I thought I might need, such as sunscreen; lip balm; a second pair of shoes, in case my feet started hurting; and a clean shirt, in case I spilled something on the front of mine.

"This is where I started out and I came by here periodically throughout the day."

The key thing about this particular spot was that it was near the main entrance, where most people passed through on their way into the festival grounds, and of course, many also passed by on their way out.

"I remember Bubba stopping by the information booth and chatting for a moment, thanking me for taking on the event and telling me how he'd appreciate my vote."

"About what time was that?" Di asked. "Was he just arriving for the day?"

I closed my eyes for a moment and tried to remember.

"I'm pretty sure it was just after the 5K had concluded. Yeah, yeah, I remember several walkers/runners walking by with their just collected race T-shirts while I was talking to Bubba."

"Did they hold the 5K on the walking track here?"

"No. All the booths were set up here. They had a circle track set up on the small field near the bridge over Tiptoe Creek," I said, gesturing to indicate the area.

"Okay, so which way did Bubba go after that and was he with anybody after he wandered away from the booth?"

"He talked to some of the 5K people. I'm pretty sure he wandered in that direction," I said nodding northward to the area that terminated in the vicinity of the open area where most people were gathered for the fireworks and the porta potties beyond that. "That would make sense, though, since most of the booths, games, and judging tents were set up between here and there."

"Good. Let's keep walking. What was set up in this area and what was going on after the 5K?" Di asked.

We talked as we walked farther up the walking track.

"The next big events were the judging of the jams, jellies, and preserves, followed by the judging of the cakes and pies, respectively."

"Any drama go on there?"

"There's always drama surrounding the kudzu jelly contest. One of the same two women has won it for the past twenty years or more. They kind of alternate and each one has her dedicated fans. It's actually so contentious it's hard to find people willing to serve as judges. They know whichever way it goes, some little group will be going home mad."

"I never knew the canning world could be so cutthroat," Di said.

"It's rough enough that my mama actually gave up on the jelly competition years ago, and she's not one to walk away from a fight."

"So was Bubba around for the canning or baking competition?"

"He was," I said, stopping in my tracks and turning to face Di. "I'd forgotten all about that. Bubba was a judge in the cakes contest. And he was a last-minute replacement, too. He filled in for another councilman, who had stepped in a gopher hole out on the golf course and twisted his ankle."

We sat down on a park bench and I stared at the empty space where the cake-judging tent had stood on the day of the festival trying to summon everything I could remember.

"I stepped into the tent entrance just as the judges were tasting the last few entries in the chocolate cake category," I said.

"How many categories are there?"

"Just two. Chocolate and nonchocolate."

"All food pretty much falls into those two categories."

I tried to envision the scene in the tent when I entered.

"I had walked past earlier, but I made a point of coming back because Mama had entered her triple chocolate cake. As I stepped into the tent, Bubba, the mayor, and Miss Hicks, the librarian, were sampling the last couple of entries. After scribbling notes on their judging sheets, the three of them huddled into a little circle and whispered for a few minutes; then Mayor Haynes handed a list to Miss Hicks and she announced the winners and presented the ribbons. Our pastor's wife, Cheryl Duncan, came in third. Mama came in second, and Bernice Halford took the blue ribbon."

"Well, I'd like a slice of the cake that could beat your mama's. Her chocolate cake is probably the best I've ever tasted. Do you think the judging was rigged, like with the beauty pageant?"

"No. Honestly, I think they just like to spread the love around and not give the blue ribbon to the same person every time," I said.

"So you don't think your mother or the preacher's

wife would have taken Bubba out over losing the blue ribbon?" Di said with a wicked smile.

"Actually I think Miss Hicks would bear the brunt of their displeasure if they were inclined to hold a grudge. I mean, what would the mayor or Bubba know about baking anyway? Besides, I think giving Cheryl Duncan a ribbon of any color was probably an act of charity. I've never tasted her chocolate cake, but I have had her banana pudding and it was no prize. I left right after the winners were announced. There didn't seem to be any controversy or hard feelings."

"Was Earl there with your mama?"

I thought for a moment. "No, I don't think he was."

"Well, all this talk about cake is making me hungry," Di said.

We walked to the ice cream stand a couple of blocks away. It's just a walk-up counter with a couple of picnic tables sitting in front of the tiny building. We each ordered a scoop on a cone—pistachio for me, Rocky Road for Di—and walked back to the park.

The calories from the ice cream probably canceled out any benefit from our walk, but there wasn't a breeze stirring and it was still pretty warm even in the shade.

"How far up the track had we made it?" Di asked.

I stopped and looked around to get my bearings.

"The contestants' tent for the Miss Dixie pageant was here," I said, pointing to a void. "But I didn't go in there. It was where the girls were getting dressed and primping. I did run off a couple of boys who looked to be in the third or fourth grade. They were trying to peer into the tent. So the little peepers would know more about what went on inside the tent than I would.

"Next to that tent, to the right here, was the winners' tent. That's where they served a barbecue dinner to all the contest winners from the day. I did go in there during the dinner. Bubba was at one of the tables. He always talks—talked—so loud he was hard to miss."

"Was he politicking or was he one of the people invited to the dinner?" Di asked.

"He was eating. In fact, most people were just getting their desserts when I came by. Nonie Jones, Cassie Latham's grandmother; and Bernice Halford were at the back of the tent cutting cakes and slicing pies, and some high school girls were carrying the desserts to the tables. I remember Bernice delivering a slice of her award-winning chocolate cake to Bubba and some pie for the mayor. I'm not sure if Bubba was at the dinner with the family because his niece won or because he had served as a judge. Or maybe all the town council members were invited. Anyway, Nonie Jones offered me some cake, which I declined. I figured I'd eaten more than my share of junk food by that time. I went around and congratulated several of the winners."

"Were Cassie and her mom at the dinner?"

"I don't recall seeing them. But I don't know if the runners-up were invited. The first and second runners-up were included later with the group on the stage when they introduced all the winners from the day to the crowd, just before the fireworks show. Of course, by the time of the dinner, Cassie's mom had already had way too much to drink and had had her tearful and very public confrontation with Bubba."

Larry Joe was still at the computer in the den when I got home.

"Have you been going over paperwork for McKay's the whole time I've been gone?"

"Yeah, just a lot of odds and ends mostly. Some of it's because of new contracts, so that's actually good news. But I'm fixin' to go upstairs and work an hour or so on the house before bedtime."

"Honey, I know you're a do-it-yourselfer, but with your dad cutting back his hours and the business growing, don't you think you should hire someone to help work on the house? You could hire Kenny. You know he's a good carpenter and hard worker— and easy to get along with. Your dad is handy, but you two would kill each other. Plus y'all spend enough time working together as it is."

"I probably will hire Kenny to help with some of the woodworking when I get to it. And I'm just about caught up on the trucking business now. Don't worry, the upstairs bath will be in full working order before Labor Day."

He put the computer in sleep mode and kissed the top of my head as he walked past. The landline rang just as he walked into the kitchen.

"It's your mama, you want me to grab it for you?"

"Yeah, might as well."

"Hi, Mama Walford, here's Liv," he said as he quickly passed the phone off to me.

"Have you talked to your sister today?"

"Why do you ask?" I said with an uneasy feeling.

"She left a message asking me to call her."

"I wouldn't call her just yet if I were you. You remember her friend from high school, Nicole?"

"I never did like her, always thought she was kind of low class."

"Well, apparently she still is. She called to tell Emma about Earl's . . . " I struggled for a moment looking for the right word. "Troubles," I said. "It might be best to give Emma a day or two to calm down before giving her a call."

"Okay. I think that's probably sage advice. By the way, Liv, the guest list for the wedding is going to be a little longer than I told you. I was just talking off the top of my head when I estimated sixty people."

"How many people are on the guest list now?"

"A hundred and forty-six."

It took me a minute to catch my breath.

"Okay. You know if it rains we'll have to move all the guests into the barn. So, I need to go out to Earl's place and do some measurements to see exactly how many people we can accommodate. We may need to make some adjustments."

"Thanks, hon. I knew you'd find a way to make it work. I'd better let you go. Earl's calling to me from the back porch."

Chapter 10

I went to the office Monday morning and got right to work—trying to clear Earl's name. I knew I was going to have to pass off some of the party-planning work to Holly, while I worked on getting to the bottom of Bubba's murder. Fortunately, I was due a nice check from the city for my work on the festival and I didn't have an event scheduled this week. I decided to think of Earl as my main client, since he had told me he was willing to write the checks for his and Mama's wedding. I had no intention, presently at least, to charge for my time, but I was more than willing to let him pay for expenses, especially the more outrageous items on Mama's wish list.

I phoned Dorothy at city hall to ask about the town council race. I needed to know if Webster Flack would have the field to himself now that Bubba was out of the picture, or if there was still time for someone else to make it onto the ballot.

"Hon, the ballot for the August primary is set," she said. "Webster's and Bubba's names will be on it. Since Webster will now be unopposed in his party, he'll be on the ballot in the general election in November, as well. But there's still time for other candidates to qualify to run in November as a candidate in the opposing party or as an independent."

"So you're saying even with Bubba out of the way Webster still may not win in November?" I asked, trying to understand the strange workings of politics.

"That's right," Dorothy said. "Probably won't do much for his self-esteem if he loses. But honestly I wouldn't be surprised. Just about anybody who gets enough certified signatures on a petition to get them on the November ballot has a better than good chance of winning. There're plenty of folks who think Webster's a nut. And people who were put off by his ugly campaign against Bubba are likely to feel even less affection for him since Bubba's murder.

"Liv, why don't you consider running? It's been a few years since we've had a woman on the council. People like you. And if you're interested, running against Webster in November would be almost like running unopposed."

"So you feel pretty certain he won't win?"

"Not a chance in Hades."

"Thanks, Dorothy."

"Will you give running for office some thought?"

"Not a chance in Hades," I said before saying good-bye.

I supposed it was flattering Dorothy wanted me to run for office, even if she suggested the only reason I'd win was because I'd practically be running unopposed.

I got up from my desk with the intention of making a pot of coffee. I have no running water upstairs but keep bottled water on hand for hydration and coffee-making purposes. The coffee bag was empty. So I grabbed my mug and headed downstairs to Sweet Deal Realty to help myself to a cup of their coffee.

I walked in the front door to hear the gurgling noise of a fresh pot brewing.

"Mornin,' sunshine," Winette said with her usual perk as she walked in from Mr. Sweet's office-cum-storeroom, carrying a "For Sale" sign.

"I just came down for some coffee. Looks like you have a new client."

"Yes, indeed. Business is booming. I have a closing scheduled on Thursday. How're things in the party-planning universe?"

"It's a bit slow in my little galaxy, but I'm not complaining. I'll be getting a nice check from the city for the festival, and Earl has asked me to keep Mama busy planning the wedding so she doesn't have time to worry over him."

"He's a nice man. I hope you're able to get him out of his current troubles."

I couldn't believe what I was hearing. Winette is

usually doling out advice about how I should keep my nose out of any murder investigation. I guess she noticed my jaw hitting the floor.

"I'm sure you're surprised to hear me encouraging your snooping. But let's be honest, you're going to do it anyway. And you can't very well stand by and let them lock up the man your mama's going to marry. What kind of daughter would you be?"

Winette said she needed to get going and I walked over to the coffeemaker just as it stopped sputtering and poured myself a cup. Mr. Sweet wandered in, probably from the barbershop across the street, where he regularly hangs out talking to other old men.

"Hi, Mr. Sweet."

"Hi, Liv. You know, if you keep pilfering our coffee I'm going to have to raise your rent."

"You know you'd be hard pressed to find another tenant willing to commute to use the restroom," I said.

He just muttered something under his breath and disappeared into his office.

With a mug of steaming coffee in hand, I went back up to my office. I needed to get a few things organized before Holly arrived later in the morning. During weeks when we had downtime, we were working on some marketing materials and a new Liv 4 Fun brochure. The brochure needed updating anyway and we were also getting ready for a big chamber of commerce business expo in Hartville in the fall, with an eye to increasing our profile on that side of the county.

After Holly arrived, we looked through scores of digital images from various events, trying to decide which ones to include in the brochure and which we might want to blow up to poster size for the expo. We wanted to be sure to include a mix of large and smaller events and venues to suit a wide variety of budgets.

We sorted through photos for events we had planned, putting our favorites into a folder on the computer desktop.

"By the way, I talked to Mama last night and she's revised her guest list for the wedding."

"I never believed for a minute she'd keep her list down to sixty people. How many people is she planning to invite now?"

"A hundred and forty-six."

"That may require an adjustment to our plans," she said.

Holly was meeting a friend for lunch at one o'clock, so we wrapped things up about a quarter till. Mama had called and wanted me to come over so we could talk more about the wedding. I managed to put her off another day. I needed to put some time into looking for a suspect to replace Earl. I wanted to ensure Mama's dream wedding day included the groom.

I drove through Wendy's and got a junior cheeseburger, which I ate in the car before driving to Earl's business. Daniels Lumber and Hardware sits at the corner of Front Street and the highway, where it had been located for thirty years. If Earl was starting his business today he would never be able to afford this parcel of land. I'd imagine it stuck in Bubba Rowland's craw that his biggest competitor's store was situated in such a prime location. The highway is a busy corridor funneling rural commuters into Memphis, Collierville, and Germantown. Dixie businesses, especially those right on the highway, profit greatly from this regular stream of traffic.

Daniels Lumber and Hardware is a flat-roofed building with a brick façade and a large window in front, next to the entrance. While it is good sized, it could in no way be mistaken for one of the big-box stores on the highway a bit farther west.

I walked inside and noticed the display of ice chests, pool noodles, and lawn chairs near the door. I knew Earl was most likely in his office in the back of the store.

This being Dixie, I ran into two people I knew on the short trek through the store. A nice older man who goes to my church was looking at glow-in-the-dark duct tape. I made a mental note to come back and look at that. There had to be some handy use for glow-in-the-dark tape I just hadn't thought of yet. He spoke and inquired after my mama's health. This is an example of one of the everyday neighborly encounters that recommends small-town life.

Next I ran into my neighbor Edna Cleats. Neighbors like her are the reason people decide to bolt from small towns in search of the blissful anonymity of big-city life.

By the time I spotted her, it was too late to hide.

"Hi, Liv," she said, giving me a tootles wave. "It's a shame we're neighbors and yet sometimes we'll go days at a time without seeing one another."

I forced a smile and a nod.

"I'm so sorry for what your mama's going through right now. Imagine having her fiancé arrested for murder."

"Mama has no doubts about Earl's innocence— and neither do I."

"Of course not, hon. Still, it has to be difficult. And expensive, too. I heard Earl had to dole out a quarter of a million dollars to get out of jail, at least temporarily. That's sure a beautiful ring he gave Virginia. I hope they don't end up having to sell it to cover Earl's legal expenses. That would be such a shame."

I was speechless. Unfortunately, I was the only one who was.

"Tell your mother to call me if she needs anything. And tell her I'm so sorry about her coming in second in the chocolate cake contest at the festival. I'm sure it was a very close call for the judges. I'd better get going. Mr. Winky will be expecting his dinner."

Mr. Winky was her cat.

I finally made it to the back of the store. Through the window behind the back counter where sales staff write up special orders, I could see Earl in his office with his feet propped up on his desk. He glanced up and motioned for me to come through.

In his gentlemanly manner, Earl stood up and waited for me to take a seat in the chair facing his desk before he sat back down in his chair.

"Hey, Liv. What can I do you for?"

"I've just been wondering about who benefits most financially as a consequence of Bubba's death. I figured you'd know, or at least have a pretty good idea, about how things stand for Bruce businesswise now that big brother's out of the picture."

"I expect they had a partnership arrangement that passes Bubba's interest in the business to Bruce, making him sole proprietor. But if the business were in financial trouble, which I don't believe it is, it wouldn't help pay the bills. If the business is solid financially, the only way it would put extra money in Bruce's pocket is if he sells, which I can't imagine he would."

"What about stuff like life insurance?" I asked.

"I don't know if Bruce is the beneficiary of that or not, to be honest. I'm sure Faye was sole beneficiary before. After she died two years ago, I don't know what changes Bubba made. He may have left it to Bruce or put it in trust for Jennifer. He may have left some or all of it to his church. There's also his house, next door to your Mama. It's a nice house, but not exactly worth a fortune."

"Okay," I said. "What about Bubba's relationship with Bruce? Was it all brotherly love or was sibling rivalry in play?"

"To the best of my knowledge they've always

gotten along well enough. In fact, if anything, I'd say they were probably closer the last couple of years. You know there was no love lost between me and Bubba Rowland. But losing his son in a car crash and then losing his wife to cancer the very next year is a tough break for anybody. And I think Bruce tried to be there for him."

"So no bad blood between the brothers, not even old jealousies, like one of them being their daddy's favorite or one of them coming out poorly on the money side when their parents passed away?"

"No . . . no, nothing like that," he said.

The long pause in Earl's answer to my last question worried me, so I pressed.

"Nothing like that, but there was something, wasn't there?"

"Maybe, but it was a long time ago and I'm pretty sure Bruce and Faye never knew about it."

He pursed his lips together and stared at his desk, obviously reluctant to continue.

"Earl Daniels," I said, feeling exasperated, "tell me what you know, no matter how long ago or how trivial you think it may be. You've been charged with murder, remember? And I'm just trying to help."

Earl leaned forward, propping his elbows on the desk, before speaking in a hushed tone.

"All right. I already told the sheriff when he pressed so I might as well tell you. Back when Bruce and Carrie were first married they had trouble, like lots of newlyweds, adjusting to married life. There was lots of fussing and fighting and tears, and Carrie running home to her mama once or twice.

"They eventually worked it out and started a family. But Bubba Rowland always was a sleazy opportunist, ready to swoop in on innocent prey if he caught a whiff of weakness.

"I was delivering lumber over on Route 3 one day and I spotted Bubba's old Cadillac parked in front of that cheap little out-of-the-way motel near Bucks Road. It's been closed for years now. Anyway, I saw Bubba come out of one of the rooms strutting like a rooster. And a minute later I saw Carrie come out of the same room, looking shamefaced.

"I may be wrong, but my guess is that was the only time it happened. Next time I saw Bruce and Carrie they were holding hands and acting more the way newlyweds should. I don't think Bruce or Faye ever knew and I certainly wasn't going to tell them. If Bruce knew, he waited an awful long time to seek revenge. Plus, as I already said, they've seemed closer since Bubba lost Faye and Bubba Jr.

"You'll keep this under your hat, right?"

"Sure. It sounds like ancient history. And besides, you said you'd already told Dave."

"Are you keeping an eye on your mama and drawing up wedding plans?"

"I'm meeting with her tomorrow."

Chapter 11

I had asked Holly to work on sourcing a gondola for Mama's wedding. I touched base with her Tuesday morning and she told me to come by her house so she could show me what she'd found so far.

I stopped in Dixie Donuts and More and picked up a thermos of brewed coffee and a box of doughnut holes. I thought Holly deserved a little treat. She was being such a good sport about helping me with Mama's crazy wedding list, as well as looking after odds and ends with the business while I took time away to clear Earl's name and babysit Mama.

The front door to Holly's handsome Tudor-style home was open. When I knocked she hollered for me to come through. Holly had inherited her parents' home, the one she grew up in, following her mother's death. After having lived all over the globe with her army general husband, who passed away shortly before her mom, Holly said coming home to Dixie just felt right. The more-than-big-enough Victorian that Larry Joe and I call home seems like a shack compared to Holly's manor house.

She hadn't changed much of the décor since she'd moved back. But she had added a few touches that her very proper mother would not have abided. Holly was in the dark-paneled traditional library with tall, stately bookcases topped with marble busts of famous writers and American statesmen, including Henry David Thoreau, Thomas Jefferson, and Benjamin Franklin. At one end of the room was a large partners desk that her daddy had used, not that he ever had a partner. A humidor, no longer stocked with contraband Cuban cigars, still stood behind the desk.

Holly was sitting in a Queen Anne chair at one end of a Ping-Pong table at the other end of the library, the game table serving as a desk for her laptop and notepad. The table was one of Holly's own special touches. They were a staple at military bases and USOs around the world, and she had become quite the table tennis fan and even played on an officers' wives' team in Germany. I would guess one of the few two-star general's wives to do so. Holly occasionally conscripts her expressionless housekeeper into playing a game or two.

"How's it going? Are you ready for a break? I brought food offerings," I said, as I set the dough-nuts and coffee thermos onto her father's leather-topped desk.

"*Mmm*, that coffee smells lovely, darlin'," she said, getting up from her chair. She said she'd be right back and went to the kitchen to retrieve plates, cups, and napkins. Renee at the doughnut shop had dropped sugars and creamers into a bag and tucked it into the box. We served ourselves, then sat in two leather reading chairs separated by a carved antique table.

"So is it possible to rent a gondola for the wedding?" I asked.

"We can rent gondolas in Ft. Lauderdale or a place near Minneapolis, but we'd have to hold the wedding there. They only provide service locally."

"Okay. Is there any place that will bring a gondola to us?"

Holly dabbed her glaze-dappled lips with a cloth napkin and took a sip of coffee before answering.

"There is a place in England that will deliver a gondola, along with a gondolier, anywhere in the world. But as you might imagine, it's pricy."

"How pricy?"

"Unless they plan to live on it, I'd describe it as cost prohibitive."

"I was afraid of that," I said.

"But I actually have an idea for an alternative. Come over here and I'll show you."

Holly left her plate but picked up her coffee cup and walked over to the makeshift desk. She tooled the mouse around and clicked open a window on the screen.

"Take a look at this. There's a man at Pickwick Lake who builds these wooden flat-bottomed boats that taper at both ends. To me, the longer ones have a gondola vibe about them. See what you think."

I leaned over to get a better look and she clicked on one of the photos to enlarge it.

"Yeah, I agree. The craftsmanship is beautiful." Suddenly having a flash of brilliance, I added, "I could buy a carved figurehead and I'm sure Kenny could figure out some way to tart up the boat and make it look a bit Viking-like."

"Awlright," Holly said. "I'll get in touch with the boat builder tomorrow and see if we can come up with a rental arrangement. If he's not amenable to renting, I'll get some price quotes on buying. Do you think Earl would consider buying a boat if it comes to it? That would be kind of expensive, but still much cheaper than bringing one in from overseas."

I thought for a moment.

"If the price isn't outrageous, I think he would. I mean, he could always turn around and sell it and get at least most of his money back. But if we can't rent one, I'll check with Earl before we buy."

"Okay, I'm on it," Holly said.

"I'm off to spend some time with our crazy bride-to-be."

"What are y'all up to today?"

"We're going to go look at some dress possibilities for the wedding. And if we finish up there, we'll go to a stationery store and look at wedding invitations. I'm going to attempt, at least, to guide some of the wedding plans out of Mama's head and into the real world."

* * *

I was scheduled to meet my mother up at her house at ten-thirty. I couldn't bear the thought of sitting at her kitchen table listening to her rattle on about whatever new outlandish ideas she might have dreamed up for the wedding since our last meeting.

So I told her we were going to do a bit of shopping in Memphis.

Mama generally likes to be in the driver's seat, except when it comes to actual driving; then she prefers to be chauffeured. She locked her front door, walked down the front steps to the driveway, and handed me her car keys. I took them without question or comment and slid behind the wheel of her Cadillac while she got in on the passenger side.

"So what're we shopping for that we have to drive all the way into Memphis instead of just going over to Hartville?"

Mama tends to not like shopping in Memphis. She thinks it's too crowded. I anticipated meeting some resistance, so I sweetened the deal by telling her we could eat lunch at one of her favorite restaurants there.

"We'll find a larger selection in Memphis, certainly in specialty items. Besides, going to Memphis gives us an excuse to eat lunch at The Arcade Restaurant. You haven't eaten there in quite a while, have you? We'll grab some lunch and then do some shopping. There are a couple of different places I'd like to stop."

Mama didn't say much, but she didn't put up a fight, so I knew she was secretly pleased about lunch. I wanted to feed her before we went shopping, so she'd be in a good mood.

We made the drive to downtown Memphis in just over an hour. It was lunchtime, so I had to circle around a couple of times to snag a parking spot on the street, just as someone was pulling away from the curb.

The Arcade Restaurant, on a busy corner on South Main, is a Memphis institution. A plaque on the building claims it's the oldest café in town. Mama and I passed through the front door under the vintage neon sign and scooted across the baby blue vinyl seats in one of the booths.

A waitress handed us menus and brought us ice water. Some of the sandwiches are named after movies that have filmed scenes in the restaurant, including 21 Grams and The Rainmaker, a vegetarian special and a turkey club, respectively. Much more unusual and particular to Memphis is the fried peanut butter and banana sandwich, a favorite of Elvis Presley back when he was a regular at The Arcade. Bacon may be added on request.

We looked over the menu even though we knew before we arrived what we'd order. Breakfast is available all day and their pancakes are tops. We both ordered the sweet potato pancakes with a side of bacon. Mama doused her pancakes in syrup while I ate mine straight up. Since the air-conditioning was heavenly cool, we sipped coffee without breaking a sweat even on a steamy July day.

"So now that you've fattened me up, where are you taking me—to market?" Mama asked.

She was still acting suspicious and a bit surly because I hadn't told her exactly where we were going. Mama isn't a woman who likes surprises, generally speaking.

"Don't you trust me? I do this for a living, you know."

"Take folks hostage?"

I decided it was best just to ignore that remark. We settled the bill and stepped out into the sizzling air. With the Caddy's AC on full force, we drove east down Poplar to a formal wear store with lots of plus-sized choices. The dresses I had in mind were marketed as mother-of-the-bride, but I thought they would also work well for a nontraditional full-figured bride of a certain age.

A bubbly salesclerk chatted us up as soon as we entered. It was easy to deduce that she worked on commission. She directed us to the plus-size section. After a quick tour, I had a sinking feeling I knew exactly which prominently displayed dress Mama was going to choose. I tried to steer her toward other options, even got her to try on a couple of other dresses. But there was no way to deny the gravitational pull this frock had on her.

"Mama, why don't you go ahead and try on *that* dress," I said, nodding toward the dress in question.

She tried to act coy.

"Well, if you really think I should," she said. "It's a bit dressier than what I originally had in mind."

"It can't hurt to check it out," I said, knowing

very well she was not leaving the store without at least trying it on.

While she disappeared behind louvered doors, I looked around for a formal dress I thought I could sell her on as an alternative.

When she marched regally out of the dressing room and turned with a flourish to face the three-way mirror, I knew the dress would be coming home with us.

It was a sequined floor-length dress with an Egyptian-inspired collar, sheer sleeves, and a short train. It was also deep purple, a favorite shade of Mama's, and honestly a good color on her.

I knew the moment I laid eyes on the dress that in Mama's head she imagined herself as Cleopatra floating down the Nile in her gondola Viking boat standing next to her Antony, or Thor—I don't pretend to understand all the machinations of Mama's mind. Admiring the image in the mirror, Mama looked as proud as a sixteen-year-old who'd just been named homecoming queen. As ridiculous as the dress was, I couldn't deny the pleasure it obviously gave her.

I wasn't lying when I told her I thought it suited her perfectly.

The "perfect" dress was more than twice as expensive as the other dresses she had tried on, which put a big smile on the saleslady's face. I wondered what kind of look Earl would have on his face when he signed the check for it. But I had a feeling when he saw how happy Mama looked wearing it, he wouldn't put up a fuss.

We had barely started the drive home to Dixie when Mama said, "By the way, Liv, I've added five or six more names to the guest list. I declare, as soon as I add a particular person who absolutely has to be invited or they'll get all in a snit, I think of someone else who will be mad if I invite that person and not them."

I decided to take another stab at trying to nail Mama down on at least a ballpark idea of the wedding date she had in mind. I knew Mama's elaborate vision of this occasion had to include a date, or at least a season. Fall leaves, spring buds, or summer bounty. But no matter how I approached it, she was being evasive.

Finally, I said, "Mama, can't you give me some idea of *when* you'd like your wedding to be? Narrow it down to a month, or a least a season for me. There are some things we can't plan without a date."

Mama teared up and started fishing in her handbag for a tissue. I suddenly felt thimble tall and wished I could disappear.

"What's wrong, Mama?"

"It's kind of hard to set a date, not knowing what's going to happen with Earl. I know perfectly well he did not kill Bubba Rowland. But if that sheriff doesn't get off his duff and find the real killer, my sweet man could end up in prison anyway. I already told Earl we could just go on down to the justice of the peace next week and get married and wait to have our wedding celebration later on. But he won't hear of it. Says he won't marry me until he can give me his name without any hint of dishonor attached to it. That blame fool."

Tears started burning my eyes, too, and I asked Mama if she had an extra tissue. I flipped on my turn signal and pulled into the parking lot of a 7-Eleven.

"Listen, Mama, I promise you that Earl is not going to spend one day in prison," I said, turning to face her with earnest eyes. "You have my word on that. So try not to worry."

She reached over, grabbed my hand, and gave it a squeeze. Then she pulled on the car door handle.

"I think I'm going to make a stop in the little girls' room while we're here. I should have gone at the dress shop. And I'm getting a Slurpee. You want me to get you one, too?"

Mama and I slurped our icy cherry drinks on the drive back to Dixie. I dropped Mama off at her house. I shut off the engine to her Cadillac, got out, and walked over to my SUV as Mama retrieved her purchase from the car. She looked so proud as she took the hanging garment bag containing her wedding dress out of the backseat. She started to walk away as I got in my car, then turned around and hollered for me to wait just a minute. She went in the house and came back out in just a couple of minutes with a Tupperware container. I rolled down my window.

"Here're some sliced peaches. I bought a quart

at the farmers market yesterday. They've already been sugared."

"Thanks, Mama."

I drove to the office, determined to get some work done. When my time isn't taken up with an impending event, I like to play catch-up on back-burner items and work on organizing my desk and supply closet and surf the Internet looking for new party ideas. I usually enjoy having time for these kinds of things. But I was so distracted I started to feel that I was actually doing more harm than good with my scattered attempts at organization.

Mama's tears over Earl refusing to marry her until he had cleared his name were still pulling at my heartstrings. I knew my time would be better spent with wholehearted attempts at finding the real killer than halfhearted attempts at organizing my supply closet.

I ran over the list of suspects in my head and decided I hadn't invested nearly enough time looking into Webster Flack. There were some violent tendencies there. The vandalism at Bubba's store and the altercation the day of the festival when it looked to me the two men might come to blows.

I decided I needed to have a little chat with Dave. I locked up the office and crossed the square to the sheriff's office.

I walked up to the front desk and asked Terry if she could buzz the sheriff for me.

"Can I say what this is concerning?" she asked with a bored look.

Just as she started to buzz his extension, the sheriff ambled in and said, "It's okay, Terry. I've got this."

He looked at me, then turned around and started walking away without a spoken greeting, much less an attempt at pleasantries, which is an egregious breach of Southern etiquette.

I followed him into his office, where he plopped down into his chair.

"Dave, can we talk for a minute?" I asked.

"We can if it's not about the murder investigation," he said with a scolding glare.

"Okay. It's not about the murder, or at least not directly. I wanted to ask you about the vandalism to the Rowland's building—which happened before the murder."

"What about it?" he said, his nostrils beginning to flare.

"My understanding is there was some indication it was done by Webster or one of his group. But you never arrested anyone. What evidence did you have pointing to them, instead of some teenage vandals or taggers? I mean, there has been other graffiti popping up around town from time to time."

Dave opened a filing cabinet drawer, pulled out a folder, walked to the copy machine in the hallway, and made a double-sided copy. I was right on his heels when he turned and handed me the paper.

"Here's the report. Knock yourself out. I don't have time for this right now."

He stormed back to his office. I decided to leave before he changed his mind and asked for the report back.

After getting the police report from Dave, I went home and set about making potato salad. I also seasoned and formed ground beef into patties for hamburgers later. I went in the den, put my feet up, closed my eyes, and thought about the festival and Bubba and Earl and hoped my mind would be able to organize my thoughts about the murder more effectively than it had about organizing my supply closet.

Not much luck on that front, so I called Larry Joe and asked what time he expected to be home. About thirty minutes before his ETA, I went into the backyard and fired up the gas grill. We hadn't cooked out much this summer and I thought some charred beef would hit the spot for my husband.

When Larry Joe got home I put the hamburger patties and some buttered buns on a platter and went out back. I put the buns on the grill just long enough for a light toasting and some grill stripes, before taking them off. I placed the thick burgers on the grill and went back in the house.

Larry Joe had made it home and was pouring us some iced tea when I walked into the kitchen.

"Hon, I can take over grill duty," he said.

"Okay, I just put them on, so you've got a few minutes. Do you want to eat out back? There's some shade, but it's still awful warm."

"No, I've had enough of the heat for one day. Let's eat in."

I sliced a red onion and some sweet pickles and placed them, along with the mayo, mustard, and ketchup, on the table. I was spooning potato salad onto our plates when Larry Joe returned with the hamburgers.

He gave thanks and we sat down to the table and began fixing our burgers.

"So how did your day go?" he asked. "You went shopping with your mama, right?"

"Yeah. I guess you could say it was successful. She bought a dress for her wedding."

"What do you think of the dress?"

"It's not any more ridiculous than the rest of her wedding wish list," I said with honesty. "I also managed to finagle the police report about the vandalism at the Rowlands' store from Dave."

Finagle might have been an exaggeration, but I decided I deserved the credit anyway.

"Impressive. So what does it say?"

"You know, I've only glanced over it. I'll read it to you after dinner."

"That's something to look forward to."

After supper, I spooned some of the sliced peaches Mama had given me into a bowl and topped them with whipped cream for Larry Joe. We retired to the den and I read him the police report while he enjoyed his dessert.

"Let me see, 'Incident Report, Reporting Officer (R/O) Ted Horton, case number . . .' blah, blah. Okay, 'at 7:25 AM on June thirty, Dispatch received a call reporting vandalism on Third Street in Dixie, Tennessee.

"'The complainant identified himself as Bruce D. Rowland, co-owner, along with his brother, Bubba Rowland, of Rowland's Building Supply. Upon arriving at the business and parking in his usual space in the rear alley, Rowland said he discovered graffiti spray painted along the rear wall wrapping around onto part of the side wall of the building. There was also broken glass on the pavement near the building that upon inspection was identified as falling from a small window on the second floor in the rear of the building.

"'Upon arriving at the scene at 7:45 AM, R/O was met by Rowland and his wife, Carrie H. Rowland, who also works in the family business and said she arrived moments after her husband and parked beside his vehicle.

"'Rowland told R/O he had locked up building and left for the night at approximately 9:00 PM the night before and was the first to arrive at the business that morning.

"'Rowland confirmed that there were no video surveillance cameras overlooking the alley. Closer inspection of the broken window indicated it had been broken by an object thrown at it, creating a small hole and shattered pattern radiating from the center. The hole was not large enough for someone to reach through to unlatch the window and there was no indication that the window had been forced open.

"'R/O photographed the scene, including the

graffiti, which included obscenities, and the broken glass and windows. R/O also collected and took into evidence a large rock, which Rowland said he had not previously noticed in the alley and which may have been used to break the upper window, and two spray paint cans: Krylon brand paint, colors smoke gray and tangerine orange.

"'When questioned about any suspicious activity or persons in the area preceding the vandalism, Rowland said there had been protesters with placards walking in front of the building the previous weekend. They were in opposition to a residential development that his brother was involved with. He said there had been some shouting, including profanities, but no violence. Rowland's brother had filed a complaint about the protest incident, stating that the protesters were harassing customers and impeding entrance into the store.'"

I laid the report on the table.

"Any thoughts?"

"Breaking a window just to be destructive, since the break wasn't big enough to let them get in, sounds like anger. Otherwise, the graffiti could just be chalked up to some kids cutting loose—not that I'm excusing that behavior. Were there any witnesses who saw someone hanging around the store?"

"No. And since there are no security cameras, they really have nothing to go on. One of the bad words on the wall was misspelled, so it probably wasn't done by a genius."

"Around Dixie that doesn't narrow the field by much," he said.

Chapter 12

I was moving pretty slow Wednesday morning for some reason and wasn't dressed until after 8:30. Instead of having my usual toast or cereal I took the time to scramble some eggs and fry a couple of slices of bacon. I checked messages and e-mail on my phone as I lingered over a cup of coffee.

Since I didn't have any meetings on the schedule I decided it would be a good time to figure out the guest capacity at Earl's place. Theoretically, it was as big as all outdoors. But since the weather doesn't always cooperate, we needed adequate space to accommodate all the guests under cover if it happened to rain.

I phoned Holly to see if she cared to join me since taking measurements is easier with two people.

"Morning, Holly. Are you up for a field trip today? And when I say field, I mean literally. I need to go out to Earl's property and take measurements, especially of the barn. Mama has more than doubled the size of her guest list and I need to figure out how many people we can actually accommodate there."

"Awlright, darlin', what time?"

"You tell me, my schedule is wide open."

"Let's go this morning and then have lunch together," she said.

"That sounds great."

I arranged to meet her in front of the office at ten o'clock.

I thought we should go ahead and check out the space in the house and on the wraparound porch for a pass-through reception if by some miracle Mama actually cut the guest list. Plus, it would be nice to have access to the indoor plumbing if we ended up being out there for a while. So I called Earl, told him what Holly and I were up to, and asked if I could swing by the store and pick up a set of house keys.

"You can if you want. But there's also a spare key under the pair of boots by the back door."

"You keep a key under your boot? Where do you put it when you wear your boots?"

"I haven't worn those boots in years. I guess you could call them decorative at this point."

When I pulled up in front of the office, I could see through the front window that Holly was inside Sweet Deal Realty chatting with Winette. Holly spotted me and hurried out the door to the car. I exchanged a wave with Winette.

Holly was wearing blue jeans, which is unusual

for her. But they were bell-bottoms, so they didn't stray completely from her signature style.

Earl lives a few miles out of town. It's a fairly smooth ride until turning off on his road, which hasn't been repaved in who knows how long. The house sits a good way back from the road. I pulled into the gravel driveway and slowly bumped along until I was beside the house.

"It's been some time since I was out here," I said. "I'd forgotten how pretty it is. Shall we check out the house or the barn first?"

"Let's measure the barn first, which I imagine is pretty warm. Then we can retreat into the air-conditioning in the house," Holly said.

"Good plan."

We walked around to the back of the white farm-house with a broad porch on three sides. The front door looked freshly painted in an emerald shade of green and I wondered if Earl had chosen the color to match Mama's eyes. But maybe I was just being sappy.

I'd estimate it was about a hundred feet from the back of the house to the faded red barn. It was another hundred feet or so from the side of the barn to the edge of a large pond with a little island in its center. Unlike the recently mowed surround-ings, the island was covered in tall grass. I made a mental note that the island would need to be mowed or weed whacked before the wedding. It wouldn't look proper for Mama to have weeds lapping up to her knees.

The double barn doors were standing open.

There was a stack of hay bales at the back, a riding mower, a small Bush Hog tractor, a rotary tiller, and various garden implements rowed up against one wall. It would need some cleaning out before the wedding, but it was pretty clean for a barn.

I stood just inside the wooden structure, took the electronic tape measure out of my purse, and pointed the laser at the back wall. Next I stood against one of the side walls and aimed the laser toward the other side.

"Okay, Holly, it looks like the barn is fifty by thirty, which is fifteen hundred square feet."

Holly entered the square footage into a space calculator that works out how many people a space can accommodate. It even refines the estimate based on how the space will be set up for the occasion—banquet tables, buffet tables, stages, dance floor, and so on.

"We'll need a stage for the band, right?" Holly asked.

"Yeah. And in case of rain, I think we'd use the platform for the ceremony, as well. And we're planning on a buffet for 150 to 160 people."

Holly entered all the pertinent information into the calculator.

"Awlright, depending on which calculator you use, we can manage 140 to 166 guests," she said.

"That's good. Mama's got 152 people on her list right now. She's bound to add a few more. But at least a few of those invited won't attend, so we should be able to make it work—just barely. I need to get a look at that list and figure out how many are likely attendees. I feel certain she's sending invitations to some out-of-towners she doesn't want to offend, but who won't actually come."

"We'll pray for good weather—but be prepared, just in case."

I nodded in agreement.

We headed to the house to check the space there, in the unlikely event that I, or Earl, could persuade Mama to trim her guest list. I retrieved the key from under the boot.

From the back porch we stepped into a large den with a fireplace. It had a decidedly masculine feel, with a well-worn leather sofa and chairs and deer trophy heads above the mantel. We took measurements in the den before moving to the living room at the front of the house. It was much more formal, with Victorian settees, or what I always think of as funeral parlor furniture, since that was how the funeral home was furnished when I was growing up.

Our measurements and calculations confirmed my assessment that we could accommodate sixty or so people circulating on the porches and through the house.

The house was surprisingly tidy for a bachelor, but then Earl wasn't exactly unattached. Some of the organization, especially in the kitchen, and the dust-free condition of the entry hall table caused me to suspect Mama's handiwork. Although the two of them spent a good deal more time at Mama's house, I suspected she made regular trips here for cleaning and maybe even a bit of romance. The thought made me smile.

Holly interrupted my reverie.

"I suppose they'll live full-time at your mama's after they're married."

"Mama hasn't said so, but I can't imagine her giving up her kitchen."

"I wonder if Earl will hang on to this place. It could be a nice retreat for them," Holly said.

We locked up the back door and replaced the key in its hiding place before driving back to town.

Holly and I had enjoyed a leisurely lunch at Taco Belles. Supper tonight at my house was going to be leftovers from lunch for me and a to-go box of fajitas I had ordered for Larry Joe.

My hungry husband smiled when he came in the back door and heard the fajitas sizzling in a cast iron skillet as I reheated them for his dinner. He gave me a quick kiss on the cheek.

"I've been slaving over a hot stove for minutes," I said. "We're just about ready to eat if you wouldn't mind pouring us some iced tea."

We took our plates to the table. After a few word-less minutes of chowing down, Larry Joe raised his head from the trough.

"Hey, Liv," he said waving his fork in my direc-tion. "I was concerned after you told me Winette thought Rankin might not be on the up-and-up. I think she may be on to something. I ate lunch at the country club today and talked to three dif-ferent golfing buddies who had invested in the new development.

"One of them gave me this," Larry Joe said, pulling a glossy, full-color brochure about the development out of his back pocket.

I leafed through the brochure before dropping it into my purse, which was sitting on the kitchen floor. On the back cover was a photo of a smiling Aaron Rankin.

"All three of them told me they had also invested in some rental properties Rankin owns in East Tennessee. He's apparently a smooth talker. Rankin told them that it will be a while before they see a return on their investment in the Dixie project because of sales and construction timelines, but that they could start lining their pockets in the meantime if they wanted in on this other deal. He told each of them to keep it under their hats because he only had a couple of openings left and made them think he was making the offer to them special. It's obvious he had at least three of those 'couple of openings,' and my guess is there were several more."

"So did they tell you any details about this rental property deal?"

"The way Jeb, who's probably the brightest of the three, explained it, Rankin's investment firm oversees these tenants-in-common securities where the investors collectively own a piece of the real estate and receive a portion of the rental income from the property. Only so far they've received a bunch of reports and very little money, from what I gathered."

"That doesn't sound quite right," I said.

"That's what I thought. So Jeb mentioned the name of the investment company for the rental property—it's different from the name of the company putting together the Dixie development. I gave the sheriff a call this afternoon and told him what I'd heard. He said it sounded fishy to him and he was going to check into it. I told him I'd appreciate it, because we don't want good people getting cheated out of their savings."

"What about bad people?" I said.

"Are you talking about Bubba?"

"Yeah. I'm thinking if the developer is dipping his hand in other people's pockets and the late councilman found out about it, Rankin might have decided to shut Bubba up permanently."

Larry Joe said he was going upstairs to work for a bit on the bathroom. Honestly, I have no idea how someone can put so much time in on something and have so little to show for it. But since his virtues far outweigh his shortcomings, I try not to complain too much.

"So is Di coming by?" he asked, pausing in the doorway.

"This is her yoga class night, so she might drop by after."

I was clearing away the dishes when my cell phone buzzed. Without as much as a hello, Di said, "I just heard some news about the case I think you'll be interested in."

"Let's hear it."

"Not on the phone. I'm just leaving my yoga class. Can I stop by?"

"Of course."

In a few minutes, Di knocked, then slipped into the kitchen through the door from the garage.

"Wine, rum?" I offered, trying to be a good hostess.

"Thanks. I'll have a rum and Coke."

I poured one for Di and one for myself, mine light on the rum.

"Okay, spill it. I'm dying to hear. What did Dave have to say?"

"I didn't hear it from Dave. He's being all tight-lipped. You know how he gets. Anyway, I was chatting up Ted and Daisy after class."

"Are they still cozy?"

"Oh, good grief, they're sickening. But that's another story. Anyway, it worked to my advantage because I think Ted likes showing off in front of Daisy. So when I asked casually about the case and tried to pretend like I knew more than I did, he volunteered some interesting information.

"They got back the lab and toxicology reports. Ted said they weren't really expecting anything unusual there since Bubba was shot, not poisoned. But, here's the thing. Bubba had ingested a heavy dose of some laxative."

"This sounds important, somehow, but I'm not sure what it means," I said.

"It would appear that somebody wanted to ensure that Bubba would be making a trip to the porta john, which, not coincidentally, is where he was shot."

"Yes! And it also means whoever gave him the laxative is either the killer or an accomplice," I said.

"Even better," Di said, "it seems unlikely to me that Earl Daniels would have had an opportunity to slip a laxative into Bubba's food or drink," Di said, raising her glass and chinking it against mine.

Suddenly my mind was teeming with suspects and possibilities.

"Bubba could have eaten junk food from any number of vendors, but several of those weren't even locals and the chance of Bubba walking up and buying their food would seem a bit random. So the most likely sources, it would seem to me, would be either the Coca-Cola and not so secret whiskey cart or the winners' dinner," I said.

"Do you remember which guys were standing around the Coke stand with Bubba?"

I closed my eyes for a moment trying to remember the scene. To my best recollection, it was a come-and-go affair, with various men at different times.

"You know, I think the whiskey and Coke cart was a serve-yourself setup, with guys helping themselves to a splash of whiskey under the counter. My thought is the dinner is a more likely spot. Billy Tucker and his Grills on Wheels crew prepared the barbecue and it was buffet style with folks serving themselves. So I don't know how that could have worked, as far as slipping a laxative to just one person." I said. "And I think we would have heard if there'd been an outbreak of diarrhea."

"Right," Di said, suddenly wide eyed with excitement. "But remember earlier, when you were walking through the park trying to remember events from the day of the festival, what was it you said about when you went in the tent? They were serving dessert? Who was it that delivered Bubba's plate to him?"

"I saw Bernice Halford set a huge slice of her award-winning chocolate cake down on the table in front of Bubba. And come to think of it, I don't think I saw her fetching cake for anybody else. There was a crew of high school girls doing the serving. That does seem a little curious, doesn't it?"

"I don't know. I guess that depends on just how good of friends Bernice Halford and Nonie Jones are. Mrs. Jones would clearly be the one with the motive—her granddaughter getting cheated out of the Miss Dixie crown. But not many people would help even their closest friend commit murder," Di said.

Chapter 13

Holly came to the office midmorning so we could finish working on the materials for the business expo. I wanted to get everything printed far enough ahead of time that we could have them reprinted if there were any problems.

At previous business fairs we had used posters on easels or vinyl banners hung on a backdrop. This time I was making an investment in a more premium display without busting the budget. We were beginning to book more business events, so I wanted to step up our game. Holly and I had been poring over trade show catalogs and online photos. We'd settled on a portable stand. The banner pulled up from the base and attached to a support bar. The banner retracted into the base for convenient transporting and storage.

"I think this looks like our best bet," Holly said, pointing to one of several retractable banners we'd been comparing. "One of the galleries shows this model with the logo for a local company. Would you like me to call their sales department and ask if they're happy with the way this product has performed for them?"

I said I thought that was a great idea. The product was well reviewed, but there's nothing like talking to a customer who's actually used it. The various retractable and pop-up banner stands ran from a few hundred to a few thousand dollars. We were definitely sticking in the few hundred range. But it was still a significant investment for my small business and I didn't want to sacrifice quality.

Holly and I had brought bagged lunches from home so we could work through lunch. I told Holly I'd run across the street and get us two large iced teas while she made the phone call.

I crossed the street and met Dave walking toward me, apparently on his way to the courthouse.

"Liv," he said, looking around to see if anyone was within earshot. "I've been giving some thought to what you said about a romantic gesture." His voice dropped to a whisper when he said "romantic."

"Yeah. What are you thinking?"

"What if I hired one of those places that do singing telegrams to send someone out to deliver a love song?"

I tried to give him credit for trying, even if he was off by a mile.

"That's sweet, Dave. But I think what you really need is something a little more personal. Something you do yourself. Don't worry, I'm sure it'll come to you."

He nodded with a confused look on his face before turning and jogging up the courthouse steps.

I thought about asking him about the case, but figured if he was actually having romantic ideas I owed it to Di not to interrupt his train of thought.

I ran into the diner and picked up two sweet teas to go. When I made it back to the office, Holly was off the phone and looking at the computer screen. I handed one of the cups to her and sat down across from her.

"Did you find out anything?"

"Yes, I talked to a nice young salesman. He said they've been very pleased with the retractable banners. He did suggest that, for transport purposes, we might be better off getting two four-feet-wide stands instead of one eight feet wide. But I was scrolling through the pictures and I think we might want to get one three feet wide and one five feet wide instead of having two side by side that are exactly the same size. What do you think?"

"I think that's a great idea."

We discussed other ideas over our brown-bag lunch. We had originally planned on having several images on the banner to represent different-sized events, suitable for a variety of budgets. But we decided to save that for the brochures and use only one large image on the bigger banner and feature just one smaller image, along with our business logo, on the smaller banner. The goal was to display images that would be attention grabbers and draw people to our booth.

After much deliberation, we made our selections.

For the smaller panel, we decided to place a photo of a giggling child holding a balloon sculpture of a giraffe under the Liv 4 Fun logo. For the large panel, we chose a gorgeous shot from an elegant riverboat gambler–themed engagement party Holly and I had staged. The photo showed a handsome couple dancing and looking very much in love. The backdrop for the couple was the expansive entry of a stately home in Dixie and featured an impressive riverboat-shaped cake, as well as poster-sized king and queen of hearts cards hanging on the stair railing above them. Guests watching from double doorways on each side of the entry looked on admiringly, some applauding. The child's photo represented pure joy. And the dancing photo exuded fun, romance, and fantasy.

We uploaded the image files and placed our order. We'd have to decide on photos and complete the design for the brochures, but we'd save that for another day since it wouldn't take as long to have those printed.

"I think we've had a productive day, Holly. I'm excited about our displays."

"I know. I can't wait to see them full size."

Holly started gathering her belongings, which included a file folder of ideas and images she had researched before coming to the office.

"Holly, you need to turn time sheets in to me, so I can get you a check."

"I already turned my time sheet in. It's on your desk there," she said, nodding.

"I saw that, but it's not complete. I know you have

more hours than that, just with the time you've spent on Mama's wedding."

"Darlin', I'm not turning in hours for your mama's wedding. You're not charging her."

"No, no, Holly. My giving Mama the family discount doesn't mean you don't get a paycheck. If anything, you should be getting hazard pay for the extra dose of crazy."

"I'm very fond of your mama. And while I agree with your decision to give up weddings as a major part of your business, it's fun to do a wedding now and again. And your mama's certainly going to keep things interesting. I won't accept a dime. My mind's made up."

Holly grabbed her purse and files and waved to me over her shoulder as she walked out.

Meals had been mostly haphazard affairs around our house lately, so I decided to put in the effort to make a nice supper. And it doesn't have to be from scratch to count as "nice" on my menu, as long as it's not simply heat and serve or takeout. I stopped by the grocery store and picked up some eggs, cheeses, a couple of varieties of mushrooms, and refrigerated pie crust dough. I had some tomatoes and zucchini from Mama's garden to make a quiche, which Larry Joe actually likes. I'd serve it with sausages on the side, which he likes even better. And I grabbed some Chubby Hubby ice cream for good measure.

I took my groceries to the checkout stands. Only

one person was ahead of me when I got in line, and she had only a handful of items in her cart. Then I noticed Cassie Latham was the cashier in the next lane. I rolled my cart over and got into the longer line.

After the cashier in my former lane finished bagging the groceries for the lady who had been in front of me, she started waving and saying, "Lane open; no waiting on register three." I put my head down and tried to avoid eye contact, thinking surely there must be other people in this store ready to check out.

The woman in line ahead of me in Cassie's lane touched my sleeve and said, "Excuse me, if you aren't moving to the open register, could you back up and let me out?"

I did and it was an awkward moment as the neighboring cashier wondered, I'm sure, what I had against her. I was hoping Cassie was too busy ringing up items to notice the shuffle.

The line seemed to slowly creep forward. As soon as there was some room on the conveyor belt I began hurriedly dumping my foodstuffs onto it. When the customer in front of me stepped away I wanted to be standing in front of Cassie, giving me as much time as possible to chat. Then I had the idea to "accidentally" leave a couple of items in the bottom of the basket, so I could spot them as she finished ringing up items to give me a little extra time with her. If I had noticed Cassie was a checker when I entered the store I would have piled more groceries into my cart. Poor planning.

"Hi, Mrs. McKay. Do you have any coupons today?" She started ringing up items without waiting for a response, so I didn't feel obliged to give one.

"Cassie, congratulations on being named first runner-up in the Miss Dixie pageant."

"Thank you. It was a lot of fun and I'm honored to have done so well," she said what I'm sure had become a well-rehearsed line since the competition.

"You have every right to be proud. Still, it had to be a bit disappointing, especially when so many people—including me, I might add—thought you should have won hands down. Jennifer's a sweet girl, but she just wasn't your match in the talent portion of the competition."

"That's very kind of you to say," she said, keeping her head down and focused on sliding items across the built-in scanner.

"Of course, it was probably harder for your mom to accept the loss than for you. Parents can't help but feel it deeply when their child suffers an injustice like that. I'm sure that's why she felt she just had to confront Bubba Rowland with the rumors about him bribing one of the judges."

Cassie finally made eye contact with me, and it wasn't a friendly glance.

"My mama tends to get emotional. I'm afraid she embarrassed herself—and me—by causing a scene. She calmed down after Grandma Nonie talked some sense into her."

"Of course, of course. I don't fault a mother for taking up for her kid. Nobody does, Cassie. Still, it was a shame she was too upset to stick around for the fireworks show. She *was* seen leaving before it started."

Cassie, visibly piqued by that last remark, simply told me my total, hoping to dispatch me quickly.

"Oh, hon, I'm so sorry. I got distracted and missed a couple of items in my cart," I said, picking them up and putting them on the belt.

This solicited that look of disdain that teenagers do so well.

"For the record, Mom didn't leave the festival after the winners were announced, despite the fact that *someone* says she did," she said, obviously referring to Earl. "She just left the stage area and went to the winners' tent to help my grandma with the cleaning. I went over and joined them myself a few minutes later to finish up."

I knew that was a bald-faced lie. I walked past the tent several times during the evening and they had finished with cleanup well before the day's winners were announced onstage. Since many more people attend the fireworks show than the various individual contests during the festival, introducing all the winners of the day just before the pyrotechnics begin has become a tradition.

I smiled at Cassie, who was once again avoiding eye contact, and I had to wonder why she felt the need to lie for her mother.

* * *

I had sliced and thrown together the ingredients for my quiche and was just popping it in the oven when Larry Joe came in from the garage.

He gave me a quick kiss and said, "Did you hear about the break-in out at the new development offices last night?"

"No, I carried my lunch today and didn't really talk to anyone except Holly. What happened?"

"The contractor's and sales office at the construction site for the new development was trashed and graffiti was spray painted all over the walls. The other trailer, which had housed offices for Bubba Rowland and another investment partner, was set on fire. A smoldering metal shell was all that was left by the time the volunteer fire department made it to the site."

"Was anyone hurt? Do they know who did it?"

"No one was hurt, thank God," Larry Joe said. "Dave hasn't arrested anybody. But the graffiti makes me wonder if it was some of Webster Flack's group."

"Vandalism is one thing—not that I'm condoning it. But arson is a whole other thing. Do you really think Webster or his crew could be involved?"

"I don't know, but you said you saw him and Bubba almost come to blows the day of the festival. And it's all but certain he or one of his group spray painted hateful things on the Rowland's building. Sometimes these things can escalate."

After we'd eaten and cleared the dishes, Larry Joe

went into the den. I joined him in there, carrying a bowl of Chubby Hubby ice cream for each of us. He turned down the volume on the TV as I walked in.

"You know how I told you I thought Dad was up to something?" he said. "I'm sure of it now."

"What is it?"

"I don't know exactly. But he's been taking phone calls on his cell phone and walking outside to talk. You know how he hates cell phones. He usually won't even leave it turned on, carries one mostly for emergencies."

"That is a little odd," I said.

"Then the other day, he walked out of the office. In a bit when he hadn't come back, I walked out the front to check on him and his truck was gone. He just drove off without saying a word to our secretary, Charlene, or me. And he was gone almost two hours. He never does that."

"Honey, that really concerns me. I know your dad would never run around on your mom, which would be one explanation for his recent behavior. I don't want to worry you, but I have to wonder if he has some health issue he's hiding from you and your mother."

Larry Joe went quiet for a moment, then put his arm around me. I laid my head on his shoulder.

"I may have to have a talk with the geezer," he said.

"If you do, go easy on him."

"Yeah, I will."

The TV had been playing a hushed laugh track along with a not very funny sitcom as we talked. Larry Joe turned up the volume just as the nine o'clock news came on and there was a reporter standing in front of a burned-out trailer.

"I'm here in Dixie where a suspected act of arson destroyed this trailer behind me. It housed offices for the large planned new development here that has stirred a lot of controversy with conservation activists," he said.

Crime scene tape separated the reporter from Dave and Ted, who were talking with the fire chief from Hartville, standing amid the ashes and scorched earth in front of the fire-ravaged trailer hull.

"Hartville Fire Chief Paul Ruby and his team have been sifting through rubble and examining the scene today. Here's what Chief Ruby had to say."

The screen cut to the fire official making a brief statement.

"Evidence of accelerants makes it likely this fire was an act of arson. We'll be taking evidence back to the lab for examination," Chief Ruby said.

"Sheriff Dave Davidson said he had no comment at this time," the reporter said.

Larry Joe shut off the TV with a click of the remote control.

"Wow. I can't believe the way that trailer was destroyed. If Webster is behind this, he has gone completely off the rails," I said.

"Yep. Whoever did it, I hope Dave catches him and puts him away," he said. "Speaking of putting away, I'm headed for bed. You coming up?"

"Yeah, in just a minute."

"Tell Di I said hello," he said, patting me on the knee before rising from the sofa.

He knows me so well, I thought.

He walked toward the staircase and I went into the kitchen and grabbed my cell phone off the counter and called Di.

"Hi. Did you see the news?"

"Yeah."

"Larry Joe said the graffiti seems to point to Webster Flack or some of his group. Do you think he's behind it?"

"I don't know, but that's a pretty ugly scene for a tree hugger who claims he just wants to preserve the natural beauty and wildlife habitat of the area," Di said.

"I know. Whoever is guilty I hope Dave catches them soon. Vandalism, murder, and arson—people in Dixie are going to have to start locking their doors.

"By the way, have you said anything to Dave about Bernice Halford being the most likely suspect to have slipped the laxatives to Bubba?"

"No. We haven't discussed Bubba's digestive issues recently," she said with her deadpan charm.

"I think I'm going to talk to Dave about it tomorrow. I'd like to think he's paying attention to someone besides Earl for a change."

Chapter 14

I had walked over to Town Square Diner to order a chef's salad to go when I spotted Nonie Jones and Bernice Halford sitting together in a corner booth. Just before I placed my order I noticed that Bernice was saying her good-byes, leaving Nonie on her own. I told Mabel to give me a moment and I went over and slid into the booth across from Nonie.

"Miss Nonie, how are you doing?"

"Other than my arthritis flare-ups I don't have much to complain about, especially for my age."

She had a friendly tone, but seemed wary of me. I decided I'd better sweeten the pot before I dropped her into hot water.

"I'm sure many people have already told you this, but I just wanted to say I thought Cassie should have been crowned Miss Dixie. The judging results were truly unfortunate. She is obviously such a talented young lady and it must have been very disappointing."

"Well, thank you. I think she's gifted, but then I'm more than a mite partial," she said.

I decided to press things a bit.

"Cassie handled the disappointment with such poise, especially for someone her age. She was a real trooper when they announced the winners and runners-up onstage. Lynn had a harder time concealing her feelings, naturally—as any mother would under the circumstances," I said.

"My daughter unfortunately deals with her emotions by drinking. I'm sorry folks saw her make a scene with Bubba Rowland. I know that was embarrassing for my granddaughter. We'll never know for sure if Bubba influenced the judges or not. And I do sincerely feel bad for Jennifer; her uncle getting killed was tragic and cast a pall over her big night."

"Oh, of course," I said. "It's so, so sad."

"If you'll excuse me, I need to harvest some things in my garden before they wilt on the vine. It's been so dry."

I said good-bye and she picked up her ticket and walked to the register to pay. Ever-efficient waitress, Margie, who is surprisingly light-footed for someone of her girth, came over with a tray and started busing the table.

"You want to order something, hon?"

I justified in my mind that a chef salad with bleu cheese wasn't exactly low calorie anyway and ordered what I really wanted.

"I'll have a slice of chess pie and a glass of sweet tea, please."

I didn't even get the chance to ask Nonie about

the cake she and Bernice served up to Bubba at the winners' dinner. But the fact she was being so guarded made me suspect she might have something to hide.

I spent a good bit of my afternoon on the phone, talking to a couple of prospective clients, getting prices for upcoming jobs, and talking twice to Mama, who was apparently feeling lonely.

Just before I left the office for the day, I finally decided to walk over to the sheriff's office and tell Dave my theory that Nonie and Bernice were most likely the ones who slipped the laxative to Bubba. If he wouldn't see me or wouldn't listen, at least I could say I tried.

Terry, the dispatcher, was at the front desk, as usual. I asked her to let Dave know I was there and would like to have a word. Before she could buzz him, he leaned around from the hallway and said, "Come on back. I can give you a minute."

He invited me to take a seat in one of the less than inviting blue vinyl straight-back chairs facing his desk.

"What's up?"

"I heard about the lab results showing that Bubba was loaded up with laxatives, ensuring that the killer would have a chance to shoot him while he was using the portable facilities."

"I won't hazard a guess as to who you heard that from," he said.

I ignored his remark and continued. "You said

yourself that as the event coordinator, roaming all over the festival grounds during the day, I was in the best position to have seen things that went on that might relate to the murder. And I recall seeing something that might be helpful."

"Okay, let's hear it."

"I went into the winners' dinner tent just as they were serving dessert. There were some high school girls bringing around cakes and pies to the tables. But I remember seeing Bernice Halford hand deliver a big piece of her prize-winning cake to Bubba. It would have been hard to know which of the festival food vendors Bubba might choose to eat at. And it would have been difficult, if not impossible, for the guys at the whiskey cart to slip something in Bubba's drink without being noticed. The winners' dinner seems like the most likely spot to have introduced laxatives into Bubba's food. And since the barbecue was served buffet style, that would have been difficult. But the cake was brought special delivery to Bubba by Nonie Jones's best friend, just hours after Nonie's granddaughter was cheated, in most people's estimation at least, out of the Miss Dixie crown."

"You're right," Dave said without enthusiasm. "The tests of the stomach contents show the cake was laced with enough laxative to give a bull the trots. I thank you for confirming that it was Bernice who served it to Bubba. Witnesses I talked to weren't in complete agreement on that point."

He started shuffling papers on his desk like he was getting ready to dismiss me.

"Doesn't this bit of information point to the killer being someone other than Earl? It's clear he couldn't have slipped the laxatives to Bubba to lure him into his rifle sights."

"That's true. But it's also possible someone told Earl about the laxatives. And we don't have any other evidence pointing to Nonie or Bernice at the moment."

"You don't seem to be looking very hard for evidence that points anywhere other than at Earl at the moment, Sheriff Davidson," I said.

"Look, Liv, this information could help Earl. It's just not the silver bullet you were hoping for. And you know very well that Ted and I are following up on every lead. We're still going through photos and video and I'm not letting Bernice or Nonie—or any other suspect—off the hook. Thanks for the information. Now back off and let me do my job."

He stood up and I turned and walked out before he had the chance to ask me to leave.

After supper, I went into the den and had just settled into the sofa when Di called.

"I just left the liquor store with a bottle of Merlot. I thought I'd drop by if you care to share a glass with me. It's Friday night and the man in my life is married to his job."

"Sure, come on by, if you don't mind listening to the man in my life bang on the pipes upstairs."

I went to the kitchen, where my purse was sitting on the counter, reached inside and pressed the garage door opener, so Di could slip in through the back door.

In a few minutes she knocked as she entered. She walked over to the kitchen table and pulled a magnum of Merlot out of a brown paper bag. I got out the wineglasses and a corkscrew. Since Di's uncorking skills are superior to mine, she did the honors.

I poured wine into the glasses and Di followed me through to the den.

"So how did the conversation with Dave go about the ex-lax-cake bakers?" she said, her feet propped up in the recliner.

"If my hope was that this would at least move Earl down the list of suspects, then I'd have to say not so good. Even though he confirmed it was the cake that contained the laxative."

"How can Dave think Earl had anything to do with that?" Di asked.

"He suggested that just because Bernice may have put laxative in the cake doesn't prove she pulled the trigger, and that Earl could have heard about the laxative from someone else and used that information for his own nefarious purposes."

"That's ridiculous."

"Yeah, well," I said. "Clearly we can't depend on Dave to follow this thread to sew up the case. We're going to have to do that ourselves."

Di suggested we try to take a look at things from Dave's perspective and see if there were any obvious holes in our theories.

"Okay, are there witnesses or photographs that

show where Nonie and Bernice were during or right before the fireworks?" Di asked.

"I don't know," I said, grabbing a junk mail envelope from the end table and scribbling a note on the back of it. "That's something we should try to find out. But for the moment, let's assume they have alibis and that's why Dave seems to be dismissing the idea that either of them is the killer. Where does that leave us?"

"It would mean, I think, that somebody or somebodies also knew about the laxative. That would mean Bernice and Nonie either told someone or someone overheard them talking about it."

"And the most obvious someone would be Lynn, right?" I said. "I can't believe her mama wouldn't have told her about it so she could enjoy watching Bubba suffer, at least a little. And even though she denies it, Earl said he saw her leaving right before the fireworks started—and he's the one person I believe."

"So if Bernice or Nonie mentioned it to someone else, Lynn is the most likely suspect. But what about other people who could have known? When Bubba got shot wasn't necessarily his first trip to the outhouse that evening. Maybe other people noticed him running to the facilities. Maybe he even mentioned the fact that his stomach was upset to someone. That also opens the possibility that whoever he told could have mentioned it to someone else," Di said.

"I guess someone could have taken note that he made more than one trip to the restroom, but that wouldn't necessarily mean he had an upset stomach to the casual observer," I said. "It could mean he just had to pee a lot, maybe prostate trouble. And that kind of pit stop would be pretty quick and might not give the shooter time to get in place and line up a shot. Plus, I don't think he'd be talking about something that personal with just anybody. But he could have mentioned it to his brother, maybe. And his brother, or anybody who overheard him telling his brother, could have told somebody else."

"I don't think so. I mean, honestly how many people talk about their own diarrhea, much less somebody else's?" Di said.

"That's a good point. So if we move Nonie and Bernice down the list for the moment, that makes either Lynn or Bruce the most likely suspects. Let's focus on them for the time being. Since it's well known I shop at Earl's maybe you could drop by Rowland's Building Supply tomorrow after work and chat with Bruce. I'll stalk Lynn at the seamstress shop. I have some pants I've been meaning to get hemmed," I said.

Di drained the remains of the wine she'd been nursing for half an hour.

"You want another glass?"

"No, I'm heading home," she said, starting for the door.

Di paused in the doorway and turned around.

"I know Bruce and most of the men around here go hunting. Do you know if Lynn or her mama can handle a gun?"

"Lynn had one sister and no brothers and grew

up on a farm. I would suspect she knows how to shoot. I never went hunting, but my daddy taught both Emma and me how to shoot cans off a fence. And when I went away to Middle Tennessee State University, he gave me a small derringer to carry in my purse for protection. He was worried about me living in the big city."

"Is Murfreesboro a big city?"

"Fairly big. I'd guess a population of about a hundred thousand. But just about any place would be a big city compared to Dixie. Don't forget to take your Merlot with you."

"No, I'll leave it here for you two, or for another time. I picked up a spare earlier at the liquor store."

After Di left, I poured myself another half glass of wine before corking the bottle and putting it in the fridge. I figured a bit more wine might give me the fortitude to handle a phone call to my sister. I hadn't talked to her since I'd hung up on her when she went all crazy on Earl and Mama's marriage, like we should have our mother committed.

I supposed I owed her an apology since I hung up on her. But then she *had* hung up on me during our previous phone call and never offered an apology. However, I decided if I was to have any chance of having an amicable conversation with my little sister about Mama's impending nuptials, I'd have to be the one to extend the olive branch.

I punched in her number.

"Hi, Emma."

"Oh, it's you," she said with a tone of disdain. I decided to ignore it. I felt my best strategy was to try to get her talking about a less touchy subject.

"How are the kids?"

"They're asleep," she said brusquely. I could tell she wasn't going to make things easy on me.

"Good. Does that mean Trey is a good sleeper now?" I asked, playing the doting aunt card, but she didn't pick it up.

"Were you calling about something in particular?"

I knew she was fishing for an apology. A knot of anger clenched in my stomach. My gut reaction was to feel like she owed me an apology at least as much as I owed her one. But I resolved to remain charitable and try to work toward getting Emma to be at least reasonable, if not supportive, of Mama's wedding plans.

"Yeah, Emma, I wanted to apologize for hanging up on you the other night. We're sisters. We should be able to talk about things, even when we disagree. I think you know Mama's going to make her own decisions, and I hope you'll give Earl a chance. But I know it's a lot to take in, and if you need time to work through your feelings, I'll try to be respectful of that."

"You sound just like Hobie. I'm tired of everybody telling me I need to work through *my* feelings and just accept the ridiculous notion of Mama getting married again and this man she plans to impose on my children as their granddaddy—who's been charged with murder. I'm the only sane person in this family."

I heard the phone go *click* as she hung up on me again.

I tried. I can honestly say I tried. And I might feel differently one day. But at the moment I couldn't imagine offering another apology to my little sister unless one of us was on her deathbed.

It had been a long day and I was ready to put it behind me and go to bed. I stormed up the stairs to the bedroom.

Larry Joe was standing in the bathroom, fiddling with some sort of pipe fittings as I walked past.

"Just so you know, I'm never speaking to my sister again."

"That should make holidays interesting," he said.

Chapter 15

We were just finishing up breakfast Saturday morning when we heard a knock at the front door. I looked out the window and saw Dave's truck parked in front of the house.

"It's Dave," I told Larry Joe.

He went to answer the door and Dave followed him through to the kitchen, while I made quick work of clearing the table.

"Mornin', Liv," he said, taking his hat off.

"Hi, Dave. Would you like some coffee or juice? I can make you some scrambled eggs and toast if you're hungry—won't take a minute."

"I'll take a glass of water, if you don't mind,"

Larry Joe, who was standing just behind Dave, reached into the cabinet beside the sink, plopped a few ice cubes from the freezer into the glass, and filled it from the tap.

I invited Dave to sit down. We joined him at the

kitchen table and he took a couple of big gulps of ice water.

"Larry Joe, I just wanted to give you an update on that information you gave me about Aaron Rankin. I checked with a pal with the Knoxville Police Department and he told me that there'd been quite a few inquiries about Rankin's dealings and that I should talk to the state bureau. So I had a nice long chat with Kelvin Duffy at the Tennessee Bureau of Investigation. He told me unofficially, of course, that Rankin's investment company is under fierce scrutiny right now. They have the resources for that kind of forensic accounting. When I told him we had some Dixie folks who had also put money into the East Tennesee property, he said he'd keep me posted if they uncovered any fraud or misappropriation."

"Dave, do you think Rankin could have been involved in Bubba's murder?"

"I'm not ruling it out, but the biggest problem with that theory is that nobody I've interviewed remembers seeing Rankin at the Fourth of July festival, and he hasn't shown up in any of the photos or video we've viewed so far. Do you recall seeing him at any point during the day?"

I thought for a moment.

"No, I can't honestly say that I do. I saw him at the town hall meeting about the development and I've spotted him a couple of times around town. But I don't remember ever speaking to him."

"We're looking into Bubba's financials. But he had a reputation for under-the-table deals, which would be hard to track. In the meantime if you two would keep mum about any possible misdeeds by Mr. Rankin, I'd appreciate it. We don't want to give him any warning. And we don't want folks to start worrying about their investments unneccesarily.

"Larry Joe, thanks again for bringing this to me."

"Thank you for checking it out," Larry Joe said.

"By the way, Liv, Bernice admitted to lacing the cake with ex-lax. She put it in the frosting. But she insists it was only to cause Bubba to suffer a little discomfort and indignity in retaliation for him robbing Cassie of the Miss Dixie crown. Bernice told Nonie about what she'd done so she could also enjoy watching his torment.

"Well, thank you kindly for the water. I'd better get back at it," Dave said, rising from his chair.

Larry Joe walked him to the door.

When my husband returned I was sitting at the table sulking over my coffee. I've never had a poker face and Larry Joe can usually read me pretty well.

"Honey, I know you're disappointed it looks like Rankin wasn't on the scene when Bubba got killed. But Dave is sharp and he's following every lead. He'll get to the truth."

"I hope so. I'd hate to go through the ordeal of planning Earl and Mama's wedding and Earl not be able to attend."

Larry Joe said he was going to play golf and then run by the office for a while. I gathered up items of clothing that would give me a plausible reason for dropping by the seamstress shop to have a chat with Lynn Latham. She was a suspect I needed to take a closer look at. I didn't like that she'd said Earl had lied about seeing her leave the festival area before the fireworks. And I found it curious that Cassie was lying to give her mom an alibi.

I had a pair of Bermuda shorts in need of hemming—they fell below my knees—and a pair of khakis belonging to Larry Joe that needed a new zipper. I placed them both in a plastic bag to take to the seamstress shop after lunch. With any luck, Lynn would be working today.

At about a quarter to one, I grabbed a quick soup and sandwich lunch at the diner before walking to All Sewn Up, about a block off the town square.

Lynn was sitting at a table in the work area behind the counter. Two sewing machines and a cutting table lined the interior wall.

I spoke as I stepped up to the counter. Lynn looked up but didn't seem glad to see me. I laid my bag on the counter and she looked resigned to the fact she'd have to wait on me.

"What can I do for you?"

I told her about the pants and shorts.

"Should have them both ready in a week, if that's okay?"

"That's fine," I said.

She filled out a ticket, ripped the numbered stub off the top, and handed it to me before turning to walk back to her workstation.

"Are you on your own today?" I asked.

"Mrs. Anderson's still out to lunch. She should be back soon."

"Does your mama do much sewing anymore?" I asked. "I remember her making some beautiful bridesmaids' dresses for a high school friend's wedding I was in ages ago."

"No. She still does a bit of mending for folks, but these days she mostly likes to knit." Changing subjects, she said, "Look, Liv, I'm sure you're really here to quiz me about seeing Earl in the parking lot as the fireworks were starting up. I've told the sheriff more than once I didn't see him. I can't help it that he thinks he saw me. Maybe he saw someone who looks a bit like me from a distance, and he assumed it was me, but it wasn't. I've always thought Earl Daniels was a decent man, and even if it turns out he killed the likes of Bubba Rowland, it won't change my opinion of him one bit."

"Actually, what I wanted to ask you was, when did your mama tell you about the ex-lax Bernice put in Bubba's dessert?"

"I already told the sheriff that, too. She didn't tell me anything," Lynn said.

"Bernice says she put the laxative in the cake just to make Bubba suffer a little. And she told your mama so she could enjoy seeing him suffer. I can't believe Nonie didn't want to share that same joy with you."

"I don't much care what you believe. I don't wish anything bad on Earl, and I hope he and your mama will be very happy together. But regardless of my feelings about Bubba, I didn't have nothing to do with killing him."

Mrs. Anderson came in through the front door, jangling the bells hanging from it as she did. Lynn put her head down and quickly slid back into her seat at the worktable and tried to look busy.

I didn't want to cause her any trouble with her boss, so I spoke to Mrs. Anderson, called out "good-bye" to Lynn, and left the shop.

It was time to put reality aside for a while and work on Mama's fantasy wedding. Honestly, trying to pull together the outrageous bits of Mama's vision into something cohesive had become a welcome respite from the ugliness and seeming futility of investigating Bubba's murder.

I had an appointment to meet with Kenny Mitchell. He was going to show me some sketches he had drawn up for the Viking ship figurehead for Mama's gondola, based on a couple of carved faces I had shown him online. Kenny is a go-to member of my Liv 4 Fun team, along with Harold. Both work for me on a part-time, as-needed basis. I had confidence in Kenny's talent, and I also appreciated the fact that he didn't laugh when I explained to him what we were going for, as ridiculous as it must have sounded.

Kenny was meeting me at Harold's house, or, more specifically, in the workshop behind Harold's house. Kenny, a young man, lives in a small apartment, and Harold, a retired electrician, lets Kenny use his well-equipped woodworking shop for projects.

I had found a couple of carved wooden faces, and Kenny was trying to figure out a way to make it blend and look like it belonged on the front of the flat-bottomed boat we were considering as a stand-in for a gondola.

Honestly, most of the drawings of Viking ships I'd seen featured a figurehead of a dragon or fearsome sea creature. But we weren't going for authenticity here and I knew Mama had something more glamorous in mind. Many of the figureheads I looked at were mermaids, but since we would be using a much smaller boat, I thought just a head or a bust would work better proportionally. When I gave the dimensions of the boat and the carved figures to Kenny, he had agreed. He had also picked out a Victorian woman's head from among the images I had sent him, saying he thought it would work best.

As Kenny flipped through his sketchpad showing me his ideas, I was grateful for the window air-conditioning unit pouring cold air into the small concrete-block building. After a couple of minutes, Harold came in wearing a stained T-shirt straining to cover his beer belly, with a Budweiser bottle in his hand to make sure it stayed full.

"Kenny's done a fine job on them sketches," Harold said, strolling over and taking a look at the drawings over my shoulders. "He's got a good head for carpentry, as well as having good hands for the work."

"You're embarrassing me in front of the boss,

man," Kenny said, his dreadlocks flopping as he shook his head.

I took some pride in the fact I had brought these two together through the work they did for my clients and me. It had been nearly a year since I met Kenny through Winette—he goes to her church—and brought him on board as a freelance employee with Liv 4 Fun. Harold obviously had a fatherly fondness for Kenny, and the admiration was mutual.

"I'll place the order for the lady head today. Buy whatever supplies you need at Earl Daniels's store and have the salesclerk put it on my account," I said. "Kenny, can I give you a lift somewhere?"

Kenny didn't have a car, or a driver's license, for that matter, because of some trouble he'd gotten into over drugs. But he'd gotten active in church and sorted himself out. In another year he hoped to be able to get a driver's license again. Having wheels would definitely make his work as a carpenter easier.

Kenny thanked me for the offer of a ride but said he was helping Harold on another project.

"He's apprenticing as my plumber's assistant and I'm apprenticing as his carpenter's helper," Harold said. "I'll take him home later."

After I left Harold's house I ran by the grocery store and picked up some peel-and-eat shrimp, a squeeze bottle of tartar sauce, hoagie rolls, and deli cole slaw for dinner—no cooking required.

I didn't see Cassie working any of the registers.

But after our uncomfortable chat the other day, I thought it would be best if I avoided contact for a bit anyway.

Back at the house, I peeled and roughly chopped the shrimp and some celery and mixed it with mayo, Old Bay Seasoning, and a bit of lemon juice. I split and lightly toasted the hoagie rolls, and dinner was ready to plate up as soon as Larry Joe made it home.

We took our plates and glasses of iced tea into the den and ate our sandwich supper while we stared at some mindless TV program.

After we finished eating, Larry Joe clicked off the television with the remote.

"Liv, are you on to anything new about the murder investigation? You haven't said much about it in a few days. It worries me when you and Di are quietly scheming."

"I don't know that there's anything new. I dropped by All Sewn Up today with some clothes in need of mending and had a chat with Lynn Latham. She insists Earl is wrong about seeing her leave the festival before the fireworks, even though Earl seems certain it was her. And when I chatted with Cassie earlier this week while she was ringing up my groceries she lied and said she and her mom were helping clean up in the winners' dinner tent during the fireworks, when I know it was already cleaned up and cleared out well before the fireworks show. It worries me that Cassie thinks her mom needs an alibi. What do you think?"

"I think you're asking the right questions and you're bound to come up with some answers eventually. I also think Earl is lucky to have you in his corner," he said.

Larry Joe patted my knee as he got up from the sofa.

"Hon, I'm going to run over to the folks' house. I promised my mama I'd help Daddy rehang a couple of doors that he's repaired, sanded, and refinished. She doesn't want him to hurt himself. And it is unwieldy to hang a door by yourself."

"Okay."

Larry Joe leaned down and gave me a quick kiss before leaving.

I refilled my glass with iced tea and sat down at the kitchen table before giving Di a call.

"So did you find out anything from Bruce today at the store?" I asked.

"Not really. But I did learn something from Ted when I ran into him and Daisy at the ice cream parlor this afternoon. We should have fixed him up with Daisy sooner. He sticks his chest out like a puffed-up pigeon and gets all chatty about his work as an officer of the law when she's around."

"We didn't exactly fix them up, but tell me what Ted said that's so interesting."

"You know we were wondering who knew about Bubba's stomach distress."

"Yeah."

"Well, in addition to Bernice, who slipped him the laxative, and Nonie, Bruce knew for sure. Apparently, Bubba told his brother that his tummy was kind of letting loose and that he thought he might need to go home. Bruce told him to hang on and he'd see if Carrie had something in her purse that might settle his stomach. Bruce said he gave Bubba an Imodium pill, but it must not have taken effect before he got killed."

"That just tells us that Bruce and Carrie and whoever was within earshot knew Bubba had stomach troubles," I said.

"According to Ted, it may tell us more than that. Bruce said that he gave Bubba the Imodium and that he and another man at the whiskey cart saw Bubba swallow it. But the lab results didn't show any Imodium or whatever its chemical name is in Bubba's system. There was some antihistamine in his system, though. They can't know for sure when Bubba took the allergy pill—he could have taken it earlier in the day. But it could be Bruce had asked Carrie for an allergy pill and just told Bubba it was a stomach pill."

"I'm not sure I understand why Bruce would do that."

"If Bubba was talking about going home—and both Bruce and that guy at the whiskey cart, I think his name was Henry, heard him say so—but Bruce didn't want Bubba to go home just yet, he could have given him a pill Bubba believed was for his stomach upset. Bubba probably would've hung around a bit after taking the pill to see if it helped. However, since it wasn't a stomach pill, Bubba still would have ended up running to the porta potty, placing him precisely where the killer wanted him to be during the fireworks," Di said.

"I get it. And that would make Bruce the prime suspect."

"So, what did you find out from Lynn?" Di asked.

I filled her in on my meager conversation with Lynn.

"So where does she fall on your list as a suspect now?"

"She has a motive, and when I chatted with Cassie in the checkout lane at the grocery store the other day, she was obviously lying about where her mom was when the fireworks began, which tells me she at least believes her mom *could* be involved in Bubba's murder."

"Holly was on the festival grounds most of the day helping out, wasn't she?" Di asked.

"Yeah, she was. Holly manned the booth off and on. A couple of volunteers took turns minding the booth most of the rest of the time," I said.

"Have you run through the day with her, like we did at the park? I'm sure Dave's interviewed her, but maybe it would help jog your memory if you went through things with Holly to see what she remembers, especially from the vantage point of the information booth," Di said. "She may have even seen Lynn or Cassie or Nonie around the time the fireworks began."

"I'll ask Holly about it when I see her on Monday. But honestly, Lynn was so upset and so drunk, at least when I saw her, I doubt she had a clear enough head or a steady enough hand to actually have shot Bubba."

Chapter 16

Larry Joe and his dad had a 10 AM tee time and they had invited Earl to join them.

I thought it was thoughtful of them to include Earl. I hoped it would take his mind off his troubles for a bit.

Since my husband and father-in-law were performing good works, I decided I should run an errand of mercy myself and check on Mama, especially since it had been a few days since I'd really talked to her. And since it was Sunday I thought it might make up for the fact I'd blown off going to church.

I knew Mama and Earl would have eaten breakfast before attending eight o'clock church services. I also knew the men would grab lunch at the country club after their game. So I called Mama and offered to pick up some muffins at Dixie Donuts and More and come keep her company for a while.

I had asked Mama if she had any special requests

before I stopped by the doughnut shop. She asked for chocolate chip and blueberry. I figured it was too late in the morning to get muffins hot out of the oven, but I knew we could always heat them in the microwave and they would taste almost as good as just baked.

I was in luck, though. Renee had just taken blueberry muffins out of the oven when I walked in the bakery.

"Hi, Renee," I said, standing in the small, empty dining area furnished with bistro tables. "I'm surprised you're baking more muffins this late in the morning."

"I'm just getting ready for my little afternoon rush. There's one group of older church ladies who always come by here for muffins or doughnuts after they eat lunch at the diner. They usually roll in here just after noon. And I get other churchgoers stopping by to pick up something on their way home. And if Mabel runs out of pie at the diner, I sometimes get a pretty big crowd."

"I never realized the dynamics of Sunday pastry sales was so complex," I said.

"So what can I get for you, Liv?"

"Just let me have two blueberry muffins and two chocolate chip muffins, please."

"Are you picking up for you and Larry Joe?"

"Actually, I'm picking up for me and Mama and then heading over to her house. Our men are out on the golf course this morning. Mama will want two muffins, one of each, and I'll leave one for Earl."

"How are your mama and Earl holding up? It

seems so unfair him having these legal difficulties just after the two of them got engaged. I think they make a cute couple, by the way. And for the record, neither Fred nor me believe for a minute that Earl Daniels could kill anybody."

"Thanks, Renee. I appreciate your support. I'm sure Dave will find the real killer. He has a good record on that front."

"With a little help from you from time to time," she said with a knowing smile as she boxed up the muffins.

"Well, I don't know about that. But, in the meantime, Larry Joe and his dad are distracting Earl with a game of golf. And I'm trying to keep Mama occupied with wedding plans."

"That sounds like a winning plan to me. You give my best to your mama."

"I will," I said as I paid Renee for my order.

As I entered through Mama's back door, I noticed the aroma of freshly brewed coffee and a pile of magazine clippings scattered on the kitchen table.

At first I felt piqued that she was ambushing me with wedding plans. But then I reasoned that looking at photographs of normal people's weddings might help guide Mama in a different direction.

I sat the box of muffins on the counter and called out to let Mama know I was there. I heard the clack of her sandals against the parquet floor as she made her way to the kitchen. She gave me a quick hug before helping herself to a muffin.

"*Mmm,* these are still warm," she said with a mouthful of blueberry muffin.

She had changed from her Sunday-go-to-meeting clothes into a sleeveless top and crop pants—frankly not a flattering look for her and one I doubted she'd leave the house in.

I retrieved mugs from the cabinet and poured us some coffee and Mama sat down at the table.

"I'm glad Larry Joe and Wayne asked Earl to go golfing with them. He won't say much, but I see him staring off in the distance and I know he's worrying. Maybe swinging clubs and hitting balls will take his mind off things."

"I hope so. That was the idea," I said.

I sat down and started commenting on magazine photos before Mama had time to start asking me questions about the investigation. Fortunately, she took the bait. She laid some photos of bouquets side by side. Not surprisingly, she didn't actually like any of them, but they sparked some ideas.

"I kind of like the shape of this one and the colors in this one," she said. "This one's pretty, but I think it'd be too small for me to carry. It's fine for the little wisp of a girl in the picture, but I probably need something that will match my size and stature better. Don't you think?"

I wasn't sure what to say, but it didn't matter because she didn't pause long enough for me to respond.

"What I'm really thinking is we should use some of the wildflowers growing on Earl's property, along with some flowers from my garden, you know, to make it personal. And I'd like to include a cotton boll or two in the bouquet, since Earl's daddy was a cotton farmer when he was growing up and they still raise cotton in a couple of fields Earl rents out in the back forty."

I couldn't remember seeing any wildflowers growing on Earl's property other than dandelions and jimsonweed, but I figured we could probably find some Queen Anne's lace or phlox or beggar-ticks if we looked hard enough. I wasn't sure how to incorporate cotton bolls, but maybe we could pin some kind of embellishments to the white fluff. I'd talk to Holly and see what we could come up with.

Mama started commenting on some shots of wedding showers. My first thought was, *I wonder what kind of stuff Mama and Earl will register for since they don't really need the typical newlywed stuff.* My second thought was, *Good grief, I hope one of her friends throws a wedding shower for her and it's not left up to my mother-in-law and me.* I knew there was no way my sister was going to cohost one with me.

"Speaking of showers, that must have added some excitement when Heather went into labor during her baby shower. Her mother-in-law was compli-menting how nice the shower was and how she was glad you and Holly were there to take charge since they were all in a tizzy with the baby coming."

I wasn't sure Heather's mom or mother-in-law appreciated us taking over at the time, but it was nice to know they did in retrospect, or at least they said they did.

"So, Liv, have you been by to see Heather and the baby?"

"No, I haven't. Heather e-mailed me a baby photo, though," I said, pulling up the image on my cell phone and showing Mama.

"What a doll. I think she favors her daddy in this one," she said.

"Speaking of babies and their daddies," I said, "I overheard a couple of women at Heather's shower gossiping. I probably shouldn't have listened, but I did. Anyway, they were saying that the Weems girl doesn't know who her baby's daddy is and there are several possibilities. I don't know if there's any truth to that, of course. But since there are a couple of different Weems families in the area, I wondered if you know who they might have been talking about."

"Yes, I do. It's Esme Weems's daughter, Taylor. She's in her early twenties and expecting any day now, I think. She's always been kind of a wild child. Anyway, Sylvia told me Esme was wanting Taylor to ask the daddy to help out some with expenses, which is only right, and Esme doesn't make a lot of money working at the drugstore. At first Taylor was acting like she just didn't want to say who the daddy was, but she later admitted that she doesn't know. So unless the baby is the spitting image of his or her father they may never know, unless they go on that Maury what's-his-name show on TV."

Caught up on local gossip and having gone through a big chunk of Mama's magazine pile as well as a chocolate chip muffin, I said I'd better get going and told her I'd give some thought to the bouquets.

* * *

I went home, browned a roast in the skillet, and threw it in the Crock-Pot, along with some carrots and onions. I could toss a salad to serve alongside it. With Mama tended to and supper taken care of, I intended to turn the remainder of my Sunday into a day of rest. I stretched out on the sofa in the den with the newspaper crossword puzzle.

At some point I nodded off, but awakened to the sound of the back door slamming, immediately followed by stamping feet and muttered curses. I got up and went through to check on my husband and found him with the fridge door open, twisting the cap off a beer bottle.

"What's wrong, honey?"

"My dad is what's wrong. I would have killed him right there on the golf course if it hadn't been for thinking how much it would upset my mama."

"What happened?"

"You know how I told you Daddy was up to something, sneaking off and making secretive phone calls? Then you mentioned he could be trying to hide a health problem from us. I couldn't bear the thought of my mama having to go through the stress of another health crisis, if he was putting off something that could be easily treated if he addressed it right away."

"Honey, sit down," I said, sitting down at the kitchen table, while he took a seat across from me. "Go on."

"I'd been looking for the right time to bring it up with him. You know how defensive Dad can be when he feels like you're questioning his motives or his good sense. So we were out on the course and he seemed to be in a good mood, laughing and joking with Earl and me. And I thought he might behave a little better with Earl being there. He's always had a lot of respect for Earl, I believe, don't you think so?"

"Yeah, I think your daddy has a fond admiration for Earl." I watched as Larry Joe absently peeled the label off his beer bottle.

"Anyway I told him I'd noticed him taking off now and then lately on his own without telling anybody and I was a little concerned. I said I'd appreciate him sharing with me what was going on, especially if it had a bearing on his health. That old man went ballistic. You would have thought I'd tinkled in his shoe and asked him to drink it."

Larry Joe paused, pursing his lips and shaking his head in disbelief. He took a big swig of beer and swallowed hard.

"He started out yelling he was a grown man who didn't need people keeping tabs on every move he made. Then he moved on to how his wife and his son look on him as some kind of invalid who needs an attendant ever since he had that one heart attack—as if the first one doesn't count. Then he grabbed his golf bag and stomped off the course without finishing our round."

"I encouraged Earl to finish the course, if he liked, but told him I thought I should go check on my dad. Earl said he shared my concern and finishing the game didn't matter. We followed Daddy to the country club, joined him at the bar and ordered some beers.

"After a few minutes of silently sipping our beers and staring at each other in the mirror behind the bar, Daddy said, 'Since it's obvious you're not going to let this go, let's get a table.'

"We sat down at a table in the back corner. He told me that he had intended to tell me about his plans as soon as he had things sorted out. He said he'd just been to the doc for a checkup a couple of weeks ago and everything was fine, adding that I could ask Mama if I didn't believe him.

"Then he said with mom and me pushing him to cut back on hours and move toward retirement, he'd decided to look into some semiretirement options and thought he'd found something," Larry Joe said. "You'll never guess what that old geezer's idea of semiretirement is."

He threw his hands up in the air and shook his head before getting up and retrieving another beer from the fridge.

"Are you ready for this? He's planning to buy a vending machine route. Can you believe it?"

I shook my head slightly. Obviously Larry Joe wasn't pleased with the idea, but I didn't know enough about it to have an informed opinion.

"Right now he spends most of his time sitting on his butt in the office, talking on the phone, and occasionally walking back to the garage or warehouse to talk to the supervisor or the truckers, and having dinner with clients. So his plan for semiretirement is to drive a truck through heavy traffic in Memphis, carry heavy cartons of snacks around to stock the machines, and haul them off to be repaired when they break down. That's his idea of taking it easy! Not to mention he'd have to dip into his retirement savings to buy these machines."

"Is that what you told your dad?"

"Yeah, that's what I told him, as well as the fact that he's being stubborn and selfish and not even thinking about what Mama might want. I suggested she might like it if they traveled a little. And that maybe instead of buying junk food machines, he might spend a little of their savings and take his wife on a cruise."

"How did he react to that?"

"Not well," Larry Joe said, getting up from the chair. "I'm going upstairs to work on the house. Mama and Daddy may have to move in with us if he runs through their life savings with his harebrained retirement scheme. You know he'd never be happy with just a few machines; he'd have to keep expanding until he'd taken over the vending machine market for all of west Tennessee."

In his current state of mind, I knew there was no point in trying to talk to Larry Joe about making nice with his dad.

I'd decided to curl up on the sofa with a book and wait for the thunder between Larry Joe and his dad to die down before I tried to orchestrate a truce.

About five minutes later the phone rang.

Chapter 17

I answered the phone and heard my mother-in-law crying.

"We have to do something to help patch things up between Larry Joe and his dad. Wayne is fit to be tied. He's even talking about not going to the office tomorrow, saying since Larry Joe knows everything he should just run the business by himself. The only times Wayne has ever missed going to the office was when he was too sick to drag himself out of bed. Liv, he's so worked up I'm worried he might have another heart attack."

I could hear her blowing her nose. I gave her a moment.

"Miss Betty, didn't Daddy Wayne just go for a checkup recently? And the doctor said everything looked fine, right?"

"Yes."

"Then stop worrying yourself that he's going to have a heart attack every time he gets mad. Did

Daddy Wayne tell you about his plans for what he calls semiretirement?"

"A little. I gathered Larry Joe pooh-poohed it as a foolish idea. He hurt his dad's feelings—and stepped on his pride."

"I know. But Larry Joe believes that instead of tapering off toward retirement and taking care of his health, his dad is planning to take on a job that's more physically demanding. His heart's in the right place but his mouth was on the wrong side of town when he heard about his daddy's vending machine plan."

"He gets that from his father, the shooting-off-his-mouth part. Liv, I know it's too soon to sit Wayne and Larry Joe down to talk to each other. But would you come over and talk to the old fool? He's always liked you and respects that you've built a business of your own. I think you could calm him down. I'd worry less about him having a heart attack if the veins in his temples weren't bulging."

This wasn't an errand I wanted to take on, but I could hardly refuse.

I texted Larry Joe to tell him I was going out for a bit, then drove to my in-laws' house.

On the way over I tried to work out a plan in my head for how to soothe Daddy Wayne. It seemed to me that the first issue I'd have to address was his wounded pride. He had put a lot of time and effort into researching the vending machine business and Larry Joe had just dismissed the idea. I decided to ask him to tell me all about it, without offering criticism. Honestly, I didn't know if it was a terrible idea or not and I wasn't sure that Larry Joe got all the facts before he jumped to that conclusion.

I parked in the driveway and entered through the kitchen door after tapping lightly. Miss Betty was standing by the sink when I came in.

"Thanks for coming over, hon," she said, giving me a shoulder hug.

"Don't thank me just yet. Is the bear in his den?"

"Yeah, he's in his recliner clicking the remote control, scrolling through the same half-dozen channels over and over. I've got some peach cobbler. I thought I'd heat up some in a bowl and take it in to him as you go in, you know, help sweeten his disposition."

"Good idea. I'll take all the help I can get. My plan is to get him talking about the vending machine business, his retirement plans, whatever, while I just listen. I think part of the problem is Larry Joe didn't hear him out. In my experience most people calm down if you just let them speak their piece."

"Sounds like a good plan. I'll just sit on the loveseat and work on my knitting. Wayne either forgets I'm there or thinks I'm not listening when I knit. I'll just be around to back you up if need be."

I declined my mother-in-law's offer of peach cobbler and followed her as she took a bowl into the den.

"Look who dropped by," she said as she handed him the dessert.

He gave me a sullen look before saying, "Hi, Liv.

If you've come to tell me to make nice with that husband of yours, you can save your breath."

"Nope, I wouldn't ask you to apologize."

This was true. Strictly speaking, I would leave any admonishment for him to apologize up to my mother-in-law, while I encouraged Larry Joe to tell his dad he was sorry.

Miss Betty took up her knitting and I turned slightly to face my father-in-law.

"I gathered that you and Larry Joe had a falling-out, but I couldn't make much sense out of what little he told me. Why don't you tell me about this vending machine business venture you're thinking about?"

"Why don't you ask him?"

"Because I'm asking you. And obviously you know more about it. I like to get information straight from the horse's mouth—cuts down on any confusion."

I fell silent and hoped he'd fill the void. After a moment, he did.

He started slowly, with a just-the-facts kind of approach, but became more animated as he went along. I nodded and *mmm-hmm*'d as he spoke.

As a party planner, I'd garnered a lot of experience arbitrating disputes between people, usually spouses, who had differing visions for an event. I'd learned if I let them talk long enough and listened closely I could usually discern the crux of the matter, what was really important to each of them. Then I could devise a plan that would include what was most important to each of them, or at least close enough to appease them.

As I listened to Daddy Wayne it became clear to me he was worried that as he cut back more and more on his hours at McKay Trucking, he'd by necessity have to turn over the reins on most matters to Larry Joe. This could lead to the awkward situation where, at least in a de facto way, his son would become his boss. I knew that would be an untenable situation for either man.

He also wasn't ready to give up what he saw as productive work for puttering around in his workshop and tending to Miss Betty's honey-do list. He needed to feel he was doing something important.

I didn't necessarily think the vending machine route was as horrible an idea as my husband did. But I also thought we could come up with something that wouldn't involve him driving into Memphis.

When he came back around to saying how Larry Joe expected him to give up real work and keep busy doing arts and crafts projects in his workshop, I seized my opportunity.

"Daddy Wayne, you really are a skilled woodworker. You've made beautiful shelves for Miss Betty's collection of salt and pepper shakers and you made that new hymnal board for the church. I think it would be wonderful if you could use those skills for important projects here in the community.

"You know what, Winette was telling me just recently how she could use a skilled craftsman to oversee some of the projects Residential Rehab takes on. Kenny Mitchell is a good carpenter, but he's

generally working paying jobs on the weekends—
often for me, in fact, for various events. You might
want to talk to her about that. You could at least try
it out and see if you think it's something you'd want
to take on. The RR volunteers are enthusiastic, but
most of them aren't skilled. They need a leader. And
there's no end to the projects that need doing,
repairs and maintenance for the elderly and disabled. In fact, just a couple of weeks ago, Winette
called Kenny and another man for an emergency
situation. A lady in a wheelchair was basically
homebound because her wheelchair ramp had col-
lapsed and she couldn't get in or out of her house on
her own. Kenny worked until well after dark finishing up the ramp. Someone who's retired or even
semiretired would be a big help in situations like
that."

He seemed to be mulling over my suggestion.

"Of course the work with RR doesn't pay anything, at least not in this life," I said, hoping to
appeal to his sense of Christian charity.

"Betty and I aren't exactly hurting for the
money," he said, taking the bait. "It's not like I'd be
making that much from the vending machines
anyway, unless I expanded the route in a big way. I
can't take on being a regular supervisor at RR projects, just yet. I'm planning on just slowly cutting
back my hours over the next couple of years. But
that's something to consider."

I looked over at Miss Betty, who gave me a discreet, knowing smile. I felt my work here was done.

So we chitchatted a few minutes about other things and I said I'd best be going.

I'd have a little talk with Larry Joe, and with any luck he and his dad would shake hands and make up by tomorrow afternoon.

Chapter 18

Monday was a scorcher. The relatively mild—for July—mid- to upper–80s temperatures we'd been enjoying most of the month spiked to the upper 90s and were forecast to touch a hundred degrees by Tuesday. Even with the air-conditioning cranked up, my blouse was clinging to my back. I stood up and stretched, pulled a bottled water out of the dorm refrigerator, and walked over to my office window.

I was gazing mindlessly across the town square below when the patrol car pulled up in front of the sheriff's office. Ted got out, opened the rear door, and helped Webster Flack, whose hands were cuffed behind his back, get out of the car.

After standing with my mouth agape for a moment, I rushed over to my desk, grabbed my phone, and punched in the number for the sheriff's office. As expected, Terry, the dispatcher, answered.

"Terry, this is Liv. Is Webster under arrest for arson or murder—or both?"

"You know very well I can't talk about that, so just—"

I cut her off.

"I guess I could come over and pester you in person. I've been meaning to lodge a complaint against my neighbor for public nuisance."

There was a brief pause.

"I haven't heard anybody mention the word *murder* this morning," she said before hanging up.

So Webster Flack has been arrested for arson.

I texted the news to Di. It's rare for her to talk on the phone when she's at work, but in just a minute my phone buzzed.

"He may not have been charged with murder yet, but there's good reason to believe the murder and the arson are connected. I mean, it was Bubba Rowland's office that was torched," she said without a perfunctory "hello."

"I hope so."

"I can't talk. Why don't you come over tonight after you feed Larry Joe, or you can call me."

"Will do."

Click.

Holly arrived at the office about nine. I told her about Mama's ideas for her bridal bouquet and asked her to come up with some ideas for making weeds and cotton bolls look pretty.

"I'll give it some thought," she said without even laughing.

I also asked her to include in her deliberation

what would be the appropriate-size bouquet for someone of Mama's proportions.

I had a meeting scheduled at 2:00 PM. Holly and I were going to work up some notes, based on what little they had told me on the phone, for prospective clients who wanted to talk to me about a high school reunion.

Before we got down to business, I decided to ask Holly what she remembered about the day of the festival.

"Holly, has Dave questioned you about the day of the festival?"

"No, but that nice young deputy came by and talked to me."

"Would you mind telling me what you told Ted? I'm still trying to get a handle on what happened that day in my feeble attempts to help Earl out."

"Of course not, darlin'. Although I doubt I can be much help. I barely saw Bubba all day."

Holly had spent a good deal more time in the information booth near the entrance on the day of the festival than I had. It had an awning, giving shade, and a battery-operated fan stirring a breeze. Plus it had a couple of chairs that allowed Holly and the volunteers manning the booth to sit down. Holly's in good health, but she's almost my mama's age and I didn't really want her running around in the hot sun all day, not to mention she and the two other older ladies helping out were gracious greeters. They were cute Southern belles, who shared in common a molasses drawl.

"Just try to tell me everything you remember.

You might even recall something that didn't occur to you when you talked to Ted."

"Awlright. You and I were manning the booth together early that morning when so many people were arriving. You left a few times to deal with vendor issues, like when the electricity wasn't working at a couple of the food booths."

"Did you see Bubba during that time?"

Biting her lip, Holly gazed up at the ceiling trying to remember.

"I don't think so. You and I saw him a bit earlier. He stopped by and chatted with us for a minute soon after the 5K had concluded."

"Yeah, I mentioned that to Dave, too," I said.

"I saw Bubba walking into a tent at some point that morning," she said. "I believe it was for the cake contest, and he had a judge's ribbon pinned to his shirt pocket."

I told her he was a fill-in judge for the cake competition.

"I find it hard to believe your mama's cake didn't take the blue ribbon again this year. I was one of the judges a couple of years ago and her chocolate cake is the best I've ever tasted."

"I think so, but I may be a tiny bit biased. Did you see Bubba again after that?"

"Yes. Late in the afternoon when I had returned to mind the booth again, Bubba Rowland came by with a face like thunder. He walked right past me without so much as a word. He went out to the parking lot by the main entrance, where I could see him talking to another man for a few minutes.

When he came back by he was smiling. He nodded to me and said, 'Good golly, Miss Holly. How's it going?' Whatever the other man told him certainly seemed to put him in a good mood."

"Did you know who this man was?"

"No, in fact I don't recall ever even seeing him around town before, which is what I told the deputy."

"Can you describe him?"

"He was a tall, well-built man. Fortyish, I'd say, with sandy brown hair and a used car salesman's smile."

A lightbulb lit up in my head. I grabbed my purse, rifled through its disorganized contents, and pulled out the brochure for the new development that Larry Joe had given me.

I flipped to the back cover and showed it to Holly. "Is this the man?"

She looked at it for a long moment.

"I believe that's him. Yes, that's definitely him," she said, tapping her index finger on the image of developer Aaron Rankin.

Chapter 19

Around noon, after Holly and I had gotten some notes together for my meeting and she had left for the day, I decided to walk over to the diner for a bite to eat. I peeked in the window at Sweet Deal Realty to see if Winette might want to join me, but she was apparently out of the office.

I crossed the street and a man held the door open for me as I entered Town Square Diner. The diner was starting to fill up with the lunch crowd. I scanned the dining room for a table and noticed Carrie Rowland sitting at a table by herself. I went over and asked if I could join her, and she motioned for me to sit down. I felt a rush of cool air from the vents overhead and was thankful Carrie had chosen a table in the direct path of a nice draft.

I knew Carrie worked part-time at Rowland's Building Supply a couple of days a week, doing bookkeeping. But her freshly cut, dyed, and curled hair caused me to suspect she had come into town for a hair salon appointment.

"Your hair looks nice," I said.

"Thanks. I guess it's a little gift to myself. Today is my nineteenth wedding anniversary."

"Congratulations," I said.

"Thanks. Under the circumstances we're not really celebrating. But Bruce and I exchanged cards at breakfast and we'll probably have a glass of wine with dinner. Next year will be a milestone anniversary, so we'll save the big celebration for then."

Normally it would have seemed appropriate to offer condolences or at least ask how the family was doing after a recent death, but knowing what Earl had told me about Carrie and Bubba's long-ago tryst I just didn't feel comfortable mentioning him. I decided to leave it to Carrie to bring up Bubba if she wanted. She didn't.

We both ordered an entrée salad. For me, at least, the idea of a hot dish on such a hot day was unappealing.

"I heard they arrested Webster Flack this morning for the arson out at the development site," I said. "Do you know if they're also charging him with the vandalism at Rowland's, since there was similar graffiti in both cases?"

"I don't know," she said. "I couldn't believe the sheriff hadn't already arrested Webster for the vandalism at the store. If he didn't actually write the words on the building, he was no doubt the instigator. Then when I saw the video on the news with some of the same words and that same tangerine color spray paint, I would have thought it was obvious, even to the sheriff, that it was the work of the same person. But then, the damage at the store was minor in comparison to that at the development. Maybe it just wasn't a priority, especially after Bubba's murder."

"Yeah. Dave and his small staff have their plates full right now," I said.

"Speaking of plates, I think I'm going to have Margie put the rest of my salad in a to-go box," Carrie said before waving over the waitress.

We chatted for a minute about the weather and such before she took her leftovers and went up to the counter to pay.

The diner was full up by this time and I was still picking absently at my salad. As soon as Margie took away Carrie's plate, a man with a scraggly beard and less than a full set of teeth took her chair, asking if I minded only after he had sat down. He was staring at me and made some odd comment about how our waitress nicely filled out her uniform. Since Margie wears at least a size 3X, I could hardly argue the point, so I ignored the remark.

Then he asked, "You run that party business, don't you?"

Clearly he had me at a disadvantage, since I had no idea who he was.

"Yes, I own a party-planning business."

I waved at Margie and motioned to my plate, indicating I'd like a to-go box.

"If you don't mind me asking, do you ever plan lingerie parties?"

"Why? Are you thinking of throwing one?"

"Oh, no," he said with an unsettling laugh. "I was just wondering."

I gathered his interest was prurient and I wanted to separate from his company as soon as possible. I picked up my plate and dumped it quickly into the box Margie had slipped onto the table, grabbed my check, and said, "I have to be going now."

He was saying something as I walked away.

As Mabel was making change for a twenty, I asked about the strange man at my table.

"Do you know him?"

"Naw, not really. He comes in from time to time." She added in a near whisper, "I don't think he's quite right."

I walked back to my office and stashed my take-out container in the mini-fridge.

At 2:00 PM my prospective clients arrived. After noting the brand names prominently displayed on their clothes I surmised mineral water would appeal to them. I offered and they accepted.

Kurt was a senior manager at some company in Memphis, and Judy, whom I knew only to speak to, lived in Dixie and owned the fitness center on the highway. What they shared in common was they had graduated from Dixie High School together and were on the committee for their thirtieth class reunion coming up in two years.

Obviously it was a bit far in advance to plan the details of the reunion at this point, but I appreciated that they wanted to get on the calendar. And for large events where a lot of people will be coming in from out of town, it's a good idea to get started early.

The pair were the local representatives of the planning committee, which included classmates from across the country, who were communicating by e-mail and had started a Facebook page to keep everyone up to date on plans, as well as solicit input.

The committee had an ambitious list of several events they wanted to schedule over a Thursday through Sunday time period. There were 108 people in their graduating class, and they were estimating based on early contacts that about 75 classmates along with their spouse or date would likely attend.

They were proposing a pub crawl tour of Memphis on Thursday evening, capping off the night on Beale Street, a touristy venue featuring blues clubs. They wanted Friday to be a family-friendly day of activities, including perhaps the Memphis Zoo, along with a catered picnic in Overton Park. And they wanted to hire a couple of nice coach buses to shuttle reuniongoers to these activities. They were proposing the big event to be a dinner at the country club on Saturday night, followed by a dance in the Dixie High School gym for nostalgic reasons. We would have to secure special permission from the school board to book an event at the school, and, of course, the date couldn't conflict with scheduled school activities. We could probably manage that since they were planning to hold the event in the summer, about mid-June.

Kurt had a square jaw and a thick head of hair. I imagined he might have been voted most handsome or most likely to succeed. And his female cohort was petite with delicate features. I could easily envision her being named in the yearbook as most beautiful. However, I was fairly certain neither of them had been named most congenial.

"If you give me a budget range, I can get back to you with some preliminary price estimates for the activities, as well as my fee."

"We were hoping you could just check out what's available as far as bus rentals and group rates and menus and bands and such, providing us a list of options on price ranges, so we can go from there," Judy said.

I bet you would.

In other words, they wanted me to do all the research and preliminary planning and then give them a contact list with price estimates without paying me a dime.

"It really wouldn't be that helpful to your committee, I'm afraid, if I gathered information without any budget parameters. I would suggest you do some kind of survey of your classmates and get an idea about what they're comfortable paying per couple.

"When you have a better idea of a budget range, I can get some preliminary estimates and plans together. At that point, if you're pleased with the overview we can draw up a contract and I can begin working on more specific plans, meeting again with you to iron out the details."

"Can't you provide us with at least *some* price quotes for the things we know we want, like the bus rentals and bands?" she asked.

I had the feeling she and square jaw wanted to be able to report a bunch of details back to their committee as if they had done the research, without actually having to do any of the legwork. I, of course, didn't mind doing the legwork as long as it was clear I was getting paid.

"I'm sorry, Judy," I said in my kindest voice. "As I said, most of these things depend on the budget, as well as the number of people we need to accommodate. For instance, we will need to know how many people are planning to participate in the Memphis events to know how big a bus or buses we'll need to reserve. And, as for booking a band, the price varies greatly depending on the type of music you want, how long you want to book them to play, and, of course, how popular and in-demand the particular band is. I just can't go very far without a budget range unless the client gives me a blank check, which I can honestly say hasn't happened so far."

Kurt grinned and Judy frowned, but they agreed to get back with me in a month or so.

"That sounds great. Just call or e-mail me and we can figure out where to go from here."

* * *

Larry Joe called about four o'clock to say they had some freight mix-up on the trucks and he didn't expect to make it home until around eight or so.

"Go ahead and eat and just save me a plate or bring me home some takeout if you go to dinner with Di."

"Is this freight problem going to cause you to miss a shipment deadline?"

"Not if I can help it."

"Okay, honey, I'll see you later," I said.

I gave Di a call and let her know I was free for dinner if she was available.

"Yeah. I was supposed to have dinner with Dave, but he had to bail because of stuff going on with Webster, I gathered."

"Does stuff going on include a murder charge?"

"He didn't say," she said dryly. "Let's go to that Chinese buffet on the highway. I know it's noisier than Taco Belles and I know we just had Chinese takeout recently, but I have a taste for it."

We arranged for me to swing by and pick her up around five-thirty.

The dragon that greeted us at the entrance to the restaurant looked more cartoonish than fearsome. The petite hostess advised us to be seated at the table of our choice and help ourselves to the buffet. A server would be around shortly to take our drink order.

I loaded my plate with Kung Pao chicken and Crab Rangoon. Di nabbed a back corner booth, which would give us a bit of privacy.

"I hope Dave is making Webster sweat it out in the interrogation room," I said. "Maybe he can charge him with murder as well as arson and Earl can put this whole nightmare behind him."

Di showed off by eating her rice with chopsticks.

"I don't know, I think Bruce looks at least as promising as a suspect as Webster," she said.

"Why is that?"

"Okay, so on my route this afternoon I ran into Kelly, one of the women in my yoga class. And when I say 'ran into' I mean that literally. I was coming down a driveway sorting mail in my hands as she came around the corner, wearing headphones, and ran smack into me. Fortunately, she was only traveling at jogging speed instead of a dead run.

"After exchanging apologies for the collision we chatted for a minute. I was saying it was such a hot day I hadn't seen many people outside, much less running. Most people were in their houses or in their cars with the air-conditioning full blast. Anyway, she mentioned that on the day of the festival she had locked her keys in her car. The long and short of it was, Bruce Rowland got a slim jim from his car and popped open her car door in a matter of seconds," Di said, punctuating her sentence with raised eyebrows.

I dropped a Crab Rangoon in my lap.

"I'd completely forgotten that Bruce is a locksmith—it's part of Rowland's business. That means he could have easily used that same slim jim to pop open the door on Earl's truck and take his rifle."

"That's what I'm thinking."

"Did you mention this to Dave yet?"

"Yes, I did. And all he said was the fact that Bruce is a locksmith doesn't mean he broke into Earl's truck."

"It doesn't mean he didn't, either. Let's face it, Dave's not going to listen to anything we say unless we hand him a smoking gun. The best we can hope for at the moment is that Webster is guilty and confesses," I said with resignation. "I'm going to make another trip to the buffet and get some of those coconut macaroons. Can I get you anything?"

"No, I'm good."

I returned with a plate of sweets. A young waiter came by and refilled our glasses with iced tea.

"So did you do anything exciting Sunday?" Di asked, shifting gears.

"I'm not sure exciting is the right word for it— exhausting would be more like it."

I filled her in on the whole set-to between Larry Joe and his dad.

"That all happened after I started the day having brunch with Mama and going over her ideas for bridal bouquets."

"What's her vision?"

"Basically, jimsonweed and cotton bolls."

"I can honestly say I never would've thought of that."

"Who else but Mama would?" I said. "Oh, but I

did hear some interesting gossip from her if you're inclined to listen to that kind of trash."

"I'm all ears."

"Do you happen to know Esme Weems or her daughter, Taylor?"

"I know who they are. They used to rent a house on my route. Why?"

I told her about the uncertain parentage of Taylor's baby.

"Or at least that's the word on the street. It could be Taylor just isn't saying because the baby's father is a married man or it could be she genuinely doesn't know."

"If she doesn't know and really wants to, she could go on the Maury show," Di offered.

"That's just what Mama said . . . oh, oh, oh," I said, nearly knocking over my glass as I gestured wildly.

"What?"

"I believe you're right about Bruce being our prime suspect—and not just because of the slim jim. He may have a big fat motive."

"Well, tell me."

Even though no one was sitting nearby, I leaned forward and talked in a hushed tone.

"Earl told me, reluctantly, that he once spotted Bubba and Carrie coming out of some seedy hotel room."

"Yuck. I can't imagine why Carrie would even consider sleeping with the likes of Bubba—unless he was blackmailing her."

"No, no. This was a long time ago. According to Earl, she and Bruce were newlyweds at the time and having newly married kinds of problems. Bubba wasn't bad looking back then and Carrie would have been vulnerable. I happened to sit with Carrie at the diner today and she mentioned she and Bruce have been married nineteen years. And Jennifer just graduated from high school, so she's about eighteen."

"Oh, I see where you're going with this. You think it's possible Bubba, not Bruce, is her daddy."

"Biologically speaking, yes."

"Even if that's true, it seems like an awful long time for Bruce to wait to take revenge on his brother," Di said.

"What if he only found out recently?"

"How?"

"That, I don't know. But when you put it all together, Bruce knew Bubba had the trots, even supposedly gave his brother an Imodium pill, which the lab tests show was really an antihistamine. It's possible he just told Bubba the pill was something for stomach upset to discourage him from going home and to ensure Bubba would still be making trips to the potty during the fireworks show. And we know Bruce had a slim jim, so he could have easily taken Earl's rifle out of his truck. So if somehow he had found out Bubba was Jennifer's biological father . . ."

"I agree that could be a powerful motive," Di said. "But we don't have anything except suspicions. Dave couldn't possibly get a warrant for a DNA test based on that."

"No, *he* couldn't. But maybe we can help him out on that score."

Chapter 20

I made it to the office before nine on Tuesday and got right to work, but as was usual lately it had nothing to do with actually running my business—a routine I was going to have to break out of soon if Liv 4 Fun was to remain solvent.

After dinner at the Chinese place last night, Di and I formulated a plan to collect DNA samples ourselves and have them tested. I dropped Di off at her place and headed home to do some research.

I checked out paternity-testing labs online to learn how to proceed. For knowing participants in DNA testing, cheek swabs, which are rubbed against the inside of the subject's cheek, are generally used. Since we were being clandestine, that wasn't really an option. However, hairs pulled from the subject's head with the root still intact were an acceptable substitute for DNA testing. And DNA testing is extremely accurate when done properly, according to the Frequently Asked Questions section.

Instructions said DNA samples should be placed in unused paper envelopes because plastic bags can promote the growth of bacteria.

Having the DNA tests done was going to be a bit pricy, especially if I paid to have them expedited. But I planned to count it as my wedding gift to Mama and Earl.

I was looking at some other lab options online when Larry Joe came in. I had quickly closed the window on the computer screen. I knew Larry Joe said he was 100 percent behind me on this investigation, but my best guess was he wouldn't be completely supportive of our covert DNA collection plans.

As much as I wanted to keep our little scheme for DNA testing under wraps, I had no choice but to enlist some help. And I was going to have to rely on someone I knew lacked discretion. But desperate times call for desperate measures, so I punched in the number for Dixie Dolls Hair Salon and asked the receptionist to put my hairdresser on the phone.

"Nell, I have a favor to ask. Is it okay if I drop by the salon right after closing this evening?" I said.

"No, hon, don't come to the shop. I've got the floor people coming in to wax tonight. Come on by the house anytime after seven. Billy's got a catering job and Billy Jr.'s friend is sleeping over, so they'll probably be holed up in his room playing video games. We should be free to talk."

"All right, sounds good. I'll see you then."

After I'd set up my after-hours appointment with Nell, I checked e-mail. Holly had already come up with some good ideas for Mama's bouquet. She suggested looking for wildflowers in shades of purple and pink and pinning rhinestone brooches or earrings to the cotton bolls to coordinate with the dress Mama had bought.

About midmorning I walked to the gift and stationery store on the next block to buy some sturdy envelopes that would fit the bill for collecting DNA samples.

With the freight mix-up Monday Larry Joe hadn't made it home until almost ten o'clock the night before and he was beat. At that point, I had decided not to ask how things were going between him and his dad or if they'd made up since their scrap at the country club on Sunday.

I hoped he'd be in a good mood when he got home from work tonight, but just to smooth the way I had picked up some catfish filets, a favorite of his, at the market.

I mixed a bag of shredded cabbage and carrots with dressing to make the slaw, then breaded and fried the catfish in a skillet.

After he came in through the back door, I gave him a big kiss. He lit up like a Christmas tree. I'd like to think it was my kiss that caused the reaction, but I felt pretty sure it was a glance over my shoulder at the catfish sizzling in the pan that had set him aglow.

He washed his hands at the kitchen sink before filling glasses with ice cubes and sweet tea. I plated up our catfish and slaw, adding some sliced tomatoes and pickles to the plates.

"*Mmm*, this is good, hon."

"It's been a while since we've had some catfish. I thought it'd be a nice change. So how were things at work today? Any fallout from that freight problem last night?"

"No, we made the shipment on time—just barely."

"How are you and your dad getting on?" I said, hoping for the best.

"Don't worry, I made nice with the old man. I decided I would just grin and bear it if he started talking about his plans to become a vending machine magnate. But I was pleasantly surprised when he started talking about how he thought he might look for ways to help out with projects around Dixie, including volunteering with Residential Rehab. How it would give him a chance to put his woodworking skills to good use."

I just smiled and said that sounded good.

"Thanks, Liv," he said, leaning over and giving me a peck on the cheek. "I felt pretty sure you're the one who put the bug in his ear about RR. It's a brilliant idea. And you're a sweetheart to put up with me and my dad."

"You both have your moments."

Larry Joe cleared the dishes and I put two scoops of Chubby Hubby ice cream in a bowl for him.

"None for you?"

"No, I'm going to run over to Nell Tucker's for

a bit. She said she wanted to talk to me about something."

That wasn't an out-and-out lie, but it wasn't exactly the truth, either. But I couldn't very well tell Larry Joe that I was going to Nell's to ask her to retrieve a DNA sample from Jennifer Rowland. Some lies fall into the category of "for the greater good." Or at least that's what I told my conscience.

I drove over to Nell's, and just to be neighborly, I brought along a six-pack of hard cider, since I knew she was partial to it.

She opened the door as I came up the front steps.

"This must be a big favor if you think you need to bribe me with alcohol," she said, holding the door open and motioning for me to go through.

"I just had some on hand and remembered you were fond of cider," I lied. I had stopped by the store to pick it up on my way over.

"Come on back to the kitchen. Can't offer any hors d'oeuvres, but I've got pretzels and brownies if you want."

"I never turn down brownies," I said.

She twisted the cap off a bottle of cider and asked me if I'd like one.

"No, thanks. But I'll take a Coke if you have one."

"Diet okay?"

"Sure. In fact, I prefer it."

She slid the six-pack into the fridge and handed me a can of Diet Coke. She opened a Tupperware container of brownies sitting on the counter and placed it on the dining table. I took a seat and she sat down across from me.

"I hate to ask . . ." I started.

"Don't be coy. I owe you at least a couple of favors with all that happened after the last murder in town. You're just calling one in."

"I'm not sure you owe me a favor, but I'll ask just the same. I know part of Jennifer Rowland's prize as the new Miss Dixie includes having her hair cut and styled at Dixie Dolls Hair Salon—"

"Permed and colored, too, if she wants," Nell interjected.

"Right. Has she had her appointment with you yet?"

"No, she's scheduled to come in tomorrow."

Billy Jr., Nell's middle school–aged son, and his best friend, Gavin, barged through the back door, stomping and laughing—and smelling foul. Billy had been over at Gavin's house and they smelled so bad I put my hand over my nose as soon as they entered the kitchen.

"What in the world?" Nell said, looking Billy up and down. "Is that manure on your shoes, son?"

"I must have stepped in a cow pie," Billy said.

"Well, both of you go outside and take your shoes off on the back porch. You're not tracking that filth through the house. Go on now."

I laughed when the kids went back outside.

"Honestly, what boys get into," she said, looking over at me.

Billy and Gavin returned a moment later in their

sock feet. Billy opened the fridge door and both boys peered into it before Billy pulled out a jug of milk and grabbed two plastic cups out of the dishwasher and filled them.

"What were you two doing out in a cow pasture anyway?"

"We were just cutting through the pasture to this place that Gavin's brother likes to get off to."

"Yeah, get off," Gavin said, and they both started snickering again.

"And just where is this place, Billy Jr.? Have you two been riding around with some of those older boys? You know you're not supposed to get in a car with anybody without me or your daddy saying it's okay."

"Don't worry, mom. Gavin and I were riding our bikes out near his house. It's just a scenic spot, that's all."

"Yeah, it's *purdy*," Gavin said. "Garrett and his girlfriend think it's the bomb."

The boys were trying without success to suppress their giggles.

"Liv, you want another brownie?"

"No, I'm good. Thanks."

"Here, Billy. You and Gavin take your milk and these brownies and go on up to your room. Miss Liv and I are trying to have a chat."

As we heard the boys bounding up the stairs she said, "I don't like him riding in cars with some of those older boys, including Gavin's brother, Garrett. I'm sure you've seen him. He's Jennifer Rowland's boyfriend. Anyway he's graduated from high school now, and I worry about him and his buddies drinking and driving with his little brother and Billy Jr. in the car."

"Billy and Gavin didn't step in cow manure on the street or in the backseat of a car. They were probably safe enough tonight."

"You're right. I'm a mom; I can't help but worry even when there's no need. So what's this favor you were going to ask me?"

"There's something I need you to get from Jennifer Rowland for me when she comes for her hair appointment. Do you think you could pull seven or eight hairs out of her head with the follicle still attached?"

"Without her noticing?"

"It might be hard to do without her noticing, unless she's unconscious," I said. "Just come up with some plausible explanation for doing it, like you're going to do a quick color test on them before you put dye on her whole head or something like that."

"I suppose I can do that. But, Liv, I've watched enough 'Who's the daddy?' shows on TV to know you're asking me to collect a DNA sample. It doesn't take much of a leap to assume you're thinking Bubba Rowland may have been Jennifer's daddy. What makes you think so?"

"Probably just desperation. I'm grasping at any straw trying to clear Earl's name, so he's free to marry my mama. She's got her heart set on it. Plus, I know Earl wouldn't kill anybody. But, for obvious reasons, you have to promise not to mention this to anyone."

"Don't worry. I admit I like to gossip as much as the next person. And it's kind of expected by some of my customers. And while I don't give a cheese sandwich for Bubba Rowland or his reputation, I think too much of Jennifer and her mom to let a rumor like that creep down the grapevine."

"Thanks. You'll need to wear gloves when you pull the hairs out, and if you use tweezers to pluck them out make sure you sterilize them first—and try not to touch the roots." After retrieving a paper sample collection envelope from my purse and handing it to her, I said, "Place the hairs in here."

Larry Joe was watching *Ice Road Truckers* when I got home. I had just settled in next to him on the sofa in the den when my cell phone buzzed. It was Mama.

"Liv, I just wanted to give you an update on the list. I've got seventeen more names we have to add."

Mama talks loudly enough that anybody in the room could hear her part of the conversation as well as mine. I looked over at Larry Joe, who had a great big smirk on his face. I elbowed him and shot him a look that said, "I'm not amused."

"Mama—"

She cut me off.

"I know I said I'd try not to add any more people to the list, but not all of these are mine. Three of 'em are people Earl wanted to add—and I can't very well tell him he can't invite who he wants."

I badly wanted to tell her to add Earl's three guests and scratch off the other fourteen she had added, but I knew it wouldn't do any good.

"We'll need to set up some more tables and chairs on the lawn, of course. But I've been thinking we should put tents up over them to keep people from getting too much sun—or in case it starts to sprinkle. Do you think it would be better to put up one big tent or several little ones?"

"I don't—"

"I'll leave that decision up to you and Holly," she said, interrupting again. "After all, you're the pros. I won't keep you, hon. Tell Larry Joe hello." Click.

"So what's the guest list total up to now?" Larry Joe asked, laughing under his breath.

"I'm not sure. What's the population of Dixie?"

Chapter 21

I got to the office a little before nine and spent most of the morning busily accomplishing not much. But I did find time to work in a coffee break with Winette. I asked her if she'd heard anything more about the developer Aaron Rankin.

"I did casually ask Mr. Sweet if there was a particular reason he decided against investing in the new development." She looked over her shoulder and through the open door of the back office, where Mr. Sweet was engaged in a phone conversation, before continuing in a hushed voice. "He said there were several things in the proposal that didn't look right. But he told me he knew he wouldn't invest before he even looked at the proposal. Said Aaron Rankin is one of those men who doesn't look you in the eye when he shakes your hand. And that always makes Mr. Sweet think they're eyeing his wallet."

I went back upstairs and looked up examples of

wildflower bouquets on the Internet. I didn't see any that featured cotton bolls, so Mama's would be original, if nothing else.

Just before noon, I was on the phone when I looked up and saw Nell standing in my doorway. I motioned for her to come in and take a seat while I wrapped up the call.

As soon as I hung up, she waved the little DNA collection envelope at me.

"You got it?"

"Yes, ma'am. Jennifer only squealed a little when I started snatching hairs off her head. But she bought the line about testing the hairs for a color match. I was worried for a minute when she wanted to see the color on the test hairs. I had to tell her I'd already thrown them away and she'd just have to trust me. When will you get the DNA results?"

"I still have to get a sample from Bubba before I can send them in. I don't suppose you're doing hair or make-up on the dearly departed councilman?"

"Bubba didn't have much hair to speak of. And that strange mortician, the younger one, likes to do the make-up himself. I only do it if the family special requests it."

"Oh, well, I'll think of something," I said.

"Update me when you know something for sure."

I insincerely told her I would, knowing I wouldn't be able to tell the results to anyone but Dave—and he wasn't going to like it.

"I'd better get back to the shop before my next appointment," Nell said before taking off.

I texted Di to let her know we had Jennifer's sample in hand, and asked if she'd like to ride with me up to Jackson, Tennessee, later on, sometime after five. She texted back, I'll drive. Pick u up 5:15.

I shot back a thumbs-up.

I had texted Larry Joe to let him know Di and I were making a quick run to Jackson. I was beginning to think I'd have to leave before he made it home when I heard the garage door open and his truck rumble into the garage. As the garage door was going down, I looked out the window and saw Di pulling into the driveway. I grabbed my purse and stood ready to tell Larry Joe a quick good-bye before I exited through the front door.

He opened the door and stepped into the kitchen.

"Whoa," he said, suddenly looking up and taking a short step back. "You startled me, hon. Why are you standing at the back door like a puppy that needs to be let out?"

"Di pulled into the drive behind you. I just wanted to give you a quick kiss before I go."

"Oh, okay. Before you leave, did you hear about Aaron Rankin?"

"No, what about him?"

"I just ran into Dave at the gas station. He said the TBI went to arrest Rankin and he did a runner. Somebody must've tipped him off. Anyway, Dave said that law enforcement statewide have been alerted to be on the lookout for him."

"I guess this has to do with him ripping off investors?"

"Yep. Why are you two off to Jackson? And does this mean I'm on my own for supper?"

"I need to pick up a gift there, and yes. There's leftover roast in the fridge you can heat up in the microwave."

He went quiet for a moment and then said, "I'm still waiting for my kiss."

He smiled and I gave him a big smack on the lips, followed by a short kiss for good measure.

I hopped in Di's 1972 Buick Riviera and buckled up. The body wasn't exactly in mint condition, but under the hood there was a rebuilt engine with only 77,000 miles on it, courtesy of Di's ex-husband. Jimmy Souther didn't have much use for it since he was currently residing in the Texas State Penitentiary.

"I'd be glad to drive, since this is my errand. Why did you want to drive tonight?"

"Because you almost always drive and I haven't put any highway miles on the Buick lately."

"Oh. Larry Joe just told me Aaron Rankin's on the run from the cops."

"Why? It's not about Bubba's murder, is it?" she asked.

"No, the Tennessee Bureau of Investigation is after him for some kind of investment fraud. But it may involve some investors in Dixie, as well as in East Tennessee."

"Wow. Okay, tell me again why we're driving to

Jackson to buy a set of salt and pepper shakers. They have those at Walmart, you know," Di said.

"Not like these. Holly met a group of old friends for lunch at the Old Country Store recently and she spotted a set of Elvis shakers. It's Elvis wearing a black leather jacket like the one he wore in the 1968 comeback special, holding a guitar. The guitar detaches; it's the pepper shaker. Elvis is the salt shaker."

Di looked at me like I had lost my mind.

"Do you need them for a party you're planning?"

"No, they're going to be a birthday gift for my mother-in-law. You know she collects salt and pepper shakers. You've been in her kitchen, haven't you? Daddy Wayne custom built those shelves behind the kitchen table to hold her collection."

"Oh, yeah, I remember. She doesn't actually use them, but she likes to look at them."

"Right. Anyway, Holly mentioned seeing these and I don't have any other ideas for a birthday present for her, so I thought I'd run up and buy them. I asked you to join me because I thought we could eat supper at the Old Country Store while we're there. Or I guess we could go somewhere else in Jackson, if you have a taste for something in particular."

"The Old Country Store sounds good. I love their cracklin' cornbread."

"Me too."

Di was driving more than ten miles over the speed limit down a two-lane back road when a flashy sports car came careening past us. I looked over to see what fool was driving. And it was Aaron Rankin.

I recognized him from the town hall meeting and his picture in the development brochure, but he had no reason to know me since we'd never actually met.

As he passed I turned to Di and said, "That's Aaron Rankin. Don't lose him. I'll call Dave and tell him where Rankin is and which direction he's heading. We'll just try to stay on his tail until the police arrive."

Di slammed her foot down on the accelerator and we lurched forward, giving me momentary whiplash.

Di knew, because her ex had told her, and I knew, because she had told me, that the seventies' muscle car had eight cylinders and could go zero to sixty miles per hour in just over eight seconds.

I hit Dave's number on my speed dial—I'm not sure what it says about me that I call the sheriff often enough that he's on speed dial.

"Dave, Di and I are heading east on the old highway and Aaron Rankin just passed us. We're trying to keep him in sight. If he turns off this road, I'll text you."

Dave started to speak, but I hung up before he launched into a sermon about keeping our distance from a fugitive and obeying posted speed limits.

At the county line, the road suddenly veered in a hard left. In his compact sports car, Rankin left his lane, crossing the double yellow line, but managed to hug the road. Di stayed in our lane but the left rear tire left the pavement as she made the turn.

If Rankin had any doubts we were following him before then, he didn't now.

There were a couple of close calls with oncoming traffic, which fortunately was sparse. Rankin put the pedal to the metal as we reached a straightaway and he nearly sideswiped a Cadillac driven by an elderly man whose driver's side tires rolled along the center line. I momentarily closed my eyes and dug my fingernails into my pants so hard I thought I was going to slash slits in them. Di edged to the right, driving with two tires on the shoulder until we were past the Caddy.

Without slowing down at all, Rankin suddenly made a hard right turn onto a narrow road with potholes as deep as gopher holes.

I texted Dave that we had turned off the old highway onto Galbreath Road. I had no idea where Galbreath Road would lead us, and unlike my SUV, Di's car didn't have GPS. My seat belt was all that was keeping my head from hitting the roof as we bounced along. The poor condition of the road did slow Rankin down just a bit.

The phone buzzed. It was Dave.

"Have you reached the bridge over the creek on Galbreath Road yet?"

"No. I don't remember seeing a bridge."

I looked over to Di, who was shaking her head "no."

"No bridge." Just as I spoke those words we hit the bridge. I tried to tell Dave, but he cut me off.

"Good. Listen up. Just past the bridge, there will be an S curve in the road."

We were swinging into the top of the S as he spoke.

"Coming out of the second curve there will be a hill with a sudden drop. . . ."

At that moment we saw Rankin just ahead of us go flying over the hill, all four tires off the road, and land on the other side of a dip before the car spun around sideways and slid several feet.

I dropped the phone as Dave was trying to warn us to slow down. Di tried too late to hit the brakes and we went airborne before bottoming out, the undercarriage of the Buick slamming hard onto the uneven pavement. The car died.

After sitting stunned for a moment, I looked up to see blue lights approaching from the other side of Rankin's car. He got out and started running through a field, but there was no place to hide and the cruiser turned onto the field road and cut him off. Two state troopers jumped out of their car, wrestled Rankin to the ground, and handcuffed him.

I retrieved the cell phone from the floorboard and heard Dave still talking.

"Liv, are you there?!" he was shouting.

"Yeah, I'm here. We bottomed out over that hill. But the good news is the state police just took Rankin into custody."

Dave said he'd call a tow truck, and one of the state troopers walked over to Di's car, which was making a hissing noise that sounded like an expensive repair. I assumed Dave had told him about us since he didn't ask us any questions other than to inquire whether we were okay.

Di and I rode back to Dixie in the tow truck. The driver dropped us off at the sheriff's office. Terry told us that we could go on back to Dave's office, that he was waiting for us. That sounded both comforting and ominous.

Fortunately, he kept the inquisition brief. I think the fact that we were on our way somewhere else and had merely happened upon Rankin instead of having tracked him down worked in our favor. He asked us to run through everything—twice, which seems to be his standard procedure.

"I understand you were just trying to keep Rankin in sight until law enforcement arrived. But what would you have done if he had suddenly stopped his car, jumped out, and came at you with a gun?"

"Run him over," Di said without missing a beat.

Dave let it pass.

"The Tennessee Bureau of Investigation will likely want to question you. They'll need to make a full report about how they captured Rankin. My guess is they'll want to downplay your role in it."

"Fine by me," Di said. "What is Rankin going down for exactly, besides speeding?"

"Kelvin Duffy with TBI only gave me a rough outline of things. This is totally the TBI's case. But it sounds to me like Rankin has been playing a shell game with investors' funds, transferring money out of bank accounts belonging to the rental property investors into operating expense accounts.

"Some of his 'operating expenses,'" Dave said, wrapping air quotes around the words *operating expenses*, "included tens of thousands of dollars in personal expenses like luxury vacations with his wife and private school tuition for his daughter. He was also making monthly rent payments on an apartment occupied by a woman who isn't his wife.

"To conceal his misappropriation of funds he provided false and misleading financial reports to investors and he perpetuated his fraud scheme by propping up the failing rental property investments using funds from other investments. Likely that included the Dixie investors, although I'm not sure exactly how they figure into this just yet."

Dave asked Ted to drive me home. I assumed the sheriff was going to personally handle transporting Di.

When Ted pulled up in our driveway, the garage door was open and Larry Joe was getting something out of his truck. Our life is such that Larry Joe didn't seem surprised when I arrived home in a patrol car. He just waved at the deputy.

"You and Di have some excitement this evening?"

"You could say that."

We went into the kitchen. He grabbed a beer and I poured myself a glass of Merlot. He was remarkably calm about the whole car-chase episode. Of course, I chose my words very carefully.

Chapter 22

At the office on Thursday, I decided to make a few calls to get some preliminary cost estimates for the thirtieth reunion group, even though I had told them I wouldn't. If they got back to me with an estimate of how much per couple their classmates were willing to fork over, I wanted to have at least some idea how much of their wish list that amount would buy.

One good thing about multiday, varied activities gatherings is that those on a tighter budget can gracefully opt out of some of the events by arriving a day or two late, or leaving a day or two early. I was certain some of the grads would come only for the dinner/dance on Saturday, while others would want to arrive before any of the scheduled events to hang out in smaller groups with some of their old pals and check out some of their old haunts.

If Kurt and Judy's estimate of 75 classmates, each with a plus-one, was accurate, that would mean 150 for the dinner/dance. But I suspected a number closer to 100 to 110 for the family day on Friday and an even smaller number on Thursday, something like 70 to 80 for the night out on the town. This was just my best guess based on experience with similar events, but it gave me a place to start.

I called a couple of charter bus businesses and got estimates on per-hour and per-day rates. The largest buses would accommodate up to sixty people and mini buses could carry from twenty-four to thirty.

I also checked with my contact at the Memphis Zoo. I had arranged a number of birthday parties there and even a wine tasting, but those had been limited to about twenty people. I chatted with her, taking notes about larger groups and private after-hours events.

Since the reunion was for the class of 1989, I called a couple of sources and asked about bands that performed eighties music. I already knew the phone number and the rates for a disc jockey that could put together an eighties mix that would be a crowd-pleaser, and would definitely be easier on the wallet than a quality live band.

Di's car was in the shop, where it had been towed the previous evening. She was still waiting to hear what the damage was pricewise.

I picked her up from the post office a little after four o'clock and drove her home.

"I hope repairs to the Buick don't end up costing too much," I said.

"Me too, but I don't want to think about that just now. It's been a long day. Why don't you entertain me by telling me the newest ideas your mom has for the wedding."

"You enjoy seeing me suffer, don't you?"

"Only a little."

"Okay, so she's added more people to the guest list. If she doesn't stop soon, Earl's acreage isn't going to be large enough to accommodate them all. And it's not enough to just set up tables on the grounds near the house; she suggested I check on renting a tent or several tents to put everyone under cover, in case it's hot or it rains."

"So have you checked with Barnum & Bailey yet to see if they'll loan you the big top?"

"No, but it may come to that if she keeps adding to her guest list. I may have to hide all her pens."

"It could be worse," Di said.

"How's that?"

"She could decide she wants the tents erected on floating docks in the pond surrounding her little fantasy island. That way everyone would have a ringside seat for the ceremony."

I squinted my eyes and gave her a mean look.

"If you mention that to Mama, they'll be burying you next to Bubba."

We both laughed. I figured I might as well laugh as cry.

"So, down to business," I said. "Getting the DNA sample from Jennifer was relatively simple. Now we have to deal with the more complicated matter of retrieving a DNA sample from Bubba."

I pulled up in front of Di's trailer and parked.

"What's the plan?" she asked as we walked to the door.

Once inside she said she was going into the bedroom to change her clothes.

"Keep talking," she said. "I can hear you."

"The medical examiner has released the body to the funeral home. My idea is that we go to the funeral home and you somehow draw the mortician away from the preparation area, while I slip in and yank some hairs off Bubba's head."

"Will hairs from a dead man still work for a DNA sample?"

"According to the information on the DNA lab's Web site they will."

"Why do I get the job of enticing the mortician? Am I supposed to flirt with him? And let me just add, *eeww*."

"How you get him out of the way is entirely up to you. You can tell him you're interested in a career in embalming, if you like."

"Double *eeww*."

"Look, if you'd prefer I'll distract the mortician and you can pluck the hairs off Bubba as he lies naked and bloodless on a metal table."

"No thanks, I'm good," she said. "But if we're going to the funeral home I guess I should put on a skirt."

* * *

My skirt-clad friend and I drove to the funeral home. There was a funeral in session when we arrived at Frank's Funeral Home. Frank Jr. is the funeral director now, carrying on after the death of his dad, Frank Sr. The family wisely chose the name Frank's for the funeral home, rather than Slaughter, which is their last name.

I hoped the funeral in progress would mean most, if not all, of the staff was occupied with the family of the deceased and their friends. We started to slip downstairs, which is accessed through a staff only door in the back, away from the public areas, when we ran into Steven Slaughter, Frank Jr.'s brother, who spends more time with the deceased than with their grieving families. Probably a wise choice, businesswise.

Di immediately started chatting him up. He looked dubious, but seemed to be enjoying the attention of a warm-bodied female. I excused myself under the pretext of going to the ladies' room.

I wasn't sure how long Di would be able to feign interest in Steven, so I hurried. There was no one on the stairs or in the hall. I spotted a heavy metal door on the right with signs that said, STAFF ONLY, NO SMOKING, KEEP DOOR CLOSED AT ALL TIMES, and GLOVES MUST BE WORN AS YOU ENTER. There was a glove dispenser on the wall beside the door. *This must be it,* I thought.

I turned the knob; it was locked. *Dang. Why didn't this obvious possibility occur to me earlier?* I dug in my purse and pulled out a nail file. After fiddling with the lock for a moment, I realized it was hopeless. I hustled back up the stairs and found Di sitting on the arm of a Victorian settee gazing down at a rather nervous-looking Steven.

"Sorry, we need to go now," I said to Steven as I tugged on Di's sleeve.

She gave him a little tootles wave.

As we neared the car, she said, "Did you get it?"

"No. The door was locked."

She threw her arms in the air.

"What now?" she asked.

"I had hoped to avoid it, but I'm going to have to enlist Mama's help. The viewing's tomorrow, with the funeral on Saturday. I think I'd better go ahead and drop by her house and tell her what we need her to do."

"Are you sure you want your mama to know what's going on?"

"I'm not going to tell her we want Bubba's hairs for DNA testing. I think I'll give her the impression that we're looking for poison or something."

"Wouldn't the medical examiner already have tested for poisoning?"

"Yeah. But with any luck, Mama won't think about that. Honestly, I think she'll be excited to feel like she's doing something to help Earl. Hopefully, she won't ask too many questions. Do you want to come with me to Mama's or do you want me to drop you off at home first?"

"Do you think your mother will have any cake or pie on offer?"

"Chances are good."

"I'll stick with you then."

* * *

Pulling up to Mama's house, I was relieved to see that Earl's truck wasn't in her driveway. I had a feeling he might not be thrilled with the little assignment I had planned for her.

I tapped on the back door and hollered, "It's me, Mama. And I have Di with me."

She called out for us to come on in. As we passed through the kitchen I spied more than half a chocolate cake sitting on the counter next to the coffeemaker. Di elbowed me and nodded toward the cake.

We walked through to the den. It was only polite to speak to Mama before we started slicing into her cake. True to her Southern upbringing, as soon as we'd exchanged hugs and hellos, Mama asked if we'd like something sweet.

"I'd love some of your chocolate cake, if it's no trouble, Mrs. Walford," Di said.

"You know you don't have to ask me twice," I said. "Mama, don't get up; I'll get the cake. Do you want some?"

"No, I'd better not. I've already had two slices today and I wouldn't want to gain weight before the wedding. But put some coffee on, Liv, if you don't mind. I could use a cup."

I went back into the kitchen and started the coffee, before cutting two generous slices of cake for Di and myself.

"Di, you want coffee or iced tea?"

"I think I'll go with coffee. Thanks."

I made use of the pause-and-pour feature on the half-full pot of coffee and poured a small mugful for Mama, doctoring it with two sugars and some cream, the way she likes it. I put a splash of milk in mine. Di takes hers black.

I carried in their coffees and went back to the kitchen to retrieve the cake plates, balancing my coffee cup on my plate.

Mama was sorting through photos of her and Earl, placing them in different stacks on the coffee table.

"Whatcha doing, Mama?"

"I got a bunch of photos of me and Earl printed at the drugstore. Some of these had been on my camera for over a year. I was thinking we'd do a display at the reception, and we might even want to use one on the front of the wedding invitations. What do you two think?"

"I think you got robbed in the cake contest, Mrs. Walford," Di said, *mmm*ing with her mouth full.

"Well, thank you, hon. But we've got so many good bakers in Dixie, it wouldn't be fair for the same person to win every year."

Paging through a stack of photos, I couldn't help but smile. Mama wearing jeans and boots, a rarity for her, at a barbecue for friends out on Earl's property. Mama and Earl all dressed up for some fancy affair at the country club. Earl standing proudly next to Mama in her prize-winning Mrs. Peacock costume, holding her trophy, at the murder mystery fund-raiser dinner last Halloween. One thing all the pictures had in common was that Mama looked

happy. This strengthened my resolve to make sure
Earl Daniels did not get packed off to prison.

After commenting on some of the photos and
telling my mother which were my favorites, I got
down to business.

"Mama, the main reason we dropped by is that
I have a little job I need you to do for me—
something that might help me track down Bubba's
real killer."

"You know I'd do anything to clear Earl's name.
What do you want me to do?"

"I need hair samples from Bubba Rowland. I
failed in my attempt to procure them while no one
was around. Now I need you to collect them at the
viewing while everyone is there without anybody
knowing what you're doing. My idea is that if you
get very emotional and bend over the casket
boohooing, you'll be able to snatch a few hairs
before anyone is the wiser."

"You need these hair samples for the lab to test
for some kind of poison or drugs?"

"Something like that. I really can't go into details
until I know for sure."

Mama quickly agreed to her assignment and I
told her I'd drive her to the viewing. I had a feeling
Earl wasn't planning to go.

I dropped Di off at her place and called Larry
Joe to see if he knew when he'd be home. He said
he already was.

"Why didn't you call or text me?"

"I figured you were busy. Besides I just walked in
a couple of minutes ago."

"Is there anything in the fridge that looks appealing or should I drive through and pick us up something to eat?"

"I'll look. *Hmm*," he said, apparently gazing into the icebox.

"What's it look like?"

"It looks like we'll be eating something from Taco Belles for supper."

On Friday, I called Holly to check in. At my behest, she had been making phone calls and responding to e-mails for Liv 4 Fun. I figured at least one of us should be taking care of business.

"Hi, Holly. Anything going on I should know about?"

"There was an e-mail about the retirement party from the CEO's secretary. She wanted to be sure you understood that attire for the dinner would be business formal, not a casual affair."

"That would have been my guess," I said. "Have you had any inspired ideas about working Mr. Clenk's passion for stamp collecting into the event?"

"Maybe he could play post office with his secretary," she said.

The thought of Miss Payne playing the post office kissing game with anyone made me laugh out loud.

I enlisted Di to go along to the funeral home with Mama and me for the viewing that evening.

We would be forming the defensive line keeping other people from getting too close to the casket once Mama launched into her mourning scene.

After we arrived at Mama's, I got into the driver's seat of her Cadillac and Di climbed into the backseat. Mama, who was dressed in a black jacket dress with a hanky tucked in the sleeve, got in on the passenger side.

"Now, Mama, remember we need six or seven hairs from Bubba. And we need them plucked out with the root end still intact. He's dead, so it's not like he's going to feel anything when you snatch them off his head."

"And drop them into this little paper envelope," Di said, passing the collection packet to Mama from the backseat.

"I've got it, hon," Mama said. "We may have to wait a bit for the crowd to clear away from the casket. I'll make a pass by to scope things out and then mingle until it seems like a good time to go back up and say my final farewells to Bubba."

"Sounds good. Once you make your move, Di and I will flank you on either side to run interference if anybody tries to approach."

We pulled into the parking lot of Frank's Funeral Home and it was packed. This gave me some cause for concern. But I hoped some people would just do a quick in and out to offer condolences to the family.

I was secretly worried that someone might be

bold enough to make a snotty remark to Mama about Earl, or even about her coming to the viewing since she's Earl's fiancée. I did see a couple of busybodies give Mama a sideways glance, but I was hoping she was too focused on her mission to notice them.

Di and I followed Mama on her first pass by the coffin. Bubba looked better than he ever looked when he was alive, wearing a blue suit with his hair neatly combed and a blush to his cheeks.

Mama sat down on a chair against the wall next to a lady in her Sunday school class. I got in line to speak to Bruce and Carrie. Di wandered over to look at a memorial display of photos.

"Bruce, I'm so sorry for your loss. I can't imagine how difficult it must be to lose your brother to violence, and so soon after the passing of your sister-in-law and nephew."

"Thanks, Liv. Yeah, it's hard to believe the whole branch of my brother's family is gone."

"If there's anything we can do . . . ," I said, using the tired line people always say at funerals.

I moved on to Carrie, standing a couple of feet beyond Bruce, to let the next person in line talk to the weary-looking brother of the deceased.

"Carrie, how is Bruce holding up? He looks tired."

"He is. It's been stressful and he hasn't been sleeping well. Maybe once we make it through the funeral tomorrow, he'll be able to rest," she said.

"I hope so."

"I'm so glad your mama came. Bubba always thought highly of her and I know she was a good neighbor to him and Faye. And, just so you know, I don't for a minute believe that Earl Daniels killed Bubba."

"Thank you, Carrie. I appreciate you saying so."

I joined Di to look over the photo collection, which included some of Bubba and Bruce as children; a wedding photo of Bubba and Faye, him holding Bubba Jr.; one of him standing between Bruce and Carrie, squeezing them to him in a big hug; and one of him being sworn in as a town councilman. The most recent was one of him standing next to his niece, Jennifer, who was wearing her sash and tiara as the newly crowned Miss Dixie.

Out of the corner of my eye, I saw Mama working the room, which had cleared out considerably since we'd arrived. Carrie walked over and gave her a hug. I saw Mama dab a tear from her eye with her hanky. I sensed she was getting ready to make her move. There was no one standing by the casket.

I gave Di a knowing look and we strolled in the general direction of the casket. In a moment Mama started soaking the handkerchief with her tears as she walked to the casket. Di and I took our places on either side of Mama, a few feet away from the casket.

Fortunately, next to the end of the coffin near Bubba's head was a large plant, which gave Mama a bit of cover. Mama leaned over the casket and her whole body shuddered as she sobbed. Just about everyone in the room was looking her way by this time. I spotted a woman from her Sunday school class approaching with a look of concern and headed her off by going over and putting my arm around Mama in a consoling embrace. In a moment Mama looked over to me and nodded.

I kept my arm around her as we walked away, and she just shook her tear-streaked face as she clasped the hanky to her considerable bosom.

I led her to the ladies' room and Di followed, keeping guard outside the door after we went in.

After making sure there was no one in the stall, I asked, "Did you get them?"

"Of course I got them," Mama said. She pulled the little envelope out of her cleavage and handed it to me. I pulled the tab off to seal it and put it in the side pocket of my purse.

Mama took a powder compact out of her purse and fixed her face. I reached over and patted her on the arm as I gave her reflection an admiring look in the mirror.

"That was an Oscar-worthy performance, Mama."

"You say that like you're surprised," she said before rubbing her lips together to even out her lipsick.

After Di and I dropped Mama off at her house, we drove to Di's. She invited me in for some refreshment in the form of strawberry daiquiris. I felt like we'd earned it.

"Your mama's a hoot. I never would've believed she could pull off a performance like that if I hadn't seen it with my own eyes. Most people didn't even look surprised."

"Mama has a history when it comes to drama."

"So are you going to pack Jennifer's and Bubba's DNA samples off to the lab in the morning?"

"No. We still need one more," I said, taking a big sip of my frosty drink.

"One more DNA sample? Whose?"

"I think we should get Bruce's, because if it turns out Bubba's not Jennifer's father we still won't know with absolute certainty that Bruce is. I think we might as well cover all our bases."

"Okay, but a hairstylist snatching a few hairs off a girl's head while she's getting her hair cut and colored and your mama ripping hairs from a dead man's head is one thing. How do you propose we get a sample from Bruce?"

"I checked the DNA lab Web site and it says high-quality samples can include shavings from an electric razor and also the person's toothbrush. We'll go to the funeral lunch tomorrow at Bruce's house. In fact, I think we should drop by during the funeral before the crowd makes it to the house for the luncheon. We can raid the master bathroom and take what we need without anyone being the wiser."

Chapter 23

It was going to be a complicated maneuver to skip the funeral without giving an explanation to Larry Joe and Mama.

I gave Di a quick call.

"Hey, are you about ready to pick me up?" she asked.

"Actually, I wanted your advice. I still haven't figured out what I'm going to tell Larry Joe about why I'm not going to the funeral. I don't like to lie to him. Any ideas?"

"Just tell him I've asked you to help me with something," Di said.

"That would be like raising a red flag to a bull. He'd immediately suspect we were snooping."

"It's not like you were close to Bubba. Why don't you tell him you already went to the viewing and offered your condolences to Bruce and Carrie, and you don't feel obligated to attend the funeral as well."

"You know, that's not half bad."

"What are you going to tell your mama? I have a feeling she won't let you off the hook so easily."

"Oh, that's easy. I'm not going to tell her anything. I'll just avoid talking to her until after the funeral. As soon as Larry Joe leaves for the funeral home, I'll drive over and pick you up."

I pulled up in front of Di's place. She jogged over and got in.

"Do you know when you'll be getting your car back from the shop?"

"Yeah. As soon as I can afford to pay for it."

"I'll pay the mechanic. Just let me know when you get the bill."

Di shook her head and simply said, "No."

"At least let me pay half of the cost of repairs since chasing after Aaron Rankin is what led to the damage. And I feel bad that it was your car we wrecked, since we were driving to Jackson for my shopping needs."

"Dave offered to pay for the repairs, too, since we aided in the capture of a fugitive. I'll tell you what I told him: 'Thank you and no.'"

"Don't let false pride keep you from having transportation."

"Between you and Dave and one of the other mail carriers, I haven't had any problem with transportation. So what's the game plan here?"

"We'll go to Bruce's house to collect some DNA

evidence before everyone goes to the house after the funeral."

"Do you know if they leave their doors unlocked, or should I get a screwdriver out of my car in case we have to break in?" Di asked.

"I don't know if they lock the doors or not, but we're not breaking in."

"No?"

"No. I'm sure people have been dropping by with food and flowers all morning. Somebody will be there, either a cousin or a neighbor," I said.

"Oh, yeah. I guess you're right," Di said. "So how do we play this?"

"We'll stop by the diner and pick up a pie. We can't very well arrive empty-handed. We'll take it into the kitchen and hand it over to whoever's looking after things. After exchanging pleasantries, one of us will excuse herself to use the restroom—the master bathroom is probably our best bet. Remember we need a toothbrush or shavings from an electric razor." Taking two envelopes out of the package in my purse and handing them to her I said, "Here're a couple of those little collection envelopes.".

"How do we know which toothbrush belongs to Bruce?"

"If one is pink and one is blue, I'd grab the blue one. Otherwise, just take them both."

"Won't they think it's weird if they come in to find their toothbrushes have been stolen?"

"Probably. But there will be a whole lot of people traipsing through the house after the funeral. They'll probably assume some kids stole them. And chances are good, if they're anything like us, they have a spare toothbrush or two in the cabinet that the dentist sent home with them after their last visit."

I pulled up in front of the diner, which was nearly empty—an unusual occurrence. But a lot of people were at the funeral and it was between normal breakfast and lunch hours. We got out of the car and walked in. The bell on the door alerted Mabel to our entrance. She emerged from the kitchen and stepped to the counter, drying her hands on her apron.

"What can I do for y'all?"

"We're picking up a pie to take over to Bruce and Carrie's," I said.

"What kind you want?"

"Well, I'm assuming some other folks have also picked up pies for the same reason. Can you suggest something that hasn't been purchased for the Rowlands, as far as you know?"

"Let me see," she said, scrolling through the cash register entries. "As far as whole pies, not slices, we've sold apple, strawberry, chocolate, and lemon icebox this morning. That would leave chess and coconut cream."

"What do you think?" I said, looking over to Di for her opinion.

"I'm leaning toward coconut."

"Okay, could you box up a coconut cream for us, Mabel?"

"Sure thing, hon."

I got my credit card out of my wallet while Mabel pulled a pie from the display case and placed it in a white cardboard box.

Bruce and Carrie Rowland live about fifteen minutes outside of town in the house where Bruce and Bubba grew up. "We have samples now from Jennifer and Bubba, so we just need the one from Bruce. How long will it take to get results from the DNA lab once we turn in the samples?" Di asked as I drove along winding roads past fields green with alfalfa.

"If I pay the expedited fee, we can have results in three business days."

"That's fast."

I pulled up the gravel driveway and onto the parched grass. The Rowlands' homestead features a foursquare house with a broad front porch, a barn and other outbuildings behind the house, and just beyond the barn a picture-postcard view of cows grazing in green pasture framed by a barbed-wire fence. The faded front door was open and the screen door unlatched. I called out, "Anybody home?" as we walked in.

"Yes, ma'am," a voice called out. In a moment a short, stout woman with a cloud of white hair stuck her head through the doorway into the front room. I recognized her as the Rowlands' neighbor Lettie Perry.

"Come on through to the kitchen," she said with a little backward wave.

Lettie thanked us as she took the pie and added it to a stack of boxed pies on the counter. On the countertops and large farm table it appeared there was enough food to feed the whole county.

"Looks like you've got more than enough food here," Di said.

"Yeah. People just want to do something for the family in times like these. Carrie already told me that whatever we don't slice into, I should wrap up and take to some of the shut-ins from my church. My husband will drop off some desserts at the volunteer fire station. So we'll try to make sure nothing goes to waste."

"Good. I'm so glad to hear it," I said. "Is there anything we can do to help? Maybe set up some chairs before the crowd arrives?"

"No, hon. I think we're good."

Just then I heard a car door slam. Lettie headed toward the front room and I told her we were going to make a quick stop in the restroom. Best I could remember the bedrooms were all on the second floor, so Di and I hurried up the back staircase before whoever had just arrived caught sight of us. I didn't want to get detained by more obligatory chitchat.

The bathroom was on the hall, on the right, and looked a lot like the bathroom at my house, except all the plumbing appeared to be operational. We went in and pushed the door to.

"You know, I think I really do have to pee," I said.

I availed myself of the toilet while Di surveyed the items on the bathroom counter. Since there were two sinks, I assumed the original bathroom had been updated at some point, but the dated fixtures suggested it had been a while.

As I washed my hands, Di bagged the tooth-brushes in separate paper envelopes and slipped them in her purse.

"Give me another envelope and I'll dump the razor shavings into it," she said. I pulled a paper envelope from my purse and handed it to her. Di was gently tapping the shavings into it when the bathroom door suddenly swung open.

Carrie was standing in the doorway pointing a gun at us.

"Ladies, you can leave the razor and that enve-lope right there. We're going to take a little walk."

She backed up a couple of paces and motioned with the gun for us to step into the hall.

"Just keep walking slowly to the end of the hall and don't try anything cute," she said. "And don't bother calling out for Mrs. Perry. I sent her on a fool's errand. When she told me the two of you were here, I had an uneasy feeling you were up to something. Listening to you through the bathroom door talking about collecting toothbrushes and razor shavings confirmed my suspicions.

"Now down the stairs slowly," she said, prodding me between the shoulder blades with the barrel of the gun.

"All right, stop right there. Di, you raise your

hands up where I can see them. Liv, you open the back door real careful like."

"Carrie, have you always known Bubba was Jennifer's father?" I asked.

She became wild eyed and agitated, waving the gun. My stomach clenched and I could hear Di's breaths become ragged and shallow.

"Shut up. You don't understand anything about this. Bruce is Jennifer's father in all the ways that matter. That child worships her daddy and he adores her. I wasn't about to let Bubba Rowland take that away from either of them. Now move it."

She instructed us to walk across the backyard and into the barn, filled mostly with tractors and tools and machinery. When we reached the middle of the barn, she called for us to stop and turn around to face her with our hands up.

I hoped I could stall her by getting her talking.

"Carrie, why now? Why after all these years would Bubba decide to tell Jennifer he was her biological father?"

"Because he's got an ego as big as all outdoors and he didn't like being without an heir after his only son died in that car crash, that's why."

It made a kind of odd sense.

"Di, I'm guessing you're the more athletic one. Here, catch," she said pulling a key from her pocket and tossing it to Di.

"Use that to open the padlock on that hatch next to your left foot."

Di knelt down and did as she was told.

"Carrie, had Bubba always known he was Jennifer's father?"

"He didn't know jack phooey. But he decided to use one of those DNA labs, like you two were trying to do. He came to me boasting he had the paternity test results to prove he was Jennifer's father and he thought she had a right to know. I begged him for Jennifer's sake and for his brother's sake not to tell her. He had the gall to tell me that he'd keep quiet in exchange for my 'womanly attention'. As disgusting as the thought of Bubba touching me was, I might have considered it if I thought I could actually trust him to keep his word. But I did talk him into waiting until after the Miss Dixie Pageant. Told him if he was any kind of a daddy he wouldn't want to spoil Jennifer's big moment."

Carrie turned the gun toward Di. "Toss the key back to me. Now open the hatch."

Di lifted the heavy metal door to reveal a ladder leading down into some kind of bunker or storm shelter.

Carrie steadied her aim, holding the gun with both hands.

"I think you two are smart enough to guess what to do now."

"Carrie, you don't have to do this. We can . . ."

"Save your breath. You can climb down that ladder or you can drop through the hatch with a bullet in you. Your choice."

We descended the ladder, first Di and then me. Looking up through the hatch opening we could

see Carrie swing out her foot, the kick causing the
heavy metal door to close with a loud thud. In a
moment, we heard her reaffixing the padlock,
securely locking us inside. We stood in complete
darkness for a moment until emergency lights
flickered on, creating a dim yellow glow.

I strained my eyes in the low light to survey our
surroundings. Rusted corrugated metal walls and
ceilings extended up from a concrete floor forming
an arch overhead. It was surprisingly cool in the
underground space, considering the current temperature above ground. Bunk beds hung from the
walls with blankets folded and stacked on the mat-
tresses. The wall behind the ladder we had just
descended was flat, as was the wall at the opposite
end of the tunnel-shaped room, which I estimated
to be about ten feet wide by fifteen or twenty feet
long. The back wall was lined with shelving units
except for a drawn curtain in one corner.

"This looks like a bunker," Di said. "Bruce and
Carrie must be preppers, waiting for the zombie
apocalypse."

"This is older than the survivalist movement, I
think. I'm guessing this is a fallout shelter from the
nineteen fifties or sixties when everybody was waiting for the communists to drop a nuclear bomb.
Bruce and Bubba's parents must have put this in."

"Oh, yeah. I've seen some of those old black-
and-white documentaries showing schoolkids hiding
under their desks, as if that would provide any protection from a nuclear attack."

"It turned out these kinds of structures wouldn't have provided much protection from nuclear fall-out, either," I said.

"Maybe not. But it looks like it'll work just fine as a dungeon."

Di pulled her phone out of her pocket.

"I'm guessing we won't be able to get cell phone reception in here, but it's worth a try."

She held the phone up to the hatch and various other points around the room. "No bars," she said. "How long do you think our oxygen will hold out?"

"Since people were supposed to be able to live in these for months, or years even, I'm assuming there's some kind of ventilation system."

Di turned on her phone's flashlight function and scanned the ceiling. "Yeah, here's what looks like a vent. Unfortunately, it's not big enough for us to crawl through to get out of here."

I walked to the far end of the room and pulled back the curtain. It was a privacy screen for the out-house toilet behind it.

"At least we're set if nature calls," I said. "And we've got months' worth of canned goods on these shelves."

I sat down on a lower bunk and Di walked over and sat on the bunk across from me.

"I can't believe we never considered Carrie as a suspect. She had access to everything Bruce did. I'm sure she had keys to his truck and had seen him use a slim jim plenty of times, probably even used one herself," I said.

"And Carrie handed Bruce the pill he gave to Bubba that turned out to be an antihistamine instead of Imodium," she said.

"Oh, crap," I said. "I just realized, it wasn't Webster who set fire to the office trailer, it was Carrie."

"How do you know that?"

"I remember when I had lunch with her at the diner the other day she said something about the tangerine color spray paint used for the graffiti on the office trailer being the same as the paint used for the graffiti on Rowland's building."

"So? She could've seen that on the news like everybody else."

"Who in the world would refer to that color as *tangerine* instead of just plain *orange*? And they didn't mention that on the news, but the police report I got from Dave said two empty spray cans were left at the scene and it listed the brand and color names. I remember one of them was tangerine. But those spray cans were bagged for evidence and the only people who would have seen them, besides the vandals and the cops, were Carrie and Bruce, who discovered the obscenities scrawled on the wall."

"So why would Carrie torch Bubba's office at the development?"

"I don't know. My best guess is she was looking for those paternity test results Bubba said he had. She certainly wouldn't want somebody running across those."

"That makes sense," Di said. "At least you were right about Bubba being Jennifer's biological father."

"Fat lot of good that does us."

"We know who killed Bubba—and who's going to kill us if we don't think of some way out of this."

"Did you try holding your cell phone up to that ventilation pipe?" I asked.

Di climbed onto the upper bunk and held the cell phone up to the vent, tilting it in different directions.

"Nothing," she said. "Maybe there's something in here we can use to pierce a hole in the hatch. That might let us get cell reception, or at least let somebody hear our desperate cries for help."

I got up and started looking around.

"That hatch is inches thick. I doubt there's anything in here strong enough to punch a hole in it. But maybe there is some stuff in here we could use as a weapon, and maybe a shield, when Carrie comes back."

"That's a plan with some potential," Di said as she joined the search of our little prison cell.

"We could lob cans of lima beans at her," I said, looking at the labels of the canned goods.

"Who would stock their shelter with lima beans? Cans wouldn't be much of a match against bullets. Wait, here're some matches," she said. "If we lit a piece of paper and fanned the flame near the ventilation pipe, maybe someone would see our smoke signals. What do you think?"

"I think if we start a fire in this enclosed space we're more likely to asphyxiate ourselves."

Di dropped the matches and dropped to her knees to look under the bunk bed. She held up something and looked at it for a moment before dropping it, recoiling, and saying, "*Eeww.*"

"What is it?"

"It looks like a used condom. It would appear Bruce and Carrie use the dungeon as a kinky romantic getaway. Or one of them uses it to get away with someone else," Di said.

"Carrie and Bruce wouldn't use condoms at this point, I wouldn't think. Wait a minute. Let me see that," I said.

"Seriously?"

"I'm not going to touch it—like you did, by the way."

I knelt down. "Shine your flashlight on it."

"Be my guest," she said, handing me her phone.

I looked at the disgusting item more closely. "Di, this is a recent discard, not an ancient relic."

"Good for them."

"No, I mean I don't think Carrie or Bruce are the ones using the dungeon for romantic encounters. My guess is this little hideaway is a private spot for Jennifer and her boyfriend. What's his name? Garrett Timbs. That's it."

"Oh, I guess that makes sense. But how does that help us?"

"Di! Nell was questioning Billy Jr. about this place just the other night."

"Billy Jr.'s been down here with Jennifer? He's kinda young for her, isn't he?"

"No, no, no. I don't know that he's been down here, at least not when Jennifer and Garrett were in here. But Billy is best buddies with Garrett's little brother, Gavin. He came in with Billy at Nell's house while I was there to talk to her about Jennifer's DNA sample. Nell got upset with the boys for tracking cow manure into the kitchen and questioned them about why they'd been out in a pasture anyhow. They were giggling and elbowing each other and giving cryptic answers. I didn't think anything about it at the time. But they said something about a special place Garrett likes to take his girlfriend and how it was 'the bomb.' I know now they must have been talking about this place. Maybe the middle schoolers have been spying on the lovers or listening to their grown-up activities through the air vent.

"But, wait a minute. They couldn't have gotten cow poop on their shoes in the tractor barn, and I don't think Jennifer and Garrett have been slipping into their love lair through the hatch in the barn, either. There'd be too great a risk of them getting caught—the kitchen window has a clear view inside if the barn door is open."

"So what are you saying?"

"I'm saying there's got to be another entrance into this space—which means there's also an exit."

"Where?" she said, looking around doubtfully at the confined space.

"I don't know, but we're going to examine every square inch of this room until we find it."

Di started scanning the ceiling, thinking if there was a second exit it was most likely a hatch like the one we'd come down through. I began feeling along the wall for any lines or breaks that might signal a door. As I stood on tiptoe, moving my hands up the wall, I spotted a small flashlight tucked under the edge of a blanket on the top bunk. I grabbed it and flipped the switch. It actually came on.

After scanning the ceiling, Di bravely shined her phone light under the bunk where we'd found the discarded condom. I knew she must be desperate to get out of this place. So was I, which is why I wasn't above crawling along the wall behind the grungy toilet.

I'd just about given up hope when the flashlight slipped out of my hand and fell to the floor. When I bent down to retrieve it, I could see an arc of scuff marks etched into the illuminated section of the floor. The scuff pattern seemed to emanate from the edge of the shelves holding the canned goods on the back wall.

I showed my find to Di.

"This must be it."

It looked like the shelving unit had been swung open and closed over a period of time, creating the marks on the floor. Di and I pushed and pulled trying to open the door. We ran our fingers along the outer perimeter of the casement trying to find a latch. Next, we pulled everything off the shelves, dumping the rations onto the floor, and pushed and pulled on each shelf and the shelf backing. Finally, I banged my fist on one of the shelves in frustration. When I did, it popped out of position, opening up a hidden space on the side of the unit and revealing a latch. I tugged at the latch and the door sprung forward slightly.

As we pulled on the door, it swung open on hidden casters along the scored arc on the floor. There was an elevated opening, slightly smaller than the opening to the hatch we had climbed in through. I shone my flashlight into the space. We scooted a crate in front of the opening and Di said, "I'll go first." I didn't argue.

She climbed in and I entered right after her. We crawled something like twenty or thirty feet until the area in front of us dead-ended. Suddenly Di stood up; the space overhead opened up, soaring what I guessed to be at least twenty feet. Di stepped onto a metal ladder attached to the metal tube ascending upward into darkness beyond the scope of what our small lights could illuminate.

Di went up the first few rungs and I followed closely behind. When she reached the top, she said, "There's some kind of lid. Here's hoping I can push it open."

I held my breath. In a moment I heard a creaking and saw a shaft of sunlight peek through as the lid began to open. Without warning, the lid dropped, shutting off the sunlight, and Di slid precipitously down several rungs of the ladder, kicking me in the jaw.

I managed to hang on, just barely, and she caught herself, keeping us both from tumbling down almost two stories onto the metal surface below.

"Are you okay?" I called up, my jaw still smarting, but no real damage done.

"I'm going to have some bruises, but I think I'm okay," she said.

"Do you think you can open the lid?"

"Yeah, I just lost my footing as I pushed up. Maybe once I get to the top again you can climb up so you're behind my back. Wrap your arms around me and hang on to the sides of the ladder to steady me and keep me from tilting backward again. If we start sliding, grab on to the the first rung you hit and hang on for dear life."

"Okay," I said.

I wasn't sure it was a great plan, but it was the only one we had at the moment. And staying in the bunker wasn't an option.

Di started back up. As she hit each rung, I heard her moaning, obviously in pain.

"What's wrong?"

"I twisted my dang ankle when I fell down the ladder. I'm trying to step up with my other foot and not put weight on it. I can make it."

When Di was up as high as she could go I kept climbing until my head was almost between her shoulder blades, hoping I could steady her as she pushed up on the lid.

I saw a small shaft of sunlight again, then a bigger wedge of light as Di thrust her arms upward. I could feel her wince from the pain every time she pushed upward, putting a strain on her injured ankle, and she was trembling trying to keep the heavy lid ajar as she struggled to push it completely open.

She took deep breaths readying herself for what we both hoped was the final heave-ho. I leaned back away from her slightly, trying to give her space to thrust upward with all the power she could muster from her muscular legs that walk more than six miles a day on her mail route. I felt her bend her knees slightly and surge upward.

We heard the thud of the lid clapping against the top edge of the metal shaft as blinding sunlight flooded in.

"You did it."

"Finally," Di said, breathless, laughing and crying at the same time.

After she sucked in a few deep breaths, she climbed to the top of the ladder and flung her upper body out of the escape hatch, pushing herself forward with her foot from the top rung. I climbed up and Di grabbed my hand and helped me climb out.

We both sat on the grass, catching our breath for a moment.

"Please tell me you didn't drop your cell phone when we slid down the ladder."

"Nope. I have it right here. Let's hope we can get reception."

She held her phone up.

"I've got three bars."

"Hallelujah," I said. "Call Dave."

Di handed me the phone. "You call him. I have a feeling I won't like his tone when I tell him where we are. Just press two."

"Does that mean I'm number one on your speed dial?"

"Don't let it go to your head."

I pressed "2" and before I could say anything Dave started barking, "Where the hell are you two?

A farmer found Liv's car abandoned in a field with the keys in the ignition. I've got volunteers combing the woods searching for you."

"Um, Dave, this is Liv. . . ."

He started yelling again and I held the phone away from my ear. Di grabbed it and shouted at the phone, "Dave, shut up and listen. Liv and I are in the cow pasture behind Bruce Rowland's tractor barn. Come pick us up. Oh, and arrest Carrie Rowland while you're at it. She killed Bubba."

Click.

"He's on his way."

"He won't be alone," I said. "Apparently, Carrie moved my car to a nearby field and Dave has a search party looking for us."

Within minutes, we saw some people emerging from the woods on the far side of the pasture. One of them carefully lifted up a slack section of barbed wire and stepped through into the field. Others followed suit.

Nell came running from the direction of the house, waving her arms wildly once she spotted us.

"You two had us scared to death. I was in Bruce and Carrie's house for the funeral lunch when one of the reserve deputies came in and said the sheriff was asking for volunteers to look for you two. Somebody had found Liv's car but no trace of either one of you.

"I stepped out on the porch and called Billy. I told him to get as many of his catering crew guys together as he could and to get out here to help with the search. Next thing I knew Ted stormed through the front door and came back out a couple of minutes later with Carrie in handcuffs.

"Before he got in the patrol car, I hollered and asked him if they'd found you two and he said you were back here in the pasture. Why are you out here stomping cow patties—and did Carrie kill Bubba?"

"It's a long story, and yes, she did," I said.

Dave pulled his truck up beside the tractor barn and parked. A crowd of searchers were approaching us from the back of the field, and the funeral lunch crowd started spilling out of the house and moving across the yard toward us. It felt like we were surrounded by half of Dixie. Dave had opened the gate and was walking our way. We started walking in his direction, with Di holding on to my shoulder, hobbling on her sprained ankle, wincing and ouching with every step.

"What happened?" Dave asked, fortunately looking more concerned than angry.

"I managed to twist my ankle as we were climbing up the ladder out of the bomb shelter," she said, nodding over to opening we'd climbed out of.

He gently laid his hands on her shoulders and looked into her eyes. "You two have any injuries other than the ankle?"

She locked in on his gaze and softly said, "I don't think so."

I decided not to mention the bruise coming up on my jaw where Di had kicked me like an ornery mule.

"We'd better get that ankle checked out. Nell, I

want you and Liv to follow me to the hospital in your car."

Without another word, Dave slipped his right arm around Di's waist, scooped her up into his arms, and carried her to his truck. The gathering crowd in the yard parted to make way. The search party started clapping and the mourners joined in the applause.

Nell gave me a wink and wrapped her arm around my shoulders.

"Sprained ankle or not, I think Di Souther is going to be just fine," she said. "Ain't romance grand."

"Speaking of romance, Nell, I think you and Billy are going to have to have a little talk with Billy Jr."

Chapter 24

Dave drove Di to the small county hospital in his truck and Nell and I followed in her car. For anything major, patients would be transported to a Memphis hospital. A nurse took Di straight back to X-ray and Dave insisted the doctor give me an exam as well, even though I told him I was fine.

I was waiting for the doctor in one of the curtained-off areas when I heard Larry Joe coming through calling out my name. He spotted me through an opening in the curtain and barreled in. A nurse made a move to prevent him, but Dave spoke to her in a hushed tone before she turned and walked away.

Larry Joe gently cupped my face in his hands and asked if I was injured.

"No, no injuries. Di twisted her ankle. She's in X-ray now."

Certain he wasn't hurting me, Larry Joe scooped me up in a tight hug and showered me with kisses.

After a few *I love yous* and *Thank God your okays*, he gave me a stern look, or at least as stern as he could manage through misty eyes.

"What am I going to have to do to keep you from chasing after killers?"

"I can assure you that wasn't the plan. It just turned out that way. We had no idea Carrie murdered Bubba until she pulled a gun on us."

"Carrie? I was meeting with a client in Memphis when they tracked me down and told me you'd been rescued after getting locked up in a bomb shelter out at Bruce Rowland's place. I assumed the killer was Bruce."

"So did we."

The doctor came in and checked my blood pressure and heartbeat and listened through a stethoscope as I took deep breaths before saying he thought I was good to go.

Larry Joe and I were making our way back to the waiting area when I heard Mama.

"Good heavens, Liv. Are you okay?" she said, grabbing my shoulders and looking me up and down before wrapping her arms around me and pressing my face to her bosom.

I struggled to breathe for a moment before breaking free.

"I'm just fine, Mama, and at worst, Di may have a broken ankle. Although I think it's just sprained. And the good news is, Earl is completely in the clear now."

"I know, Nell told me about Carrie's arrest when she called to tell me that you and Di were at the hospital getting checked out. Earl's parking the car."

Di emerged from the hallway hobbling on crutches with her ankle wrapped. Dave was walking slowly beside her.

"What did the doctor say?" I asked.

"It's a mild sprain. I'm supposed to ice it for the next couple of days and not put any weight on it for about a week."

"Dave, we can see Di home if you like. I understand you've got a murderer waiting for you at the jail," Larry Joe said.

"No thanks. I've got this," he said, looking adoringly over at Di. "Carrie will keep for a bit. Besides, I think she's smart enough to keep her mouth shut until her attorney arrives.

"And for the record, we were closing in on Carrie before you two decided to put yourself in harm's way—again. Going through Bubba's financials we found a recent credit card charge to a DNA-testing lab. We'd just served the lab with a subpoena for the test results, but I had a sneaking suspicion it had to do with Jennifer—what with the accusations of Bubba fixing the pageant in her favor."

I started to say, "Now you tell us," but decided to keep my big mouth shut.

I gave Di a quick hug and told her to call if she needed anything.

"You do what the doctor says and stay off that ankle so it heals right," Mama admonished as Di began to limp toward the exit with Dave close behind. They passed Earl coming in as they were going out.

"Congratulations, Earl," Larry Joe said as they shook hands.

I gave Earl a big hug. "I'm glad you and Mama can put this nightmare behind you now."

"Well, thank you. I'm just happy to see you and your friend are safe. I'm still having trouble wrapping my head around Carrie being the murderer. But then, I suppose parents will do pretty much anything to protect their children."

"This is going to be awful rough on Jennifer, losing her uncle and learning that her daddy isn't her biological father. And now with her mom going to prison," I said.

"True. I'm going to put Jennifer and her dad on the prayer list," Mama said. "But tomorrow is all about Earl and celebrating having his name cleared. I know you two probably won't make it to church, but come over for Sunday dinner. I plan to cook all of Earl's favorites."

"Now, Virginia. Liv might want a quiet day at home after her ordeal," Earl said.

"No. This is one celebration we wouldn't want to miss," I said, glancing over at Larry Joe, who nodded his assent. "We'll see you two tomorrow."

"Okay, hon," Mama said, giving me one more windpipe-crushing hug. "Earl, while we're here at the hospital there's a lady in my Sunday school class who just had minor surgery. I'm going to run up and see her for a minute. You want to come with me or hang out here and stare at that TV on the wall?"

"I'll walk up with you," he said, giving Mama an affectionate look and placing his hand gently at her back as they made their way to the elevators.

"I think those two are going to do just fine as old married folks," Larry Joe said.

"Yeah, Earl's a keeper. And things are looking pretty rosy for Di and Dave right now, too. I'll tell you about Dave's grand romantic gesture when we get home."

"Taco Belles?" he said.

"That sounds good. But let's pick up to-go plates for us, please. I'm ready to get home."

Larry Joe and I walked through the automatic doors into the blinding sunlight holding hands. He opened the passenger door for me and I climbed into his truck. Dave told me my SUV was in the police garage in Hartville. When it was discovered in the field with Di and me missing, Ted gave it a preliminary going-over and then called to have it towed to Hartville so a forensics team could examine it for fingerprints and other evidence to help in the search for us. Larry Joe and I would go fetch it on Monday.

After picking up to-go plates at Taco Belles we drove home. I walked into the house and headed straight to the shower. Crawling around in the bomb shelter and the escape hatch left me looking and feeling grimy. I spurned the cool showers I'd been taking during the heat wave in favor of hot water pulsating on my neck and shoulders.

Stepping onto the cool tile floor from the steam that had enveloped me behind the shower curtain felt good. I wiped the fog from the mirror over the sink and looked at my jaw. I could see a bruise starting to form, but it didn't look swollen.

I pulled on the robe that was hanging on the bathroom door and went upstairs. I slipped into some shorts and a T-shirt and pulled my hair back into a ponytail. Larry Joe called from the foot of the staircase that dinner was served.

Catfish tacos never tasted so good. Di and I had missed the funeral lunch, or any lunch at all. I guess we could have opened a can of lima beans in the dungeon, but on the whole I was just as glad we didn't.

Larry Joe filled our glasses with iced tea, kissed me on the forehead, and told me to tell him the whole story.

"Don't leave anything out," he said.

I told him more or less everything, including Mama's performance at the funeral home when she was collecting DNA samples from Bubba in his casket.

"If Di and I had just waited to go out to Carrie and Bruce's house when it was full of mourners, she wouldn't have been able to march us to the bomb shelter and we wouldn't have been in any real danger."

"Or, if you'd just shared your suspicions with

Dave and let him handle things, you wouldn't have had a murderer holding a gun to your head."

Sure, it all sounds so obvious in hindsight.

After a moment of silence he changed the subject.

"So, you said something earlier about Dave and Di having a big romantic moment. Did he give her a big smooch right in front of everybody when he saw you two were still alive?"

"Better than that. Di was hobbling on her bum ankle and he picked her up and carried her over-the-threshold style all the way to his truck. The crowd started clapping."

He gave me a big smile, showing off both his dimples. A grin only brings out the left one.

I stood up and cleared away our takeout containers, dropping them in the trash can, and put our glasses in the sink. He slipped up behind me at the sink, wrapped his arms around my waist, and started nibbling on my neck and earlobes. I put my hand under the running tap and flicked my fingers at him, sprinkling him with cold water.

He spun me around and started tickling me. He suddenly stopped and gently lifted my chin with his right hand.

"How'd you get that bruise?"

"Di accidentally kicked me as we were climbing out of the hatch."

I decided there was no point in worrying him with the fact we had started sliding down a twenty-plus-foot ladder and could have fallen to our deaths.

He cupped my face in his hands and showered my face and lips with a gentle flurry of kisses. Then

he surprised me by gathering me up into his arms,
bride style, and carrying me toward the stairs.

"Larry Joe McKay, you put me down before you
throw your back out."

"Don't worry. I plan to put you down on the bed
just as soon as we get upstairs."

Chapter 25

Sunday morning, Larry Joe and I slept in and snuggled for a bit before finally climbing out of bed around nine-thirty. We spent the rest of the morning leisurely reading the newspaper over coffee and toast before getting dressed and driving to Mama's.

We walked in through Mama's front door, which was open with only the unlocked screen door pushed to, keeping the flies and mosquitoes at bay.

We walked through to the den and spoke to Earl. Larry Joe started talking sports and I went into the kitchen, where Mama was frying chicken. She had corn on the cob from Earl's garden cooking in the microwave and baked beans in the oven. She asked me to slice some perfectly ripe tomatoes from her own backyard. She took the baked beans out of the oven and popped in some homemade biscuits to warm them up.

Mama and Earl were still wearing their church clothes. She told me my in-laws were also expected.

They had run home after church to change clothes. No doubt Daddy Wayne wanted to change into some more comfortable pants and a golf shirt.

I finished setting the table as I heard Larry Joe's parents come in the front door. I couldn't help thinking how the last time we were all here for Sunday dinner, Mama and Earl had announced their engagement, and how just a few days later Earl had been arrested for murder. I was so relieved to have that all behind us now.

Mama and I started putting food on the table to pass and serve family style and Mama hollered for everybody to gather around.

We stood behind our chairs at the table. Earl reached over and took Mama by the hand, she reached over and grabbed my hand, and that chain reaction continued until the circle was unbroken.

After Earl said grace we all took our seats and dug in. Like most of her cooking, Mama's fried chicken was top notch, moist inside and crispy outside.

After we'd cleared the dinner dishes and taken our desserts into the den, Mama and Earl popped up from the sofa and held hands just like they did for their engagement news. The rest of us suspended our forks halfway between our plates and our mouths and looked up at them, wondering what they were about to say now. I was hoping they were going to tell us they had set a date for the wedding.

They had—but that wasn't the big news.

This time Mama made the announcement instead of Earl.

"Earl and I have decided to get married in Las Vegas—and we're flying all of you out for the wedding on our dime."

I was truly speechless and apparently so were my in-laws. Larry Joe was the first to find his voice.

"Well, that sounds like fun," he said, getting up and going over to give Mama a hug and shake hands with Earl. "And while I appreciate the offer for airfare, we'll pay our own way."

"Oh no you won't," Earl said. "We're paying airfare and hotel rooms for everyone."

"That's right," Mama chimed in. "Larry Joe, you and Wayne can feel free to throw a little bachelor's party for Earl, if you like."

I got up and went over to hug Mama. She took my hand and led me into the kitchen.

"Liv, I hope you're not mad that we're switching gears on the wedding after all the time you and Holly have already put into planning it."

"No, of course not. I just want you and Earl to be happy. I have to admit I'm a little surprised about the change in plans. I mean, you could have the wedding here and still go to Vegas for the honeymoon."

"No, darlin'. After Earl got arrested, I had the chance to see just who my real friends were. I realized there were plenty of people on the wedding invitation list who weren't genuine friends at all. And the way the McKays, all of you, rallied around

Earl reminded me just how important family is—your little sister not withstanding."

"Aw, Mama, you know we're always here for you two. And Emma will come around. She just doesn't always live in the real world, as Daddy used to say."

"He did, didn't he?" Mama said. "I'll invite her and Hobie to come out to Las Vegas for the wedding if they'd like. But I don't expect they'll come. The baby will give her an easy out not to. And we'll also invite Earl's son, Luke, in Miami to come for the wedding, but he won't come, either. He didn't even come up to check on his daddy after Earl had been arrested for murder—and I had called to let him know.

"But we also want to invite Di and the sheriff to come to Las Vegas as our guests. Di was right there with you trying to clear Earl's name, even got injured in the process. And Sheriff Davidson came through in the end."

"That's very generous, Mama. So tell me what you're thinking about for the Vegas trip and wedding and Holly and I will get busy on the phone working out the details."

"Oh no you won't. It's already taken care of. Earl called a travel agent he's used in the past and she's arranging a whole wedding package deal. And Earl and I have decided after we get hitched in Vegas, we're going to buy or rent a Winnebago there and hit the road out west for our honeymoon. We're not going to plan too much, just go where the road leads us.

"What you *can* do is help me with shopping and packing. I'm going to need a whole new wardrobe. And you've got three weeks. We plan to get married on Earl's birthday, August sixth. I figure that way he'll never forget our anniversary."

Epilogue

Monday morning I called Di and told her I'd pick up breakfast from Town Square Diner for the two of us and bring it over if she was up for the company.

She requested muffins and hash browns. An odd combo, but she was convalescing, so I figured whatever made her feel better.

After swinging by the diner to pick up our to-go orders, I knocked before letting myself in through the unlocked front door of Di's trailer. She was stretched out on the sofa with her foot propped up on a pillow.

"Is your ankle hurting much?" I asked as I unpacked our takeout containers.

"It was throbbing pretty good last night after the pain pill they gave me at the hospital wore off. But it's not too bad this morning."

Di had a nearly empty mug of coffee sitting on

the coffee table. I refilled it and brought over her plate and some cutlery.

"So you'll be off from work all week, at least," I said.

"Actually, I could go in and have them put me on light duty, sitting at a desk sorting things or filling out paperwork. But the thought bores me to tears, so I decided to just take the week off."

"Don't use up all your vacation time. Mama and Earl have decided to get hitched in Las Vegas. And in addition to Larry Joe and me and my in-laws, Earl and Mama want to treat you and Dave to a trip as a thank-you for your help in clearing Earl's name. I hope you'll go. It'll be fun."

"I can't believe your Mama is giving up on her fantasy island wedding. You must be disappointed."

"Whatever makes her happy," I said, savoring a bite of a warm chocolate chip muffin.

"I'm not opposed to the idea of a trip to Vegas, especially on someone else's dime. But your mama seems to be making some assumptions if she's inviting Dave and me as a couple."

"Actually, I told her I didn't know what kind of room arrangements would be convenient. So she said she'd book connecting rooms and let the two of you work it out for yourselves. Do you think Dave will actually take the time away from work to go?"

"Oh, he'll go. I can assure you he'll go," she said with a sly smile.

Tips for a Fourth of July Block Party on a Budget

A Fourth of July celebration doesn't have to be a community-wide extravaganza like the one Liv coordinated for the town of Dixie in the book. A neighborhood bash can be a whole lot of fun and provides the perfect opportunity to get together with neighbors and catch up on everything they missed out on during the busy school year.

Invites

Free printable invitations can be downloaded from the Internet, or a group of neighborhood kids can make a project of drawing on trimmed sheets of card stock with their own red, white, and blue designs and then hand deliver them, passing them out to neighbors or slipping them under doors.

If your neighborhood is well connected via e-mail (for instance, your community has a neighborhood watch and neighbors share e-mails and phone numbers), choose to go paperless and send e-vites.

Paper or paperless, be sure invitations include a way to sign up for food, shopping, setup, entertainment, and any other necessary details. Include an e-mail address for RSVPs and questions, or, alternately, set up a Facebook event page or an online sign-up page (SignUpGenius has a basic version that's free).

Food

For the meats, it might be easier, and more cost effective, to have everyone pitch in a few dollars and buy the ground beef, hot dogs, and so on in larger quantities from a warehouse club.

A few of the neighbors can gather their grills into a row of grilling stations and cook to order. The grill masters will enjoy the camaraderie and will have a chance to talk to everyone in the neighborhood as they stop by to pick up a burger or brat.

Side dishes can be potluck, although it's a good idea to have people sign up indicating what they're bringing, so you don't end up with ten bowls of potato salad and no fruit platter.

At any potluck affair it's a good idea to place index cards and pens on the table and ask people to write their name and the name of their food item. This way neighbors will know who to ask if they have food allergy concerns, such as gluten, dairy, or nut allergies. Those who don't cook can bring paper plates, napkins, utensils, cups, potato chips, and so forth.

Bonus Recipe

Southern Potato Salad

2 pounds potatoes, peeled and cubed
6 hard-boiled eggs, chopped
1 cup mayo
1 tablespoon yellow mustard
4 tablespoons chopped sweet pickles
Salt and pepper to taste
Smoked paprika

Instructions:
Place eggs in pan and cover with cold water. When water starts to boil, reduce heat to a low simmer uncovered for one minute. Remove from heat and cover. Let stand for 12 minutes. Move eggs to an ice bath to cool.

Peel and dice the potatoes into 1-inch cubes. Cover them with water in a large pot and bring to a boil for 15–20 minutes or until tender. Drain in a colander. Let potatoes cool completely before mixing, so they don't crumble.

Peel and roughly chop hard-boiled eggs.

In a separate bowl, mix together all the other ingredients except the paprika. Add potatoes and eggs and stir gently until the dressing coats the potatoes. Sprinkle paprika liberally on top.

Beverages

In addition to beer, don't forget the nonalcoholic beverages, including soft drinks, juices, lemonade, iced tea—and lots of water. Hanging out with neighbors on a hot summer afternoon means everyone needs to stay hydrated. And be sure to have some sunscreen on hand to share. Coolers, galvanized tubs, and even kiddie pools filled with ice will keep beverages icy cold.

Set up a lemonade stand and let the neighborhood kids man it. Neighbors can toss a nickel or a dime in the payment jar. And at the end of the day, divvy up the shiny money among the kids who took a shift at the stand.

Desserts

Include ice cream cones, sundaes with fixings—fun for the kids—and ice cream cakes. All are great for a hot summer day—and don't require turning on an oven.

Kids' Activities

Kick off the day with a "Patriotic Bike and Wagon" parade. Deck out those red wagons, tricycles, and bicycles—including the ones sporting training wheels—with patriotic swag. It doesn't need to be expensive. Load the cart at the dollar store with streamers, ribbons, and pinwheels. And don't forget

the red, white, and blue balloons! Even paper plates
with Fourth of July designs cut into star shapes will
look good adorning the spokes and baskets of kids'
bikes. All you need is tape or florist wire!

Keep it simple. Just put out jump ropes, hula
hoops, Slip 'N Slides. Include water balloons and
water pistols—if you dare.

Entertainment

Let all those brave enough to sign up for a talent
show in on the fun—but limit their time in the
spotlight by scheduling every performer ahead of
time. The local garage band, the pint-sized baton
twirler, the budding ballerinas, the guy who plays
the harmonica, the neighbor who fancies himself
a magician—these acts can all provide memorable
moments for your block party and strengthen
bonds among neighbors. This is a chance to learn
something you never knew about your neighbors—
for better or worse! And if the sign-up sheet is
mostly blank, you can always go with karaoke!

Fireworks

July 4th isn't complete for many people without a
fireworks show. If there's a safe area from which to
launch fireworks, and someone in the neighborhood has a fireworks display operator's license
(often needed to get a fireworks display permit for
larger shows), then by all means go big. Everyone

can pitch in to pay for the pyrotechnic display. Otherwise, it's probably best to keep it simple—and safe. Load up the kids and carpool to your town's fireworks show. Or at dusk, hand out glow-in-the-dark sticks or glow bracelets to all the youngsters, and sparklers for the older kids and kids at heart.

Fireworks that don't explode or shoot up into the air are sometimes referred to as "safe and sane" fireworks. But even these fireworks require safety precautions and adult supervision. Setting off any fireworks at a crowded block party with lots of kids around is risky. Families who wish to set off small fireworks with their own children may choose to retreat to their own enclosed backyard to do so.

Don't Forget the Photos

Keep the memories. Create a social media hashtag so neighbors can find each other's photos on Facebook, Instagram, and Twitter.

Create a private folder in the cloud on Dropbox or Amazon Cloud Drive where everyone can upload—and download—the best photos from the day.

Bonus Tip

Be sure to check with the city before setting up barricades. Regulations will vary. For example, in some cities a petition signed by a certain percentage of residents may be required.

Tips for a Fabulous Baby Shower

Heather's Gender-Reveal Baby Shower (featured in the book)

Decorations

- Clothesline strung across a curtain rod with small toys and some baby socks and onesies hanging from it. As the mom-to-be opens gifts, adorable little outfits are added to the line.

- Stuffed animals placed on the gift table and occasional tables.

- Cake featuring a pink marzipan ballet slipper and a blue sneaker. Underneath the footwear are alternating blue and pink letters that read, "It's a . . ." When the cake is sliced, a luscious pink shade of strawberry cake hidden under the frosting reveals it's a girl. (Obviously, the cake can be changed to blueberry, or any flavor along with blue food coloring, if the reveal is for a boy.)

Brunch Menu

Ham with mini biscuits
Cheesy grits
Granola and Greek yogurt parfaits topped
with fresh strawberries and blueberries
Mini bagels with assorted flavored cream
cheese spreads
Made-to-order omelets
Juices and coffee

Bonus Recipe

Cheesy Grits

4 cups water
1 cup uncooked grits
½ cup half-and-half
¼ cup butter, melted
2 large eggs, lightly beaten
1 cup (4 ounces) shredded cheddar cheese
½ cup (2 ounces) shredded Parmesan
   cheese
1 tablespoon Worcestershire sauce
⅛ teaspoon cayenne pepper (optional)
Salt and pepper to taste

Instructions:
Preheat oven to 350 degrees. In a large saucepan,
bring water to a boil. Slowly stir in grits. Reduce heat;
cover and simmer for 5–8 minutes or until thickened.

Let cool a bit. Gradually whisk in half-and-half, butter, and eggs. Stir in cheeses, Worcestershire sauce, and cayenne pepper. Add salt and pepper to taste.

Transfer to a greased 2-quart baking dish. Bake uncovered for 30–40 minutes or until bubbly. Let stand about 10 minutes before serving. Yield: 8 servings.

Games

- Bags containing baby items (some unusual) are passed around and guests have to guess what the items are merely by touch—no peeking!

- My Water Broke game: Ice trays containing a miniature baby doll in each slot are filled to varying degrees and dropped into juice or other chilled beverages. When a cube completely melts, releasing the baby, the person calls out, "My water broke!" The first one to do so wins a prize.

Party Favors

- Heavy-duty white lunch sacks decorated with pink tulle tutus and ballerina tops fashioned from pink cardboard. Pink and white ribbon threaded through holes punched in the tops of the bags secures the bags once they are filled. (For a blue design, you could use gauze for a diaper attached with a blue diaper pin. Or you could go with a gender-neutral adornment in green and yellow.)

- Gift bag contents: baby food–sized jars filled with pink and white jelly beans (or blue and white, if appropriate) labeled "Heather's (mom's name) Baby Shower" along with the date, and rubber ducky–shaped soaps.

- Slices of cake wrapped in plastic or foil could also be dropped into the gift bags for guests to take home.

Bonus Baby Shower Idea

The gender-reveal shower was for Heather. When it's time for a shower for her sister, Tiffany, a "Breakfast at Tiffany's Baby Shower" would be great fun. (This is a fun idea for any mom-to-be who likes a bit of glam—even if her name isn't Tiffany!)

Obviously, it would feature a breakfast or brunch menu, including juices served in champagne flutes. It should include fabulous iced cupcakes topped with classic baby motif decorations, such as rattles, in metallic silver or black-and-white-striped cupcake liners.

All the guests would receive a party favor box with "Tiffany's" stenciled across the top. And, of course, each guest would be issued a party store tiara to wear at the shower!

If you enjoyed *One Fete in the Grave*,
be sure not to miss the first book
in Vickie Fee's Liv & Di in Dixie Mystery series

DEATH CRASHES THE PARTY

In the quirky, close-knit town of Dixie,
Tennessee, party planner Liv McKay has a knack
for throwing Southern-style soirées, from
diamonds-and-denim to black tie affairs, and her
best friend Di Souther mixes a mean daiquiri.
While planning a Moonshine and Magnolias
bash for high maintenance clients,
Liv inconveniently discovers a corpse in the
freezer and turns her attention from fabulous
fêtes to finding a murderer. Together,
Liv and Di follow a trail of sinister secrets
in their sweet little town that leads them
from drug smugglers to a Civil War battlefield,
and just when they think they're whistling Dixie,
Liv and Di will find themselves squarely in the
crosshairs of the least likely killer of all . . .

Keep reading for a special excerpt.

A Kensington mass-market paperback and
e-book on sale now!

Chapter 1

Monday was a scorching August day that had turned into hell for me when the Farrell brothers crashed a party that already had disaster written all over it.

I was repeating the dreadful details for the umpteenth time to Sheriff Eulyse "Dave" Davidson.

At 10:00 a.m. I met yet again with the Erdmans to continue negotiations for their fortieth-anniversary party. Making all Mrs. Erdman's peculiar dreams come true, while still pacifying her husband, was a complicated balancing act—like spinning plates on poles. This is a skill every good party planner must learn.

Mrs. Erdman, her red hair sticking out in barbed curls, sat on a chintz sofa in the couple's expansive living room. We discussed every tedious detail of a moonshine- and magnolias-themed party. Mr. Erdman sat in a recliner, paying scant attention to anything that didn't require personal effort on his part.

In a nutshell—the Erdmans being the nuts—she wanted an elegant party with frills, fancy foods, and elaborate decorations. Mr. Erdman wanted to wear comfortable clothes and drink lots of liquor. So he and his buddies would sample generous servings of different whiskeys, including moonshine from his cousin Vern's still. The ladies would dress as Southern belles, sip mint juleps, and listen to a Dixieland band on the veranda. The men, at the insistence of Mr. Erdman, would be dressed as bootleggers. Picture *O Brother, Where Art Thou?* We finally ironed out a major wrinkle when Mr. Erdman acquiesced to one dance with his wife. Hopefully, the other husbands would follow suit.

Mrs. Erdman's most recent vision for the party—and she'd had many—included ice sculptures. She wanted a giant forty perched atop a 1973 Plymouth Barracuda carved in ice, which would be displayed on the buffet table, with icy bare-butted cherubs to either side. The Barracuda was the car they took on their honeymoon. Not sure about the cherubs, but ours is not to reason why. After consulting with the ice sculptor, I now had to figure out how to store 250 pounds of ice—in August—so it wouldn't melt before the party. Although the Erdmans had two refrigerators with freezers in their kitchen, they were nowhere near large enough to accommodate the sculptures.

Mrs. Erdman offered that they had a deep freezer in the garage, which stored her husband's bounty of venison and catfish from his hunting and fishing exploits. She assured me that any game left in the freezer could be given away to friends and neighbors to make way for the sculptures. Mr. Erdman didn't dispute her assertion. I followed them into the garage, with tape measure in hand, to make sure the freezer could contain the ice sculptures.

"And . . . well, you know what happened next."

"Humor me," Dave said, with absolutely no sympathy for the day I was having. So I went through it—again.

I opened the freezer to measure the interior. Unfortunately, what we beheld was the frosty remains of Darrell Farrell, staring up at us like a fresh-caught walleye.

Mrs. Erdman screamed and ran back into the house. Her rotund husband stood for a moment, stunned. I backed away from the freezer, looking at a still slack-jawed Walter Erdman, trying to think of something to say. Instead, I tripped, knocking over a big green garbage can, and found myself sprawled on top of Darrell's very dead brother, Duane, who had toppled out with the trash. He was wearing what for the life of me looked like a Confederate uniform.

Walter Erdman screamed like a young girl and ran across the three-car garage and back into the house. I'd never seen anyone haul that much ass in one load. The Erdmans, who had the nerve of a bad tooth, had left me to deal with the problem at hand, despite the fact that it was not my house and it was definitely not my party. I dialed 911.

After phoning the police, I went into the house to let my clients know the sheriff was on his way.

I found Mr. Erdman in his study, stretched out on a leather sofa, staring at the ceiling and clutching a bottle of Scotch. Sobs from the hallway indicated Mrs. Erdman had locked herself in the powder room.

"I went to the entry hall and sat on the stairs, waiting to open the door when you arrived."

The only fortunate aspect of this tiresome inquisition was that Sheriff Dave was conducting it in the air-conditioned comfort of the Erdmans' roomy kitchen, appointed with gleaming commercial-grade appliances and marble countertops. I helped myself to a Diet Coke from the under-counter fridge stocked with bottled water and soft drinks.

"Dave, you want something to drink?"

"No, ma'am. I'm good."

Presumably to emphasize that this was official business, Dave made a point of calling me "Mrs. McKay" and "ma'am," instead of "Liv," despite the fact that we'd long been on a first-name basis. Tall, lean, and not bad looking, our normally genial sheriff could, nonetheless, present an imposing demeanor when he had a mind to.

"I know you didn't ask me, Sheriff Davidson," I said, following his cue on formality, "but, despite the fact the bodies were found at their house, which would naturally make them prime suspects, I can honestly testify that the Erdmans were both completely shocked by the discovery."

"Can't rule anything or anyone out at this juncture, but I take your point," he said.

After he finally stopped probing my brain for

details, I had to ask, "Dave, do you have any idea why Duane was wearing a Confederate uniform?"

"He and his brother were both involved with one of those Civil War reenactment units," he said. "As to why he was dressed out in uniform, I can't say. They've got some big reenactment event coming up in a few weeks." He went on. "Now, let me ask you a question, Ms. McKay. You seem to keep your ear to the ground. Do you have any idea who might have had a reason to kill the Farrell boys?"

"Seems obvious to me, Sheriff," I said. "It must have been some damn Yankee."

Dave did not seem at all amused.

Connect with Us

Visit us online at
KensingtonBooks.com
to read more from your favorite authors, see books
by series, view reading group guides, and more.

Join us on social media

for sneak peeks, chances to win books and prize packs,
and to share your thoughts with other readers.

facebook.com/kensingtonpublishing
twitter.com/kensingtonbooks

Tell us what you think!

To share your thoughts, submit a review,
or sign up for our eNewsletters, please visit:
KensingtonBooks.com/TellUs.

Grab These Cozy Mysteries
from
Kensington Books